UNMASKING

Inside, the masquerade was at its height of revelry. But here in the warm darkness of the garden, Justin St. Clair gently but firmly removed Diana's mask.

He reached out a hand to trace the line of her jaw. The hand brushed softly across her lips, then tilted her chin. "I find you are rapidly becoming an obsession with me," he murmered against the softness of her mouth, kissing her gently at first, and then more deeply.

It was not as though Diana had never been kissed before. But this was different. Diana felt weak and breathless, excited and exhilarated all at the same time. Her lips parted, and she could feel his breath mingle with hers. His hands felt warm on her back as he moved them slowly down her shoulders to her waist. The silk of her costume was so thin that it felt as if he were caressing her bare skin as he pressed her closer to him. Diana slid her arms around his neck and pulled his lips down on hers again as his hands moved from her waist to her hips, and she pressed against him.

Diana did not know what kind of shocking game Justin was playing with her. But now she could be sure how skillful he was at winning. . . .

The Willful Widow

by

Evelyn Richardson

A SIGNET BOOK

SIGNET
Published by the Penguin Group
Penguin Books USA Inc., 375 Hudson Street,
New York, New York 10014, U.S.A.
Penguin Books Ltd, 27 Wrights Lane,
London W8 5TZ, England
Penguin Books Australia Ltd, Ringwood,
Victoria, Australia
Penguin Books Canada Ltd, 10 Alcorn Avenue,
Toronto, Ontario, Canada M4V 3B2
Penguin Books (N.Z.) Ltd, 182–190 Wairau Road,
Auckland 10, New Zealand

Penguin Books Ltd, Registered Offices:
Harmondsworth, Middlesex, England

First published by Signet, an imprint of Dutton Signet,
a division of Penguin Books USA Inc.

First Printing, January, 1994
10 9 8 7 6 5 4 3 2 1

Copyright © Cynthia Johnson, 1994
All rights reserved

 REGISTERED TRADEMARK—MARCA REGISTRADA

Printed in the United States of America

to
Madeleine and Daniel

Chapter 1

A BRILLIANT ray of sunlight poured through a long narrow gap in the curtains and illuminated the tumbled bedclothes at the foot of the bed. Lord Justin St. Clair awoke and shook himself groggily. Lord, he didn't think he'd been that foxed when he had stumbled home in the early hours of the morning, but his head was simply pounding. No it wasn't! Someone else was pounding, and fortunately, they had stopped, let in no doubt by the inestimable Preston, his servant whose soothing accents appeared to be having a calming effect on the importunate visitor. For importunate he was to be calling at this hour of the morning. Justin rolled over and peered at the clock on the mantel. Nine o'clock. Boney must have invaded or the king had died—or something equally earthshaking. No one would think of calling at such an hour for any lesser reason.

"It's your brother, sir," a quiet voice announced from the doorway.

Justin groaned. No one, that is, except his brother Alfred, he thought to himself. It was outside of enough that the Earl of Winterbourne insisted on keeping country hours in town, but that he should inflict them on others was, well, it was just like his brother. Alfred, Earl of Winterbourne, had been born convinced of the rightness of his views on every possible subject and with the assumption that the rest of the world naturally agreed with him. For how could it not look to someone of his social stature and rectitude for its guidance. Unfortunately, nothing and no one, not even his reckless, obstinate, and clever younger brother Justin, try though he would, had been able to change his mind during the past forty years. Having started out as a stolid, humorless child, Alfred had progressed into a pompous and overbearing adult who had stepped perfectly and easily into his equally pompous father's shoes, managing at the same time, in his usual overbearing way to tread upon everyone else's toes.

Justin sighed and gazed longingly out the window. More than once he had wished for a handy tree or vine to escape onto—usually from a jealous husband—but now with his brother in the next room wishing to talk about something uncomfortable, such a convenience would truly have stood him in good stead. The last person on earth he wished to speak to at this hour of the morning and in this disordered state of mind was Alfred.

Still, to give the earl his due, Alfred never bothered his younger brother except in the most dire of situations and, for his part, Justin could never be grateful enough for Alfred's having been the firstborn, thereby sparing him a lifetime of responsibility and sobriety, as befitted the one inheriting such a revered and ancient title. He and Alfred had recognized early on—after a few of Justin's amorous forays with village maidens and several exuberant pranks at university—that the two of them were bound to disagree on every point. They had long accepted their differences and had gone their separate ways. Alfred had become Earl of Winterbourne, married a girl with a portion handsome enough to cause everyone to forget her lack of a truly illustrious lineage and less than prepossessing countenance. He had fathered a son whose soberness of mind and conservative spirit made him the perfect heir to the Earls of Winterbourne who had always been more noted for their ability to remain unchanged by the tides of fashion and history than for anything else.

Justin, on the other hand, fulfilling the promise of his rackety youth, had embarked on an erratic but brilliant career at university, where he was at the same time the despair and the pride of his tutors. To a man, they could never understand how one who studied so little and played so much could excel in all his studies, much less hold his own among scholars of considerable stature and renown.

After a time on the town, during which he had cut a swathe among each Season's new offerings—as well as among its more dashing matrons—Justin became intolerably bored with the *ton*. He had begun casting about for something that would serve as an outlet for his pent-up energy, and a challenge for the intellect that was chafing at the mindless rounds of society.

The military life certainly offered enough excitement to gratify his adventurous spirit, what with Bonaparte laying waste to all of Europe. Various friends had done their best to entice him with stirring tales of glorious charges and deeds of valor. However, Justin, though fond of Captain Wrotham and Lieutenant Danforth, remembered them from days of yore. They appeared to have remained unchanged from the brash schoolboys who were always up for a lark despite the world-shaking nature of the events in which they were participating. Not that there was anything in the least wrong in that, Justin enjoyed a bit of fun as much, if not more than the next fellow, but even the most exuberant spirits could soon appear tedious if they did nothing but fall from one scrape to the next. Their hearty enthusiasm, which remained unaffected by even the most serious reverses, their own or the army's, soon began to pall on their more thoughtful comrade. Having refused to ac-company them back to the Peninsula when they returned to their regiments, Justin found that life now seemed even more empty after their departure, and in an attempt to keep himself from dying of boredom, had embarked on a course of excess that, while it kept him tolerably amused for the moment, was not likely to do so for long. One could only enrich oneself so much at faro and hazard, break the record for driving to Brighton in a curricle, and dally with so many beautiful women before it all began to seem almost as monotonous as his brother's staid existence.

Fortunately, before he had been forced to seek even more dangerous sport, Justin had crossed paths with Sir Charles Stewart, another choice spirit. Forced to leave the turmoil of the Peninsula, Stewart had been suffering from the boredom of his own enforced inaction and had been charmed to discover that someone else who demonstrated his own reckless disre-gard for life and limb still remained in London. In the course of their budding friendship, it slowly dawned on the dashing peer that his new acquaintance was possessed of a clever mind that was going to waste in the social round of the *ton*. Though not particularly bright himself, Sir Charles had spent enough time in the company of his half brother Castlereagh to recog-nize brilliance in others and to appreciate its value. Thus, he invited Justin to accompany him when he was posted as adviser to the allied sovereigns in Berlin. From there Justin had followed him to Vienna, where in the heady atmosphere of the Congress, he had found his true métier.

The women were beautiful, clever, and willing, and some of the finest minds in all of Europe were competing for stakes that made even as veteran a gamester as St. Clair nervous. He had worked unobtrusively as Stewart's envoy, gathering and dispensing information, and smoothing feathers that his mentor was all too inclined to ruffle.

But at long last the Congress had finished its business, too soon for Justin's tastes and the tastes of several illustrious ladies. Having discovered his flair for things diplomatic and political, he had sought out Castlereagh upon his return to London and had soon made himself as indispensable to the foreign minister as he had to his half brother. In addition to this budding career, he found himself heir to his Great-Uncle Theobald, who had scandalized the entire family by amassing a fortune in trade and speculation and had left it all to the only St. Clair who had had anything to do with him. To honor his benefactor, Justin attempted to manage his inheritance with the same skill by which it had been made. He had found himself highly intrigued by the world of finance, and had plunged into this new area of endeavor with his usual energy. It was not long before he was as well-known around the 'Change as he was in the ballrooms of the Upper Ten Thousand.

"Enough, enough, I'm coming," Justin muttered testily as he splashed some water on his face and allowed Preston to help him into a fantastically embroidered dressing gown. "I suppose I must see him, but do arrange for some breakfast if you will, Preston. A man can't take someone like my brother on an empty stomach."

"Yes, sir, very good, sir." Preston's face remained impassive, but he was very much in agreement with his master. Facing the Earl of Winterbourne did require some fortification, self-important fool that he was. It seemed the greatest shame that Mr. Justin hadn't been born to the title. Now *he* would have brought the right sort of air to it, but Mr. Alfred . . . Preston shook his head. Becoming the Earl of Winterbourne had only increased Master Alfred's self-consequence and had made him more self-centered and overbearing than he had been.

Years of looking after the two boys had given the old retainer a unique perspective and, unlike the rest of the household who had lavished all the attention on the heir, Preston had never had the least use for him. He had preferred the exhausting task of keeping up with the escapades of the younger brother to ministering to the older. While it was true that Alfred had never caused anyone an anxious moment while Justin proceeded from one life-threatening adventure to the next, the younger boy had at least acknowledged his caretaker as a human being. No matter how much trouble the lad might embroil Preston in, he was always aware of its effect on the older man. "I'm most dreadfully sorry, Preston. I didn't mean to put you in a tight spot," he would apologize with his charming grin when he had been doing something he shouldn't—riding his father's favorite hunter, playing with the gypsies camped nearby, or dallying with a local barmaid. And Preston, well aware that his charge's reckless ways sprang more from a wish to enliven a very constrained existence, would forgive him as he accounted yet again for his charge's whereabouts to some disapproving superior.

More and more, the lad, ignored by the rest of the household, had come to rely on Preston for companionship, and thus it was natural that Justin should take him with him when he set up his own establishment, a move Alfred could never comprehend. The earl knew what was owing to his family's consequence, and felt it keenly that his younger brother employed only a manservant instead of a proper butler or, at the very least, an imposing valet.

In fact, Alfred was ushered in with yet another complaint about Preston on his lips. "Really, Justin, I do not know why you do not get yourself a proper butler. Preston is getting quite above his station. Why, he kept me cooling my heels as though I were some common caller."

"No, no, Alfred," his brother soothed, "*I* kept you waiting."

"You?" Lord Winterbourne's already beefy countenance flushed with annoyance.

"Yes. I really can't in good conscience encourage you to call at such an hour. It's dreadfully bad *ton*, you know. Besides, I was a moment waking up. Rousing time last night, you know." Justin grinned reminiscently.

The earl's face was apoplectic. "You mean you were in bed? At this hour?"

Justin's eyes glinted with amusement. "But of course. You wouldn't expect me to be abroad before noon like some greasy country squire would you?"

Alfred was speechless as he thought to himself that really, Justin had only become more infuriating as he had grown older. Here he, Earl of Winterbourne, had taken the trouble to come to town expressly to call on him, and Justin just sat there mocking him in that absurd dressing gown, his lanky frame draped carelessly in the chair. It was beyond all that was annoying. Alfred knew his brother to be possessed of a restless energy that on the rare occasions when he visited the family seat, had him up and out riding almost before the stable boys were awake, yet now he had the effrontery to play the bored man about town. The earl fumed helplessly, then, remembering the original purpose of his visit, gathered himself together with considerable effort.

With a placating laugh, he began, "Well, those of us whose responsibilities keep us in the country are not accustomed to your town hours." Try though he would, the earl could not keep the resentful note from his voice, though actually he would have died rather than change places with his younger brother. The fact was that he quite gloried in those responsibilities, but it would not do to let that on to Justin, who refused to accord such things their proper respect. No, it was all very well for a younger brother to go gallivanting around Europe, flirting with women who were no better than harlots despite their high stations; but he, Alfred, was head of an important family and bore the burden of his hereditary duties with great solemnity. "Well, never mind that," the earl continued. "What I really came for was to discuss a most delicate matter with you."

"Ah yes, the purpose of your visit," Justin murmured. "I was wondering when we would get around to that, it being inconceivable that you should call on me simply for the charm of my company."

"If you're going to talk fustian, Justin, I can see I had best take myself elsewhere," the earl began ponderously.

His younger brother's eyes widened, "Fustian, I?" Then,

recognizing that the earl truly was laboring with some weighty problem, he relented. "What is it, then, Alfred?"

"It's Reginald."

"Reginald? That pattern card of perfection? I thought he was every parent's dream, the model child," Justin replied sardonically. Difficult though it was to believe such a thing, he found the earl's heir more boring than the earl himself.

"He is," Alfred rose swiftly to his son's defense, "and he has done nothing wrong. It's that harpy."

"Harpy?" Justin uncoiled himself and leaned forward. "This sounds interesting. Why, I had no idea that the lad had it in him." He grinned wickedly.

Choosing to ignore this sally, Alfred continued. "Well, it was not his fault. During the holidays, he came to London with some friends from school, the Duke of Bellingrath's son," Alfred could not refrain from adding proudly. "And, like the good lad he is, he very properly called upon his Great-Aunt Seraphina in Brook Street, just as he knew I would wish. It was there that he met *her*."

"Who?" Justin looked blank. "Oh, the harpy. At Great-Aunt Seraphina's? How intriguing. I must become better acquainted with Great-Aunt Seraphina if that's the sort of company she keeps." In fact, Justin only had the dimmest memory of the lady, she being a distant relative of his brother's wife who only recommended herself to the earl by the size of her fortune, her widowhood, and her lack of heirs. It was Alfred who had dubbed her "great-aunt" in the hopes of securing this fortune for his son. Beyond that, all Justin could recall hearing of her was that she was a bluestocking who had married a nabob late in life, none of which fit the lurid picture his brother was now painting.

"I'm glad you find it so amusing," the earl responded stiffly. "You would not if your son were about to throw away his good name on a, on a . . ." Words failed him.

"By that, I conclude you to mean that the fool intends to offer her marriage. Any son of mine would know how to enjoy a little dalliance for what it was."

Too upset to respond to this comment, Alfred nodded glumly.

"But how did such a person make the acquaintance of Great-Aunt Seraphina?" Justin wondered.

"Great-Aunt Seraphina had business to attend to in town, and as she does not keep an establishment in London, she was invited by her niece to stay with her at her house in Brook Street."

"Well, then, how is it that this niece allowed such a harpy near her aunt?" Justin continued patiently.

"You don't understand, it's the great-niece who is the harpy." Alfred was thoroughly exasperated. Really, for someone who had recently been helping to rearrange the map of Europe, Justin could sometimes be singularly obtuse. "She asked Great-Aunt Seraphina to visit simply because she wants to cozen the old lady into leaving her her fortune, and now she puts her hooks into my son as well. I tell you, Justin, it doesn't bear thinking of."

Privately, Justin thought that the infamous niece had a great deal more claim on Great-Aunt Seraphina and her fortune than Reginald did, but he tactfully refrained from saying so, merely asking her name instead.

"It's Lady Diana Hatherill," the earl snapped.

"What, Ferdie Hatherill's sister? That connection seems unexceptionable enough."

"Not his sister, his widow and an older woman," Alfred moaned.

"Well then, she does have need of the fortune. The last time I saw Ferdie, he was going through his at a merry pace," Justin remarked reasonably.

The earl glared at him.

"But I fail to see what all this has to do with me, for I am sure if it didn't, you wouldn't be here. I daresay you'll get around to it eventually. Perhaps we should fortify ourselves with some coffee, as I have the distinct feeling I am about to be asked to do something unpleasant." Justin stretched out a languid hand toward the bellpull and was just giving it a tug, when there was a knock on the door and Preston entered bearing a steaming pot and two cups. "A man past price. You divine my every thought. Thank you, Preston."

"Thank you, sir." Standing between his master and the earl, only Preston was able to see Justin's rueful grimace, and he winked sympathetically before turning to leave.

"Justin! Have you no family feeling? You must extricate

Reginald from this woman's lures," Alfred continued the moment the door was closed.

"Forgive me for appearing slow-witted, Alfred, but I quite fail to see what I have to do with the situation at all. He's *your* son. Simply tell him that you disapprove."

"He won't listen," the unhappy parent groaned.

"What, the peerless Reginald?" Justin could barely conceal a wicked grin. "The lad has more to him than I thought."

"And the lady is dead to all sense of decorum. I offered her a hundred pounds to stop seeing Reginald, and she absolutely refused."

"I should hope so. A hundred pounds compared to Reginald's expectations is paltry indeed. Didn't she press you for more? I should have. Besides, if she is after Reginald, the lad stands a better chance of getting his hands on Great-Aunt Seraphina's fortune." Justin was beginning to enjoy himself.

"Really, Justin, you are the most . . ." The earl was beside himself with exasperation. "This is no laughing matter. No, she did not press for more, but showed me to the door in the rudest way and said that friendship could not be bought, and besides, they are both of age. So you see, she means to have him willy-nilly."

The fact that the lady in question appeared to have the very principles in which Alfred judged her so lacking, only served to amuse Justin all the more. But he merely commented, "Well, then, you had best resign yourself to it. After all, Reginald is his own master, she is connected to a perfectly acceptable family, and though Hatherill ran completely through his inheritance, she must not be completely in dun territory if she is still at the Hatherill's house in Brook Street." Justin refrained from observing that the real cause of Alfred's annoyance was that Reginald's interest in a lady of good but unremarkable antecedents and with only the prospect rather than the certainty of a fortune kept Reginald from making a truly brilliant match. Knowing full well the height of his brother's ambition, Justin did not doubt that Alfred had singled out several dukes' daughters as suitable partners for his son and heir.

"Faugh, that is very likely why she fell all over herself inviting Great-Aunt Seraphina, for Ferdie Hatherill's wife must be well enough versed in the ways of creditors to know they will let her alone if she is expecting an inheritance, especially now that they see she has every hope of leg-shackling Reginald," he concluded gloomily. "I tell you, Justin, only you can save the situation now."

"I rather thought we were coming to that," the earl's brother replied sardonically. "And, pray tell me, how do you propose that I should succeed where you have failed?"

"Damn it, Justin, how do I know?" Alfred leapt from his chair and began to pace the room. "It's you who is supposed to be the diplomat—haring off to Vienna with Metternich and Talleyrand and those fellows. Though, I can't see that all that talking you did was to any purpose. When it came right down to it, it was decent men, men of action like Wellington who put the stop to that monster. Politicians, faugh, why all they are good for . . ." the earl continued, warming to his theme. Then, realizing the infelicitous nature of his remarks, he gave a discreet cough. "Well, all water under the bridge, as they say. What I mean is that I should be most obliged to you, Justin, if you could see the lady . . . ah, er, woman, and try if you can make her see that this is a most unsuitable match."

Justin raised a cynical eyebrow, "And you expect me to be more persuasive than a hundred pounds? You flatter me."

"Not at all." The earl failed entirely to detect the ironic undertone. "Everyone knows you have a way with women. Lord knows why, but they appear to find you irresistible. You might as well put your fatal charm to good use."

"Oh, but I do, brother, I do," Justin assured him smiling broadly as he rose to look dreamily out the window at the beautiful morning.

"There, if that isn't just like you. I knew it was useless to come. You have no family feeling," the earl responded bitterly. He snatched up his hat and made for the door.

His brother held up a restraining hand. "Relax, Alfred. I shall see what I can do. I daresay it will be quite amusing if nothing else. And as to family feeling, I may lack the proper amount of it, but I do owe you a debt of gratitude for having kept me from having to inherit it."

"I daresay." Thoroughly annoyed, but knowing that Justin, once challenged, would do his best despite his irritating manner, the earl bid him good day and hurried back to his hotel, eager to give orders for his immediate departure. Though possessor of an imposing residence in Grosvenor Square, he preferred to let to others for an enormous sum while he remained secure in the comfort of Winterbourne Hall, absolute master of all he surveyed.

Chapter 2

THE next morning, doing his best to continue considering his mission in the light in which he had pictured it to himself, Justin St. Clair was making every effort to feel amused as he raised the brilliantly polished knocker at an elegant residence in Brook Street. He had only a moment to reflect before a venerable butler answered the door, that its owner must not be in such desperate straits, it being one of the largest houses in the neighborhood and in excellent repair.

"Lady Diana Hatherill, please," he responded to that individual's inquiry as to what he might do for him. Justin continued to take mental note of the quality and conditions of the furnishings as he followed the butler to the drawing room. The interior gave as pleasing an appearance as the exterior, proclaiming its mistress to be a person of taste and refinement. The draperies, rugs, and chair coverings showed no signs of wear and were of recent design, confirming his original impression that the staff was large enough to maintain the establishment. If nothing else, he could assure his brother that the lady was not yet at the *point non plus* because staff was always the first thing to go in such cases.

For his part, Finchley, butler to Lady Diana and her father before her, had subjected Lord Justin St. Clair to a scrutiny that was equally as critical, and it was this ancient retainer's considered opinion that this newest caller was a sight better than the lovesick youth who had recently been wearing out his mistress's doorstep. Not that there was anything amiss with Viscount Chalford, he was a nice enough lad, if a trifle serious, but he was a mere boy, not up to Lady Diana's measure by any means. Finchley had already seen his mistress through one disastrous marriage with an overgrown boy. It was time she had someone to look after her instead of the other way around. Ferdie Hatherill had been charming enough to twist anyone around his finger, even the unwilling Finchley, but he had been wild to a fault, and in the end it was this recklessness that had been the cause of his early demise.

He had been more than a trifle disguised when he had challenged young Anthony Washburne to a curricle race over a country lane that would have tested the skills of even a sober driver, and it had not come as a great surprise to the household when his lordship had been brought home on a hurdle. Lady Diana had borne up magnificently. Two years of marriage to Ferdie had taught her to expect anything. What she had not expected was that he would have made such inroads on his considerable fortune in such a short period of time. If it had not been for the house in Brook Street and a meager income derived from renting out the land she had inherited from her father, Lady Diana would have been in a most desperate situation.

This gentleman was more the thing, Finchley thought to himself as he closed the drawing room doors behind him. Well over six feet with broad shoulders and a sportsman's physique, he had an air of distinction that Lord Hatherill, despite the constant and devoted attentions of his tailor and his valet— both geniuses in their own particular domains—could never have hoped to attain. Finchley allowed himself a sigh of satisfaction as he went off in search of his mistress.

Left to himself, Justin continued his inspection of the harpy's abode and was forced to admit that he was pleasantly surprised. Decorated in a soothing shade of gray that called attention to the Adam fireplace and plasterwork delicately traced in white, it was serene and comfortable in the fashion of a previous generation. That the style employed was a result of taste rather than economic necessity was proclaimed by the newness of the upholstery and the draperies. Justin was in complete agreement with its owner, finding the prevailing rage for ormolu, gilt, and fantastic animals as excessive as the prince who had introduced it.

"Hello," a raspy voice greeted him. Justin whirled around in surprise. He had not heard any approaching footsteps, and his senses were acute. His gaze was met by the blank panels of the drawing doors. "Hello!" The voice was more insistent this time. Feeling a complete fool, Justin looked this way and that, with no success. "Hello." A slight motion behind the clock on the mantel caught his attention, and he laughed with relief as a gray bird emerged and made its way around the corner of the clock to perch there, cocking its head and fixing him with a ruminative stare.

"Who are you?" Justin asked without thinking.

"Bonaparte, Bonaparte," the bird chanted as it sidled along the mantel to get a better view of the visitor.

"Well hello, then, Bonaparte," Justin replied.

"Hello?" This time the voice was low and musical with the hint of a question in it.

The door had opened behind him, and Justin, having failed to detect any approaching footsteps, found himself discovered in mid-conversation with a bird—a humiliating situation for anyone, especially one who had come to establish a superior position over the bird's owner.

He turned around with as much dignity as he could muster to face the woman who had entered. She was as lovely as her voice, tall and graceful with hair so dark it was almost black, a small straight nose, delicately sculpted lips, and deep blue eyes under gently arched brows. There was a decided twinkle in these eyes as she took in her visitor's discomfiture.

For her part, Lady Diana was equally impressed. Of sufficient height to make her feel short, St. Clair was a man whose face was as commanding as his physique. It was lean and intelligent with penetrating gray eyes set under heavy dark brows, which more often than not were raised in the ironic contemplation of his fellow creatures' follies. At the moment, though, the ordinarily mocking expression was softened by the sheepish look that, try though he would, Justin was unable to banish completely, and it made him appear younger and more approachable than usual.

Disarmed by this, Diana, who had at first been wary of such an imposing individual, smiled in a friendly fashion. "I see you have made the acquaintance of Bonaparte. He is an African gray parrot, and he insists on introducing himself to all our visitors whether they will or no, do you not, Boney?" She stroked the bird who, now perched on her shoulder, was pecking thoughtfully at one dark strand of hair that had escaped her coiffure and curled enticingly behind her ear. "But, sir, though you have become acquainted with Boney, you have the advantage of me."

Recovering himself in an instant, Justin straightened to his full height announcing, "I am St. Clair."

The lady's expression remained open and friendly, but there was no recognition.

"Viscount Chalford's uncle, you know." Lord, he sounded as pompous as Alfred! Justin fumed. It was too bad of the earl to embroil him in this. After all, the lad was of age. He had every right to entangle himself in any affair that he wished to, though who would have thought Reginald would have such taste, his uncle wondered as he took in the elegant figure revealed under the simple but highly becoming morning dress of striped jaconet. Truly the lady was quite beautiful, and quite wasted on his nephew.

"I see." The blue eyes were wary now, and a hint of reserve had crept into her voice.

"It won't do, you know," he continued in a more conciliatory manner. "His father is quite set against it."

"His father is quite set against *me*, you mean. It's just that he cannot decide which he is more set against, the possibility of my inheriting my aunt Seraphina's fortune away from his son or the possibility of my marrying his heir, neither being an event over which he has any control, Aunt Seraphina being in full possession of her faculties, and Reginald having attained his majority." A distinctly frosty note had crept into her voice.

Her logic was irrefutable, and the more he considered it, the more Justin resented being thrust into the awkward situation in which he found himself. Damn Alfred! "Nevertheless, it is most uncomfortable to be in the position of upsetting one's future relations, whatever their reservations," Justin continued in what he hoped was a reasonable tone.

Diana was seething. What right did this arrogant gentleman have to invade her drawing room and dictate her life to her—not that she had the least intention of marrying Reginald, a dear boy, but wet behind the ears and so slavishly devoted to her that it made her uncomfortable? What right did he have to stand there looking at her as though she were no more than a bug on the carpet, when all she had done was take pity on his awkward young nephew and befriend him. First there had been the Earl of Winterbourne—pompous fool and selfish to boot—and now this St. Clair person looking her up and down with a detachment so cool that it verged on the disdainful. The indignity of it all made Diana want to throttle her visitor. Instead, clasping her hands tightly together in front of her, she smiled sweetly. "But, you see, I don't mind upsetting my future relations at all, as I dislike you all quite as much as you dislike me. So, in fact, I should find it awkward indeed if you choose to welcome me into the family, for I don't think I wish to have anything to do with such a grasping selfish bunch as you appear to be."

The devil! If he had not been so infuriated at being relegated to the stuffy ranks of Alfred and the family, Justin would have been highly diverted by someone who had so deftly outmaneuvered him. The lady had spirit, there was no doubt about that, but if she thought she could get the best of Justin St. Clair, she was fair and far-off.

Before he could muster up a suitably stinging rejoinder, Diana had rung for the butler, adding serenely, "And now that we have made our positions clear to one another, I see no reason to prolong this discussion. I bid you good day, sir." Still wearing that sweetly superior smile, she swept from the room, Bonaparte still clinging to her shoulder, and leaving her caller rigid with pent-up frustration. There was nothing for it but to depart with as good grace as he could muster. "I shall be back, Lady Diana," Justin growled to himself. "And next time we shall see who is the victor. You may have won the battle, but you have certainly not won the war. I will be damned if I allow some chit to best me when the likes of Talleyrand and Metternich have failed."

With that, he mounted his horse and trotted off down Brook Street. Lady Diana Hatherill might have had the feckless Ferdie under the cat's foot—obviously the hapless Reginald was in her thrall—and she had even sent Alfred to the right about, but she had yet to discover what it was to lock horns with a worthy opponent. Such dealings had left her with a false sense of security, and it was high time someone taught her a lesson. It was not that she was so superior, merely that she had been dealing with men all of whom were notably lacking in character and resolution.

Justin smiled grimly to himself as he headed toward the park. Life had just become interesting again, and he relished the thought of the next encounter. No doubt Lady Diana thought that she had seen the last of Justin St. Clair. She couldn't have been more wrong. Her dealings with him were only just beginning, for there was nothing Justin liked more than a challenge, and the cleverer, the more determined the adversary, the better he liked it. The fact that he had been bested in the first round only served to spur him on. By the time Justin had reached the park, he had quite forgotten that he had originally undertaken the errand at his brother's behest, and unwillingly at that. He now had a personal stake in the affair, which made his nephew's and his brother's roles in it immaterial. He began to plot his next move as he skillfully maneuvered his horse among the press of carriages and riders, all taking advantage of the fineness of the day after weeks of inclement weather.

Chapter 3

WHILE Justin was relieving some of his spleen with a ride through the park spent conjuring up visions of future contretemps from which he would emerge incontrovertibly victorious, the other disputant had marched upstairs and was now pacing furiously around her boudoir muttering angrily to herself. "The arrogance of it all! Coming to persuade me to release Reginald as though I were going to ruin him. Ruin him, I don't even *want* their precious Reginald! Oh, if I were a man, I should have called him out. Insufferable, arrogant man!"

"Insufferable, arrogant man!" Boney agreed, happily tweaking her ear.

"Well, you saw how he was, staring down his haughty nose at me, as though I were the veriest trollop. It was beyond all bearing! It would serve them right if I were to agree to all Reginald's protestations of undying affection and run off with him." Diana took another turn around the room.

"Run off with whom, dear?" a gentle voice inquired from behind her.

"Reginald, the puppy!" Diana fumed as she looked up to see her great-aunt standing in the doorway.

"I can't think that would be a very good idea, my love. Then you would be forever saddled with him, and though he is a very sweet boy, I don't think he has a great deal of dash, poor lad. Takes after his father," Seraphina sighed sinking into a comfortable-looking *bergère* by the fire. "I beg your pardon for intruding, but I did knock, though I don't expect you heard me."

"No, I'm sorry, Aunt Seraphina." Diana laughed ruefully. "I was far too busy thinking of what I should like to do to that insolent, interfering, intolerable . . ." Diana was forced to pause for breath.

"Who, dear?" Seraphina was highly intrigued. She couldn't remember a time when she had seen her great-niece so upset— not when her father had died and certainly not when that good-for-nothing husband of hers had stuck his spoon in the wall.

"The Lord Justin St. Clair," Diana hissed. "He had the effrontery to call on me and tell me in no uncertain terms that it 'would not do.' " Diana's voice dripped pure scorn.

"What would not do?" Seraphina was bewildered. She had left her great-niece not long ago happily perusing the *Times*, and had returned to find her beside herself with rage. It was quite unlike her. As far back as Seraphina could remember, Diana had been a self-possessed little thing, largely owing to the vagaries of her absentminded father.

Geoffrey, Marquess of Buckland, had been an affectionate parent whenever he stopped to remember his little daughter, but for the better part of his life, his mind had been elsewhere—strolling the streets of ancient Athens with its most enlightened citizens, and reveling in all the glory that was ancient Greece. If he emerged from his books at all, it was to partake of some meal that his daughter insisted that he eat. Bucklands had been masters of their particular corner of Surrey since the days of the Conqueror, and it was only for the sake of the line that Geoffrey had married the daughter of Sir Hugh Fitzwilliam, successor to an equally ancient and distinguished lineage. But his heart had not been in it, and he had hardly noticed when his young wife had been carried off by an inflammation of the lungs, leaving him alone with a child of two.

Since that moment, Lady Diana had been in the nominal care of a series of nurses. However, being possessed of an independent nature, and having learned to take care of herself at an early age, she had, to all intents and purposes, raised herself. The one aspect of his daughter's life in which the marquess had interested himself, classicist that he was, had been her education.

He had hired the local vicar, a scholar of some stature himself, to give his Lady Diana her lessons. Not infrequently, the marquess would wander in during these, and the lessons would degenerate into a lively discussion of Sophocles and Epictetus.

Diana would sit wide-eyed, listening and trying to absorb as best she could all that they were saying. As she was eager to learn and a quick pupil, it was not very many years before she was beginning to make some sense of these digressions. Gradually she had come to be included, as the vicar, recognizing the quality of his student's mind, began to address remarks to her from time to time.

Diana had been allowed free access to her father's excellent library, and as she had little else to do—her father not having much social intercourse with the rest of the neighborhood— she had spent much of her days there reading and exploring whatever had happened to catch her interest.

Slowly it was borne in on the marquess that he had raised himself an excellent companion, and from the time that Diana was sixteen, he began to notice his daughter and—and as much as a man of his reclusive habits could do—took pleasure in her company. Also at that point, he made another surprising discovery: that his daughter had learned to run his household without the least bit of help from him and had been the nominal head of Buckland for some time.

The few servants who took care of Buckland for their erratic master had felt sorry for the lonely little girl and often invited her to sit and talk while they completed their tasks. By the time Lady Diana's father began to recognize her as a presence, she had gained considerable knowledge as to the functioning of Buckland. She had learned household management from Cook and the housekeeper, Mrs. Tottington. From Mr. Tottington, who was the butler, the steward, and the general factotum, she had picked up everything else in the administration of the estate, which, according to him, was not all that it should be; but without the interest of the master, his hands were tied.

Gradually, the young lady of the house began to discover that ancient as her title was and comfortable as the manor could be in its own shabby way, Lady Diana's inheritance was less than one might expect from such a place as Buckland. The fields had run fallow as the marquess was not interested in farming them or paying others to do so. He was such an indifferent landlord, that the rents he could charge the tenants in the few cottages on the estate were minimum. "For to put it to you straight, my lady," Tottington had been forced to admit one day, "he is generating precious little income, and has spent most of what was left to him by his father on building that library of his."

Diana had promised to do what she could to improve things. She had gotten her father to spend some of his remaining inheritance on repairs to the cottages, but it had been too little too late. The marquess, emerging for once from his perpetually abstracted state, had taken stock of his affairs and realized that unless he were to do something, and do it soon—even though his estate was not entailed—his daughter would be left with nothing except the rapidly decaying manor and some untilled fields.

Casting about for a solution, he had determined that he should marry her to someone who could provide for her. That decided, he suddenly began to take an interest in local affairs. Much to his neighbors' surprise, he was soon often seen in the village or attending church with his daughter—both locales where he had been only the rarest of visitors.

The marquess had dimly remembered from days gone by that Lord Hatherill had had a son just a little before Diana was born. Inquiries revealed that the Viscount Hatherill was still unmarried, and further investigation proved that his widowed mother was hoping that he could be made to offer for someone who could act as a settling influence on him.

Armed with this information, the marquess called on the Hatherills, who had been delighted by his proposition. Even Ferdie himself was taken with the idea. A good-natured, but feckless youth, he was uneasily aware that his duty lay in choosing a wife and providing a Hatherill heir, especially now that his father was gone. Such a course of action seemed a most uncomfortable fate to one who spent his days drifting pleasantly from one sporting event to another and his evenings at the gambling table. He had known however, that sooner or later his mother would make it impossible to avoid the inevitable marriage issue. So he was rather pleased that she had selected someone as comfortable as Diana, a girl he had known all his life, and someone so accustomed to a quiet existence in the country that she was unlikely to demand that he take her to town.

Nor had Diana objected. She had always liked Ferdie, for who could not enjoy being around a person so determined to take pleasure from life? If he did not possess the intelligence of the Marquess of Buckland, he was at least better acquainted with worldly affairs. Diana had never had any friends other than her father, and certainly Ferdie, amiable fellow that he was, paid more attention to her than her abstracted parent ever had. Completely unaware of the existence of such things as novels from the circulating library, she had never cherished any hopes of falling in love. The hope of added companionship and the freedom from financial worry that life with Ferdie would bring offered a pleasant change from her lonely existence at Buckland.

At first, Diana had enjoyed herself thoroughly. She quite delighted in having Ferdie's mother and younger sister to talk to, so much that Ferdie's frequent absences in town or at race meetings did not distress her, while the prospect of waking up every morning in a place where everything was not crying out for repair was delightful.

Diana would have been more than content to spend her days in the country, but her mother-in-law would not hear of it. Within six months of her marriage, the young viscountess was being introduced to the *ton*, which, confronted with an attractive newcomer who was already married and thus posed no threat to eligible bachelors or matchmaking mamas, welcomed her graciously.

For her part, Diana was less impressed with the Upper Ten Thousand then they were with her. After a life spent pursuing her own interests, she found much of the fashionable routine both constricting and dull. One ball or rout was so very much like another, and the latest *on-dit* so very similar to the last. But she kept these opinions to herself so well that no one could ever have suspected her of harboring such seditious thoughts.

Besides, there were definite compensations for having left the country. She attended the theater and the opera so frequently that Ferdie was heard to complain in his good-natured way, "Don't see what there is to like in a bunch of fellows standing onstage screaming their heads off. You won't catch me listening to it, but if it pleases you, go all you like."

In fact, Ferdie had been pleasantly surprised at his biddable bride. She was less demanding than his mother, and could always be counted upon to make excuses for him if a riotous evening left him a bit under the weather the next day. She was a taking thing and well liked by everyone, a fact which he could see had elevated his consequence even among his sporting friends. All in all, it was quite agreeable to have someone watching out for one and making sure that life was comfortable as Diana did. His mother always made him feel guiltily aware of his shortcomings—a tendency to play deep and to bet on anything and everything—but his wife never did, nor did she ever hint in the slightest way that she would have appreciated more than the occasional escort he offered her to some of the *ton* functions. All in all, Ferdie couldn't remember when life had been so pleasant. If only he could hit a winning streak to pay back some of the money he owed, but he felt certain that his luck was bound to change sooner or later.

On her side, Diana, though not as pleased as Ferdie, was well satisfied. Having looked after one helpless male for most of her life, she moved easily into taking care of another. He was far more companionable than her father, whom she now saw so rarely that when he succumbed to pleurisy a year after Diana's marriage, she hardly knew he was gone. And in many ways attending to Ferdie was much easier. He was like an overgrown child. If he arrived home in his cups singing at the top of his lungs and weaving from one solid object to another, he was invariably smilingly apologetic. If he had a disastrous evening at the gaming tables, he was always blithely certain he would recoup his losses.

As time went on, Ferdie actually began to enjoy taking his wife to some of the routs and ridottos that were such a necessary part of any fashionable gentleman's existence, and Diana always took pleasure in his escort, for he was such genial company

However, increasingly his customary exuberance had begun to fall away, and a worried frown was often seen to flit across the viscount's jovial countenance. "Nothing, 'tis nothing," he would always disclaim quickly when taxed with this unusual state of affairs, but a hunted look had begun to lurk at the back of his eyes that Diana could not fathom until several days after his groom had brought his master's body home.

Ferdie, in a desperate attempt to keep up his spirits and improve his fortunes had challenged his closest crony, Anthony Washborne, to a curricle race, betting a hundred pounds that he would make it to Brighton before his friend did. A stray

dog had blighted all his hopes and turned Diana into a widow
by ambling into the road as Ferdie came around a particularly
sharp corner at a slapping pace.

Once again, Diana had discovered, as she had when examining accounts at Buckland, that she was left with nothing so
much as a pile of debts. She had been aghast. How could
somebody have lost so much money in so little time—especially someone like Ferdie, who never seemed to put that
much effort into anything? Even his mother, more conversant
with her son's ruinous tendencies, had been appalled.

The disastrous state of Ferdie's fiscal affairs was left to the
new heir, a distant cousin, to sort out and to try to recoup the
estate's finances—which, Diana, already left with Buckland
and all its attendant headaches, handed over to him with relief.
The new viscount, a sober pleasant man, was more distressed
to think of the entail depriving the dowager viscountess and
her daughter-in-law of a home, but Ferdie's mother had been
only too happy to go live with her newly married daughter,
while Diana had withdrawn contentedly enough to the house
on Brook Street, which Ferdie, with uncharacteristic forethought, had left to her. As it was one of the few possessions
untouched by creditors, Diana was able to take up residence
quietly and comfortably while renting out the fields at Buckland to a local farmer in an effort to recover some of the estate's losses over the years.

Only the question of companionship remained, for it was
unthinkable that a young widow should remain all by herself
in London, regardless of the fact that to all intents and purposes, she had lived virtually alone all her life.

With the exception of Boney, who had been a constant companion since he had been sent as a twelfth birthday present by
Aunt Seraphina, Diana had often gone for days with nothing
more than desultory intercourse with the servants, while her
father had immured himself in the library. She had become accustomed to solitude and since coming to town, had discovered that much of the social interaction she had missed was
merely vapid conversation and empty-headed gossip.

The task now was to find someone who would satisfy the
dictates of society without threatening Diana's sanity or independence. It had actually been Boney who solved the problem,
for one morning as Diana, gazing blankly out the window, had

wondered out loud what to do, he had flown over, perched on her shoulder, and begun nibbling her ear. His mistress had stroked him absentmindedly. "Yes, Boney, you have been a good and faithful friend since Aunt Seraphina sent you, but somehow I do not think you would satisfy the *ton's* idea of suitable companionship. Good heavens, Aunt Seraphina!" And with this happy thought, Diana had rushed to her escritoire and penned an invitation to her father's one remaining relative.

That lady's reply had been gratifyingly swift in arriving. She would be enchanted to come, she wrote. Since her dear Thomas's death, she quite lacked for any intelligent conversation and felt certain that her powers of rational discourse were deteriorating rapidly. This was a most delightful opportunity to put a stop to their further decline, and she looked forward to seeing her great-niece, who, she trusted, had changed since she had last seen her ten years ago.

In what seemed no time at all, Lady Thomas Walden's elegant traveling carriage had pulled up in front of the house in Brook Street, and a tall, woman, still handsome despite her gray hair and her advanced years, alighted to walk briskly up the steps where Finchley was holding open the door for her.

Chapter 4

GREETING her aunt in the drawing room, Diana reflected that she had changed very little since they had last seen each other. The dark eyes still sparkled with penetrating intelligence softened by a gleam of humor. In her youth the long straight nose, determined chin, and prominent cheekbones had robbed her of any pretense to beauty, but now they lent character. Hers was a distinguished face, and one that radiated vitality and interest in the world around her. It was not difficult to see why she had been the scholarly Marquess of Buckland's favorite relation. And he had been hers.

Unappreciated in a household of a father who had longed for a boy and a mother who had wished equally for a dainty feminine daughter, Seraphina had been neither, and as such, largely ignored. The only person who had paid her any attention at all had been a local squire's son, Thomas Walden, with whom she had played and ridden in the forests near her home.

Blessed with a bright inquiring mind and a keen understanding, Thomas had felt as out of place in his family as she did in hers, for the squire, a bluff genial man, had no patience with books or learning and did his best to discourage his son from indulging in such wasteful pursuits.

Fortunately Seraphina's father possessed a remarkably fine library, untouched since his father had died. Unbeknownst to adults on both sides, the two had indulged their passion for knowledge to the top of their bent. And it was only natural that such close companions should develop a deep affection for each other that, when it finally came to their notice, shocked and alarmed both families. Thomas was instantly packed off to India, and Seraphina was dragged to London for a disastrous Season.

It was while in London that she had met the head of the

family, her cousin, the Marquess of Buckland, who was as uncomfortable in the ballrooms of the *ton* as she was. Forced by his mother to abandon his books and take his proper place in society, the young marquess had been miserable and had soon discovered in Seraphina an ally and a kindred spirit.

When at long last they had both returned rejoicing to their respective homes in the country, the cousins had remained regular correspondents, sharing ideas and recommending books to each other. It was the marquess who, spineless in the face of his mother's determination, supported Seraphina in her continuing attachment to the absent Thomas. Soon after his grateful return to the country and his books, the marquess had succumbed to his mother's dying wish and married the younger daughter of a local family of ancient and illustrious lineage. Marianne, the new Marchioness of Buckland, was a sweet girl, but they had had little in common, and Seraphina continued to be the recipient of the marquess's deeper thoughts and interests.

Their friendship by correspondence lessened only with the triumphant return of Thomas Walden, now Sir Thomas, fabulously wealthy and a man with powerful influence in the city. This time Seraphina had turned the tables, ignoring her parents as energetically as they had ignored her, and run off with her childhood friend.

They had been enormously content together, a happiness diminished only slightly by the lack of children. The advent of Lady Diana had been an event of great interest to Seraphina, and, busy as she was with her husband's active life and her own charitable projects, Lady Walden had kept up with the little girl's progress. She had shown such an interest in her that they had become more like aunt and niece rather than second cousins, and had addressed each other accordingly.

Under no illusions as to her cousin's reclusive nature, Seraphina had done her best to see that her great-niece had some source of affection and interest, even if it were hampered by distance and infrequent visits. For her part, Diana was forever grateful for the marvelous toys and, later on, letters and books that had been showered on her. Any package that arrived from Aunt Seraphina was certain to be intriguing. And on the rare occasions when the Waldens did visit, she had reveled in the interest of the rather forbidding-looking lady and her jovial husband.

As Sir Thomas's vast business interests had increased, the couple had traveled more and more. Their letters and visits became less frequent, though none the less warm, and Diana had always felt the love and support they conveyed no matter what part of the globe they arrived from.

Sir Thomas's death and Diana's marriage, occurring at roughly the same time, had focused both ladies' attentions elsewhere, but now on this fine spring morning, they found themselves gazing at each other again with mutual satisfaction.

For her part, Seraphina was no less pleased with her niece than Diana was with her. The promise of beauty last seen in the ten-year-old girl had been fulfilled, and Seraphina was highly gratified to discover that it had also been accompanied by an equal development of character and intelligence. For behind the deep blue eyes, which sparkled with curiosity, there was obviously an active mind that added to a charming manner. Lady Diana welcomed her aunt joyfully, recognizing at a glance that the arrangement that had begun as an accommodation to propriety was going to enrich her life and provide her with the human companionship she had never had.

Diana's first impression had proven correct, and as the days sped by, each of them discovered more and more to like and admire in the other. They read together, discussed their views endlessly, haunted museums and historic monuments, and made up for the many lost hours of youth each of them had spent buried in the country.

As time wore on, Diana came to rely on the older woman not only for friendship, but for advice. Sir Thomas had left everything, including his business interests, to his wife. Aunt Seraphina appeared, to Diana at least, to be managing it all with ease and a good deal of success—if the respectful looks on the faces of men from the city who occasionally called on her were any indication.

Diana was intrigued. Heretofore, she had only been familiar with one means of gaining a livelihood—through the land— and her experience with that had been by default, her father only serving as an example of how not to conduct such an endeavor.

Cautiously at first, Diana had posed an occasional question concerning her aunt's affairs. Aunt Seraphina, delighted by the genuine curiosity and interest behind these delicate inquiries, was more than happy to explain and expand on her activities, while her niece was astonished to learn that by spending money, carefully of course, one could make more money. Soon she began to read beyond the political news, recorded in the flood of papers and reviews that appeared in Brook Street, to the prices of shares and consols and the general tide in the economic interests of the nation.

For her part, Aunt Seraphina was highly gratified by her niece's increasing enthusiasm. Knowing how poor a man of affairs the marquess had been, she had a fair idea of the dire financial straits in which he had left his daughter, and the few comments that Diana had inadvertently let fall had given her shrewd companion an accurate picture of Diana's precarious economic situation. Lady Walden wanted desperately to help the girl, but knowing Diana's proud and independent spirit, she had been at a loss as to how to go about it, until one early morning discussion of Lady Walden's business with the stock exchange had revealed her niece's eagerness to learn more about what many considered to be a highly speculative, disreputable, and even diabolical way of improving one's finances.

Now her path was clear to Seraphina. If Diana would not accept outright gifts of money, she was more than willing to accept advice, and Seraphina had set about teaching her all she knew. Diana was a quick and keen pupil, and in no time at all had mastered her lessons well enough to accompany her aunt in one of her discreet visits to the Stock Exchange. There Diana had purchased her own shares in the consols, which had then risen in a most satisfactory fashion while still paying out at three percent. This was all the more gratifying, as agricultural prices, which heretofore had been her only source of income, had fallen wretchedly.

Thus rewarded for her first tentative efforts, the young widow had plunged herself earnestly into study of the finer points of finance, intent on recouping her fortunes and restoring Buckland to its former state of elegance. Soon, Lady Diana

Hatherill's heavily veiled figure became as well-known in the 'Change as was Lady Walden's, and her growing acuity almost as respected by the hardheaded men of affairs, who flourished there, as Lady Walden's.

Chapter 5

"WHAT would not do," Aunt Seraphina reiterated, abruptly emerging from her reverie as Diana began furiously pacing the floor, Boney clinging to her shoulder for dear life as she made ever increasing turns about the room.

"*I* would not do," Diana muttered savagely. "*I* would not do for the Earl of Winterbourne's precious son and heir, as though the Bucklands hadn't been landholders centuries before those mushrooms began their toadying rise to the top. There is nothing I have to apologize for in *my* lineage." She halted her angry perambulations long enough to glare fiercely at her reflection in the looking glass.

"No," her aunt agreed, "but then, you do not set any store by such things in the first place," she continued mildly, her eyes twinkling.

"No I do not." Her niece sighed ruefully as she sank into a chair. "And if that . . .that man hadn't put me in such a passion, I shouldn't even have thought of it. It's just that it's so unfair. I don't even *want* Reginald, but he *will* keep coming around. He is always so eager that denying oneself to him is rather like kicking a hopeful puppy. And after all, he is a good lad, if a trifle prosy, and a perfectly unexceptionable escort for two such widow ladies as ourselves. But it could never be claimed that he is the world's most stimulating companion. He does his best, poor boy, and it is entirely to his credit that he pursues his studies so assiduously. He is just not what one would call a formidable intellect. However, at the very least, he has more to contribute to a conversation than the cut of his coat or the way he ties his cravat. Now to be informed that I am bringing about his ruination . . . Oh, it is beyond all bearing!" Diana leapt up and began pacing again.

"Never say so, my dear!" her aunt gasped. "No wonder you

are in such a rare taking. St. Clair had the audacity to say that to you?"

"Well, not in so many words," her niece admitted cautiously. "But that is the meaning he wished to convey, all the same. I shall show him. I am not made of such poor stuff as that. Lord Justin St. Clair will see that Lady Diana Hatherill is not to be trifled with." Diana's chin had a stubborn tilt to it, and the blue eyes glinted dangerously.

"Oh? And precisely how do you propose to correct the mistaken perceptions of that gentleman?" Seraphina wondered. Having witnessed firsthand the energy with which Diana had thrown herself into recovering her fortunes, she felt certain that her niece was already formulating a plan to deal summarily with the interfering St. Clair. She would certainly be a formidable opponent. Lady Walden had not been long on the town, nor was she a dealer in the latest *on-dits*, but even she was aware of Justin St. Clair's reputation where women were concerned. It was said that there was hardly a lady at the Congress of Vienna who had not succumbed to his charms, and it was even rumored that he had been a frequent visitor at the Palm Palace, using both the staircase leading to the apartments of Princess Bagration and the staircase leading to those of the Duchess of Sagan in the house that these two renowned beauties had been forced to share so unwillingly.

It seemed, however, that perhaps for the first time in his life, he was about to encounter some resistance from the fairer sex. And Lady Diana Hatherill was the one to do it. Seraphina had spent enough time as a guest in Brook Street to appreciate the rare qualities her niece possessed: a keen mind, boundless energy, and a resolution not often seen in most men.

In general Diana was the kindest of friends, with a delicious sense of humor and a ready and active sympathy for those around her, be they servants, scholars, society's starchiest matrons, or parrots. Even the irascible Boney adored her, though he certainly had little enough patience with anyone else. But when her niece's wrath was aroused, usually over some injustice—a mistreated horse, the desperate plight of climbing boys, the inadequacy of the poor rates—she was unrelenting and tireless in her efforts to remedy the situation. Well, Lady Diana was more exercised than her aunt had ever seen her, and this lady silently begging her niece's pardon for extracting amusement from her discomfort, eagerly awaited further developments.

At the moment, however, the only development to appear was in the form of Finchley, who knocked on the door to inform his mistress that the cause of all her exasperation was eagerly awaiting her presence below.

"Oh, dear," Diana sighed, "I suppose you told Viscount Chalford that I was at home."

Finchley nodded apologetically. He had nothing against Lord Chalford, a nice enough young man, but anyone could see that his adoration and his constant attentions to Lady Diana were a drain on her. Finchley knew his mistress to be kindhearted to a fault, and she often suffered because of it. She was a busy lady with two households to run and her own interests to pursue. His young lordship, though he participated in some of those interests, had nothing particular of his own to contribute. As far as the butler could see, Lady Diana, always awake on all suits, was way ahead of Reginald. In Finchley's opinion, it was high time that someone else took care of his mistress. From all that he had seen and heard, she had spent her entire life looking after the men around her, and she did not need another such a one.

"Well, then I'd best see him." Diana sighed again, stealing a glance in the looking glass to restore the curl that Boney had pulled out of place, then, a resigned look on her face, she followed the butler to the drawing room.

Watching her niece's retreating back, Lady Walden echoed her sigh. How she wished Diana would find a partner worthy of her, but if she had declared it once, her niece had declared it a thousand times, "No, dear aunt, I intend never to marry again. I have had my fill of looking out after men—such helpless creatures as they are. It is time I looked after myself."

When Seraphina had ventured to suggest that perhaps Diana had had the ill luck to be encumbered with two rather poor examples of the male sex, her niece had merely raised an incredulous eyebrow and returned without comment to whatever was occupying her attention.

And Seraphina was forced to agree that Diana's latest and most frequent admirer seemed not to offer a great deal more than the other men in her life. Though far more responsible than either the Marquess of Buckland or Ferdie Hatherill, and far more attentive to Diana, Reginald had only a particle of her character. To be fair, though, one had to admit that he had shown some resolve in patently ignoring the wishes of his parent. Seraphina cocked her head ruminating—perhaps over time? No, it would not do. The Viscount Chalford would never be equal to Diana.

The older woman frowned. It was high time she took a hand in things. Diana must be made to go out and about where she could be appreciated. Whenever the two of them made one of their rare appearances, the young widow never lacked for admiring glances, and Ferdie's friends were quick to seek her out. She was charming, clever, and quite ravishing really, though not in the usual way. Her nose was straight rather than fashionably retroussé. Her lips were beautifully sculpted rather than kissable, and she was witty where most of her contemporaries were flirtatious, but there was an air about her which captured the attention and interest of everyone—men and women, young and old. The quality of her mind and conversation fulfilled the promise of her elegant appearance—a condition that was all too rare in the fashionable world of the *ton*.

Seraphina shook herself briskly and reached for the paper her niece had discarded so abruptly. She turned to the theater announcements and noted with satisfaction the performance of *La Clemenza di Tito*. Diana was fond of Mozart, and this seemed a likely inducement to bring her out into the world. Knowing the viscount's predilection for more serious entertainment, especially if Diana were involved, her aunt felt certain they could count on his escort. Though it seemed a trifle churlish to take advantage of the lad, it behooved them to have an eligible man in attendance. Seraphina had seen enough of society to know that males were far more likely to pay attention to a woman in whom one man already demonstrated interest than if the woman were alone—men being such creatures of habit. Her dearest Thomas was a notable exception, of course. Lord, how she missed him. Gathering her skirts, Lady Walden prepared to make her way downstairs and relieve her niece of the tête-à-tête that she had gone to with such reluctance.

Meanwhile, in the drawing room, Diana was trying to show her appreciation of her visitor's latest offering in a way least likely to encourage the viscount. Reginald was a sweet boy, but she did wish he would stop staring at her as though she were a goddess. Truly, it was most tiresome having someone hanging on one's every word as though one were an oracle. "How thoughtful of you to bring me the new edition of *Alcest*. I am not as familiar with it as I am with Euripides' other works, but this looks to be a most complete edition," Diana thanked him, eyeing the eight leather-bound volumes with some misgiving.

"I do hope you like them," her caller responded eagerly. "I was worried lest they appear too frivolous to someone of your serious tone of mind, but it was either that or *Ovidii Opera Omnia*, which I felt certain you already possess."

Recalling the plethora of Ovid's works in multiple editions of multiple works cramming the bookshelves in the library at Buckland, Diana nodded gratefully. But when on earth was she to have the time to do justice to this latest gift? Glancing at the viscount's hopeful countenance, she suppressed a sigh. He did try so very hard to please that she loathed herself for the creeping boredom she felt setting in whenever she was in his company. Then, remembering her earlier interview with his uncle, Diana quickly forgot his dullness, banished as it was by a fresh spurt of indignation at the high-handed ways of Justin St. Clair. It would not do, a hateful voice echoed in her head. No, it most certainly would *not* do. She, Diana would be dead of boredom in a fortnight if forced to spend it in Reginald's company, but there was no need for anyone else to know that.

Summoning up a brilliant smile, she continued, "How clever of you to divine that. Yes, Papa was a great admirer of Ovid, and thus he is disproportionately represented in our collection."

Reginald blushed with pleasure. "How fortunate you were to have a parent who understood your interests," he remarked wistfully. Then, realizing the heresy his statement implied, he hastened to defend the Earl of Winterbourne. "Father is all that is excellent, and I could never respect him enough. It is just that he has so many responsibilities that he has no time for such things."

And no patience either, I'll warrant, Diana thought to herself as she conjured up the sanctimonious expression of the earl's face as, forcing himself to look at her, he had offered her one hundred pounds to free his son from her *grasping toils*.

She did feel sorry for the viscount. He was an estimable young man who was clearly in complete awe of his father—desperate for his approval on one hand and yet longing for something more than the pedestrian existence that the earl so obviously expected of him.

At the moment, Reginald's pleasant though unremarkable countenance had a touch of pathos about it. Diana sympathized, but at the same time she wanted to shake him, to put a spark of defiance in the mild blue eyes or some determination in the cherubic features. Inadvertently, the harsh angles of St. Clair's swarthy face came to mind to be quickly banished. "My father merely made certain that my interests coincided with his," she responded dryly. "Come, don't repine. Parents never understand their children, after all. It is the way of the world."

The viscount brightened. "Is it? Naturally I am glad that Father is so occupied with important matters, but I wish we shared more. You always see things so clearly, Lady Diana. I wish I had your perspicacity. I can't tell you how enlightening I find our every conversation."

Before Diana could think of a way to cut short these encomiums, the door opened and Aunt Seraphina burst in clutching the *Times.* "You see, Diana, I was sure I had heard they were presenting *La Clemenza di Tito*. Oh!" Catching sight of the viscount, she executed an admirable start that did not fool her niece in the least. "I do beg your pardon. I did not know you had a visitor."

"*La Clemenza di Tito?* I would be most honored if you ladies would allow me the pleasure of escorting you." Reginald grabbed the proffered bait with alacrity.

"I, well . . ." Diana began helplessly.

"Thank you. You are most kind," her aunt accepted briskly.

"Most kind, most kind," Boney echoed groggily. The minute he had discovered the identity of his mistress's visitor, he had promptly fallen asleep on her shoulder; but with the entrance of the more stimulating Lady Walden, he had awakened and was lazily surveying the proceedings out of one eye.

"I shall look forward to it. I cannot think why the idea had not occurred before, as I knew Lady Diana to be as interested in the arts as she is in literature. I am most grateful to you

Great Aunt Seraphina . . ." Boney promptly put his head under his wing and went back to sleep.

"Very good, then. We shall see you tomorrow evening, but you must excuse me, the post has just arrived and I must consult with Diana about something."

"Yes, yes, of course. I only wished to deliver this parcel to Lady Diana, but I must be on my way. Until tomorrow." The viscount emerged abruptly from his rapt contemplation of an entire evening spent at his adored one's side and grabbed for his hat, worried lest he had overstayed his welcome or that the length of his visit had extended beyond the bounds of propriety. "Good-bye. I look forward to escorting you," he reiterated as he hurried out the door leaving Diana to stare suspiciously at her relative.

"Well, I had to do something. I could see you and Boney were like to perish of boredom," Aunt Seraphina defended herself.

"After consigning me to an entire evening in his company." Her niece was not to be mollified.

"Pooh! You know you will enjoy the opera, and he won't dare interrupt your intense concentration," her aunt replied not the least abashed.

Diana laughed. "You are a dreadful conniver, Aunt Seraphina. No wonder the men of the city quake in their boots when you enter their domain."

Seraphina chuckled ruefully. "Now that my poor Thomas is gone, I am afraid I do rather manage everyone who comes in my path."

Chapter 6

LADY Diana was not the only one suffering the afflic-
tion of managing relatives. The very next day after his
visit to the "harpy," Justin was enduring yet another visit from
his brother. Though it had only been two days since their conversation, Alfred, unable to wait any longer, had called on his
brother at an hour only slightly more fashionable than that of
his first visit. Close on the heels of Preston, he burst into the
room demanding, "Well? Have you seen her? What did she
say?"

"Alfred, what a surprise. I had thought you so eager to be
off to the country." Justin, just back from an invigorating ride
in the park, glanced idly through the morning post before turning to greet his brother.

Still puffing from his hurried climb up the stairs, the earl reiterated impatiently, "Well? What do you think?"

His brother cocked his head speculatively. "What do I
think?" he paused ruminating, "I think brown is unbecoming
to a man of your complexion, Alfred. You would do better to
wear dark blue or green."

"Damn it, Justin, you are the most exasperating . . ."

"I know. I apologize, but the temptation was irresistible,
you know." The gray eyes glinted with amusement. "You
asked what the . . . er . . . harpy said. To put it bluntly, she
doesn't give a rap whether the family approves or not. Says
she and Reginald are both of age, and as she doesn't care for
his relations above half, she prefers it that she is not acceptable
to them."

"But, but . . ." the earl was speechless with the effrontery of
it all. Not wish to be honored by the Earl of Winterbourne?
The idea of such a thing was impossible to grasp. "But she

cannot! To risk being unacknowledged by the Earl of Winter-bourne? She must be mad!"

His brother's amusement deepened. "Difficult as it is for you to accept, Alfred, the cachet of easy intimacy with the Earl of Winterbourne is not the height of everyone's aspirations. I don't think she'll cry off."

"Never say she is in love with my son?" Alfred was incred-ulous.

"No, I don't think she is the least bit in love with him. Judg-ing from what little I saw of the lady, she could have Reginald for breakfast. I would venture so much as to say that she can run rings around him and most probably finds him rather dull." He held up an admonitory hand. "Now don't fly up in the boughs. Reginald is all that one could wish in the future Earl of Winterbourne, but even you must admit that he is rather a dull dog." The earl subsided, glowering. "No," Justin contin-ued, "I think that she had not the least idea in the world of marrying Reginald until you put the notion into her head by kicking up such a dust. Really Alfred, you must admit, you have behaved rather foolishly over the entire affair. But the lady has no more taste than I do for being ordered about. I don't blame her in the least for wishing us all at the devil."

The earl, who had been rocking back and forth on his toes in an agony of impatience burst forth, "But what am I to do? She will make the lad miserable!"

Justin could not fail to note the desperation in his brother's tone, nor was he unmoved by the genuine concern he detected in his worried frown. "What can you do? Why, nothing."

"Nothing?" The earl's voice rose to what almost might have been called a shriek. "I cannot just sit by and do nothing while my son ruins his life."

"Relax, Alfred," Justin laid a placating hand on his brother's sleeve. "Reginald will not ruin himself. He will soon discover that she is not the lady for him. He will select a biddable and, one hopes, a suitably dowered young miss from the Season's crop of eager young ladies, and live happily ever after."

"I wish I shared your optimism," the earl muttered gloomily. "But you haven't heard him speak of her. Faugh, the lad talks of nothing else. I tell you, Justin, something must be done. If we can't appeal to her honor, then we must appeal to her baser instincts."

"I thought she had already spurned your filthy lucre."

"Not *those* baser instincts, the other kind."

"Other kind?" Justin's lips twitched in amusement.

"Don't be so obtuse, Justin, you know what I mean. They say no woman can resist you. Frankly, I can't see it, but . . ."

"It's my tailor, Alfred. He absolutely refuses to let me wear brown. Women detest brown."

"Really, if that isn't just like you! Never a serious thought in your head. Amelia says . . ."

"That is unkind in you, Alfred. I give a great deal of serious thought to my appearance. And what does Amelia say? I am willing to wager that she doesn't care for brown above half either."

Alfred restrained himself with an effort. "Amelia likes all my clothes. Besides, my wife is above such things."

His brother remained unconvinced. "Have you asked her?"

"No, but . . ."

"Well, perhaps you should."

"Never *mind* that, just say you will."

Justin looked blank, "Will what?"

"Seduce the wench, of course. That's the only way she'll leave Reginald alone."

"Seduce her? But what will I do with her?" Justin wondered, his eyes dancing with suppressed laughter.

"Lord, how should I know? Whatever you do with all of the others."

"You forget, dear brother, she wishes to have nothing to do with the rest of the family, including me."

"Surely such paltry objections never weighed with you before," the earl replied sarcastically.

His brother grinned. "How true."

"Then I fail to see why they should do so now."

"Especially when my familial duty stands so clear before me, eh, Alfred?"

"Just so." Failing entirely to catch his brother's ironic undertone, the earl looked to be relieved. Justin was a rare trial. To be sure, he would have his bit of fun, but he always did come through in the end when the situation warranted it, and for his part, Alfred could not imagine a more serious state of affairs than those now facing the future of the Winterbourne inheritance.

"Almost you tempt me," Justin pretended to hesitate while cynically observing the variety of emotions that flitted over his elder brother's florid countenance. "Oh, very well," he relented. "I never was one to resist a challenge, especially where a pretty woman is concerned. But now, pray excuse me as I have a pressing appointment with another pretty woman, and I must change into something more suitable."

"Opera dancers," Alfred snorted in disgust.

Justin held up one beautifully shaped hand, "Not opera dancers, Alfred, *the* opera dancer. Mademoiselle de Charenton is not to be mentioned in the same breath as her sisters."

If he were a man given to reflection, Alfred would undoubtedly have asked himself why it irked him that an opera dancer so celebrated for her beauty that her name was known even to the Earl of Winterbourne should have chosen to bestow her much sought after favors on his brother. To be sure, Justin was plump enough in the pocket, but he was not precisely the Golden Ball, and he was a younger son besides.

Had Alfred cared to ask, the lady in question could have enlightened him. Sometime later that afternoon, disengaging herself from a passionate embrace, Suzette de Charenton, shining star of the corps de ballet and toast of all of masculine London, gazed appreciatively at her caller. La, the man was handsome! She couldn't remember when she had last had a lover who could rival Justin's dark good looks and athletic build. One had only to look into the enigmatic gray eyes under their straight dark brows to be lost.

Suzette had done just that one evening. Several months ago, despite the glare of the footlights, she had singled Justin St. Clair out among the audience. With his square-cut jaw and powerful shoulders, he exuded an energy and determination that set him apart from the other town beaux who were whiling away the evening leering at pretty legs. When she had first caught sight of him, he had been surveying his fellows with amused detachment, but later, unlike the others, he actually appeared to pay attention to the figures of the dance, applauding at those which revealed skill and artistry rather than a well-turned ankle or an enticing calf.

Initially attracted by his mere physical presence, Suzette had been intrigued by his interest and, hoping against hope that he would appear at her dressing room door after the performance.

She had instructed her maid to deny all others access, no matter how importunate they became.

Mrs. Huggins, grim champion of the opera's leading attraction, had had her work cut out for her. More tenderhearted than most of her sister artists who only wanted to snare the richest lord as soon as possible, Suzette customarily allowed an audience with all her admirers after a performance, leaving no one disappointed. Thus, there were howls of protest when Mrs. Huggins informed the crowd of her mistress's previous engagement. Mrs. Huggins remained gracious but firm, accepting the floral tributes without moving an inch from her position in front of the danseuse's door.

Convinced at last of the lady's determination to deny them even the briefest glimpse of her exquisite form and radiant smile, her admirers had drifted away in search of the inferior companionship of the other dancers. It was then that Justin St. Clair had appeared, and Mrs. Huggins needed no further explanation of her mistress's quixotic behavior. Even Suzette's rather enthusiastic description had not done him justice. Mrs. Huggins's heart, long dead to any masculine attractions, fluttered inside her ample bosom.

It was not just St. Clair's splendid physique or handsome profile that caused all women, young and old, to sneak a second glance, it was the way he carried himself: erect, but without self-consciousness; alert, his glance taking in everything around him. And then there was his smile and his expression when he looked at someone, focusing all his attention on her as though he truly were interested.

"Does Mademoiselle de Charenton have a moment to acknowledge a devoted admirer," he inquired flashing a singularly charming smile at the dancer's grim defender.

"Well, she . . .that is, I expect . . .I shall inquire of her." And blushing like a schoolgirl, Mrs. Huggins disappeared to inform her mistress that *he* had at last arrived.

Justin leaned against the door, a gleam of satisfaction in his eyes. He had known how it would be the minute he caught the dancer's attention. She had seen him immediately, and her gaze had quickly shifted to the boxes above him; but he had caught her sneaking glances at him as she pirouetted across the stage, and as she had stopped to acknowledge the thunderous applause and caught sight of him, she had allowed the tiniest of smiles to flit across her full red lips. Wise in the ways of sought-after women, he had waited until the others had left, certain of his admission to her dressing room.

For her part, from the moment Justin St. Clair had stepped through the door that night at the opera, Suzette, experienced as she was, had wanted him more than she had ever wanted any man in her life. She had emerged breathless and shaking from their first embrace with a desire that had only increased during their liaison. It was not just his practiced lovemaking or his ability to make a woman feel as though she were the most exquisite creature in the world that made him so irresistible, but it was his genuine interest in her, Suzette de Charenton, that had caused the premiere ballerina to single him out among all her would-be admirers. "Ah, *mon chéri*, you are more handsome every time I see you," she now sighed, sliding one tiny hand down his chest.

Justin laughed. "Doing it much too brown aren't you, my love?"

The dancer fixed him with her emerald eyes, "Alas no. You know, Justin, my heart is of the most jaded, and ordinarily I am *très ennuyée* with all you silly men. But you, you are something different, *non*?"

"I should like to think so, at least where you are concerned."

She smiled, flashing a charming dimple at him. "Yes, you are, I am sad to say. I should so much prefer to be indifferent to you."

"Indifferent, sweetheart, but why, when it is so much more charming for both of us that you are not?"

"Because, odious man, I should like for one woman at least to be immune to your devastating attractions, and I have yet to see anyone who is. Even my poor Huggins has a certain air about her when you are around. It would be good for your character to meet someone who does not cast herself at your feet." The lady sniffed, but her eyes twinkled up at him.

"Then you may lay your fears for my character to rest, because I have discovered the very female you seek. Not only does she resist my, er 'charms,' she has assured me that she wishes to have nothing to do with me."

Suzette was intrigued. "I had not known that such a person existed. Is she an ape-leader?" For only a hardened and embittered old maid could resist the lurking smile in those gray eyes.

"No. In fact, some would say she is rather attractive, my nephew Reginald for one. It is his ridiculous infatuation with her that has been the cause of a great deal of bother, and sent my brother Alfred running to me like the old woman he is." Justin sighed bitterly. "But, I did not come here to talk about me. I came to feast my eyes on your beautiful countenance and to see if I could persuade you to allow me to purchase you a new bonnet from Celeste, since you confided in me how much you admired her creations. 'Tis such a fine spring day that one feels one should celebrate somehow, and this seems a most appropriate way to enjoy it."

Suzette smiled. "You are too generous, sir. Why only last week you insisted on bestowing that beautiful shawl on me, which was shockingly dear." So he would not discuss this latest contretemps with her, but she could tell by the furrow in his brow that something was bothering him. Ordinarily, Justin blithely wrote off his family as a group of dullards with more hair than wit, who were better off in the country where they usually obliged him by remaining. There must be something more to this than met the eye. Perhaps there was something to this woman who seemed to dislike him. The opera dancer resolved to discover what she could. Confident of her own beauty and power to attract, Suzette did not fear any female competition, but she was curious as to what sort of person could inspire the determined look now darkening her lover's eyes.

Chapter 7

SUZETTE was to have her curiosity satisfied sooner than she had expected as the next evening all of the parties concerned appeared at the opera.

Ascending the stairs, Diana admitted she had good reason to bless Aunt Seraphina's managing ways. It had been ages since she had been to anything more elaborate than a musicale, and she surveyed the brilliant crowd around her with lively interest. Lady Jersey, in her box, was chatting busily to an attentive gentleman whose identity was concealed by the enormous turban of the dowager unabashedly eavesdropping in front of him. Sally glanced up just as Reginald's little party entered their own box and smiled at Diana who nodded back in a friendly fashion. Good, Sally thought to herself, the young widow was finally enjoying herself again and in the process seemed to have bewitched the young Viscount Chalford.

It was vastly amusing to Sally, who, never able to resist a challenge, had once tried her best to flirt with his father, the Earl of Winterbourne, and had found him to be as stiff and humorless as one of Madame Tussaud's wax figures. He must be furious at his son's attention to an older woman, and a penniless one at that. Sally had a fondness for the gal. As Ferdie's viscountess, Diana had handled her charming wastrel of a husband with grace and dignity. Now she deserved a little gaiety for the anxiety she must have suffered; but Sally vowed she would find Diana someone more lively than Reginald.

Another member of the audience was also surveying that particular corner of the opera house. Glancing idly up at the boxes, Justin St. Clair ground his teeth as he intercepted the interchange between the two women. There was no doubt the chit had nerve. Here she was, barely a twenty-four hours after his visit, flaunting her connection with his family for all the world to see. Not that she didn't look quite lovely in a short-waisted robe of striped French gauze over a white satin slip. The décolletage and the short full sleeves showed off the graceful neck and arms to perfection. Her dark hair was pulled off the forehead with the dusky curls falling to one side emphasizing the beautifully sculpted shoulders, white skin, and unusual sapphire eyes. Impoverished though she might be, the widow somehow managed to appear elegant, as did the handsome woman next to her. Aunt Seraphina, Justin decided as he peered through his quizzing glass at the high-bridged Roman nose and determined jaw, did not look to be the type to be taken by the likes of either the Viscount Chalford or Lady Diana Hatherill.

Justin continued to stare at the box. They had barely settled themselves in their gilt chairs, before a group of exquisites eagerly entered the box. Though most of their backs were to him, Justin thought he recognized the carrot-colored hair of Tony Washburne, Ferdie's crony and challenger in the fatal race. Here was competition, Justin thought to himself hopefully. Ferdie's crowd, though as devoid of anything in their cocklofts as their departed companion, were of a sophistication and an age more likely to interest Diana than his nephew. Justin scrutinized Reginald, trying to read the lad's reaction, which, to his disgust, appeared to be blatant pleasure in his adored's surrounding court of admirers.

There was a shout of laughter, and he returned his gaze to the beaux around Diana, who, eyes sparkling, had apparently just delivered some witticism or other that even Aunt Seraphina appeared to find highly diverting. Thoroughly revolted, Justin turned his attention to the stage as the orchestra began to tune up.

Unconscious of both critical observers scrutinizing her, Diana was enjoying herself hugely. She had forgotten the excitement she always felt in the opulent theater, filled with gorgeously dressed women, and the anticipation that welled up in her as she gazed down at the brilliantly lit stage. After so much time spent quietly in Brook Street, she would have been content simply to sit silently absorbing it all, but the door to the box had opened and the chorused "Lady Diana" had warned her that the inseparable trio of Ferdie's sporting-mad friends—Tony Washburne, Sir Ralph Grinstead, and the Honorable

Henry Throckmorton—had come to greet her in their customary exuberant fashion.

She had never shared much with Ferdie's friends, caring little about their absurd bets, and even less for their determined consumption of quantities of port. But she had always appreciated their breezy, friendly manner, their warm acceptance of her into their coterie, and their way of making her feel as though they were the brothers she had never had. It had not hurt either that they considered her a veritable paragon of cleverness and, following Ferdie's lead, had consulted her from time to time on their most ticklish problems.

"Lady Diana, you must help me. I am in the most devilish coil," Tony Washburne burst out as soon as the acknowledgments and introductions were concluded satisfactorily.

Diana chuckled. "When weren't you in a 'devilish coil,' Tony? Come tell me that you are not in one, and then I shall be concerned. Besides, I haven't a feather to fly with, so I daresay I shall be of no use to you whatsoever."

"Oh no, you have it all wrong," Sir Ralph interjected, "the man truly is in desperate straits. His mama is convinced it is time he married."

"And what is worse, she has picked out a bride for me." Tony's dismay was so patent that the others could not help laughing.

"And who is this fortunate young lady? Her parents must be all about in the head if they would take you for a match for their daughter."

If possible, Tony looked even more woebegone. "It's Lady Amanda Felthorpe. Her mama and my mama were at school together, so you see it is a hopeless case. They have always been thick as thieves and of course mama now expects *me* to escort her daughter, dance with daughter and . . ." Tony shuddered and could not go on.

Diana frowned as she conjured up a picture of Lady Amanda, a mousy young lady with the strictest of principles. "Yes, I see, it does rather give one pause. Perhaps I should warn her of the life that she is likely to lead as the partner of such a rattle as you. And you, Tony, would do well to point out to your mama, in the most delicate possible manner of course, that a wife would naturally require so much attention that you would not have time to dance attendance on her as she now demands. For with the best will in the world, you cannot desert a wife to escort your mama to any of the routs and balls in town, or to take the waters in Bath, or to flit from one friend's estate to another, as she is so accustomed to doing."

Tony beamed. "There, lads, didn't I tell you she would know what to do?" He grabbed Diana's hand and kissed it effusively. "You are a woman beyond price, Lady Diana. Thank you. But, it begins, we shall not bother you any longer."

"What you mean is that you wish to return to your seats in time to catch a good glimpse of the dancers," Diana retorted smiling.

They all grinned good-naturedly and left the box as precipitately as they had entered it.

Witnessing this byplay, Justin snorted in disgust. Reginald was even more a fool than he thought if he couldn't see that the lady was a hardened flirt as well as a fortune hunter. It was high time the lad was given a talking to, but now the audience was applauding and for the moment, Justin gave himself up to the appreciation of his mistress's considerable charms and talents as she and the ballet appeared onstage to a vociferously enthusiastic audience.

At the end of the first act, the sight of Reginald again gazing fervently on as Diana chatted with a group of young men reinforced his uncle in his resolve to do something. That this particular set of admirers, remarkable only for their rather sober dress and serious demeanor, appeared to be friends of Reginald's made not the least bit of difference to Justin nor, it appeared, to Lady Diana Hatherill. The hussy smiled and laughed just as gaily as she had with Ferdie's confreres, and St. Clair fumed all the more at the laughs and attention she was drawing.

With no very clear idea of what he was going to do or how he was going to proceed, Justin grimly made his way to the box, too preoccupied to acknowledge the languishing looks cast at him by some of the ladies in the surrounding boxes. Even Sally Jersey failed to attract a glimmer of a smile, causing her to comment to her companion, "Whatever do you suppose is ailing St. Clair? He looks positively blue-deviled."

Fortunately, Reginald was just leaving the box to go in search of refreshment for the ladies, thus sparing his uncle the necessity of resorting to some devious stratagem for getting him alone.

"Uncle Justin, I am delighted to see you here. I had hoped perhaps we might . . ."

His uncle sighed inwardly at the welcoming smile on his nephew's ingenuous face, which betrayed not the slightest hint of consciousness. A man in some doubt about the appropriateness of his choice of a life companion or properly respectful of his parents' strictures would have revealed some small sign of discomfort, but not Reginald.

"I am so glad you have come," Reginald reiterated. "You must meet Lady Diana Hatherill." The name was whispered so reverently that Justin felt he was like to be sick. Such romantic infatuation would have made him queasy at any time, but coming from a former young sobersides and in reference to a woman who was no better than she should be, it was positively nauseating.

"You will like her, I know you will," his nephew continued eagerly. "She is quite out of the common way, not like so many women one meets who can speak of nothing but fashion and dress. Her father was a notable scholar and raised her without any of the silly notions you find among the rest of her sex. Her mind is most well-informed, and she is quite without vanity."

Justin restrained himself with considerable effort.

"I know Papa would approve of her if he could only rid himself of the notion that she is after Great-Aunt Seraphina's fortune. You can see that she and her great-aunt are the dearest of friends, and Diana has confided to me that she wishes to make her own way in the world. In general, Papa's opinions are well considered, but I fear that this time his judgment is outweighed by worldly concerns." The viscount dismissed his parents' worries with a shake of his head. "But come, meet her."

That's what you get, Alfred, for prosing on forever at the lad, Justin thought gloomily. He's been so filled with moral platitudes that he has become too high-minded for his own good. A young man who had been allowed to sow his wild oats in a proper fashion would have recognized the lady and the situation for what they were, and would not be in the mess that Reginald found himself in.

"No, I do not agree with you. Handel is, of course, inspiring, but his oratorio's inspire by overwhelming the audience rather than enchanting it. I believe Mozart to be the better composer. His harmony is far more deftly woven, and the listener is influenced subtly without being aware of it. I find that to be a greater art," a silvery voice caught his ear as Justin followed his nephew into the box.

He glanced over to see Lady Diana deep in conversation with one of the earnest young men surrounding her, and the picture she made, her smooth white forehead wrinkled in thought, head tilted speculatively, a look of deep concentration in her blue eyes, forced Justin into the unwilling recognition that this was a serious conversation. There was nothing the least bit flirtatious about her or the situation.

"Perhaps, Lady Diana, but do you not agree that this is not a work that is truly illustrative of Mozart's particular abilities?" Her companion was as immersed in the topic as she was, and his expression was one more of respect than admiration for the lovely picture she made.

"You see what I mean?" Reginald whispered in his ear, "Denby is a brilliant fellow—a first-rate scholar—but he's so shy, he barely talks to us, let alone to women. Lady Diana is always so interested and so stimulating that she puts anyone at his ease, unlike so many ladies who smile and laugh and make a fellow feel awkward and foolish if he doesn't know how to offer them pretty speeches."

However loath he was to revise his opinion of the lady, Justin, judging by the evidence at hand, had to admit to the truth of his nephew's remarks; but appearances could be deceiving, and there was no doubt that Lady Diana was remarkably clever. There was no more time for speculation as Reginald, grasping his uncle's arm, urged him forward to meet his companions.

Justin bowed low before the two ladies, wondering ruefully to himself when, if ever, he had impressed two women less. Lady Walden was friendly enough, but he could see her sizing him up as though he were the veriest schoolboy, and somehow he felt he did not quite measure up—a most uncomfortable sensation for one accustomed to charming ladies of all ages and degrees.

There was no doubt as to the hostility of Lady Diana's expression. She was all that was polite—soliciting his opinion of the opera, admitting to having heard a great deal about him from his nephew—but the eyes that swept over him, while they blessedly did not reveal the slightest hint of recognition, were distinctly unfriendly, and there was an unmistakably frosty note in her voice. It was abundantly clear to all and sundry that Lady Diana Hatherill remained unimpressed by Justin St. Clair. Even Suzette de Charenton, trying unashamedly to catch a glimpse of her lover through a crack in the curtains backstage, could tell from that distance that her wishes had been granted and one woman at least appeared to be immune to Justin's considerable charms.

Not only was the woman immune to them, she actually seemed to dislike him, if the rigidity of her posture and the defiant tilt of her head were any indication. Suzette could not help smiling to herself. Personally, she could not understand such an absurd reaction, but it would be great fun to tease Justin about it later. Irresistible as he was, there was just the slightest bit of arrogance about him that made her want to see him taken down a peg. No, it was not arrogance precisely, it was colossal self-assurance. Woman had been falling at his feet for so long, herself included, that he simply never entertained the possibility that they wouldn't succumb to his considerable attractions.

Suzette was intrigued. It was from a distance, of course, but the lady in question did not appear to be an antidote or an apeleader or one of those women who were so unattractive that they hated men out of self-defense. It seemed quite the contrary, if the eager crowd around her were any indication. Suzette pulled the curtain together and hurried back to her dressing room to check herself in the looking glass before reappearing onstage. The dancer was highly amused. She hoped that Reginald would force his uncle to endure the lady's company, as it was bound to have a salutary effect. At the same time, she was curious about a woman who remained unmoved by such a splendid specimen of manhood as Justin St. Clair.

Suzette was not the only one to be puzzled by Diana's reaction. Once again outside the box, as he returned to his original quest of refreshment, Reginald could not help remarking on the strange coldness between his uncle and his ladylove. "You must have overwhelmed Lady Diana. Ordinarily she is all that is charming, but I could see that she was somewhat shy in your presence. Perhaps it is that she has been in mourning so long that she is unaccustomed to all this attention. But is she not lovely, Uncle Justin? With so many who admire her, I cannot believe that she allows me to call on her and escort her occasionally. In most cases, I would not have the audacity to ask someone like her to be my wife, but I cannot help myself. However, it is hopeless, for she will never marry again."

"Oh?" Justin's ears pricked up at this piece of news.

"Yes. Unfortunate, is it not, for she would make a splendid viscountess, or a duchess for that matter. Her husband did not leave her with a feather to fly with, but she says she has had her fill of looking after men, and now she intends to look after herself. I suppose one cannot wonder at it with an absent-minded recluse for a father and a wastrel for a husband, both of whom were utterly irresponsible and let their inheritances slip through their fingers without a thought for her. It is a great shame." Reginald sighed gustily. "But excuse me, I must procure something to drink for the ladies." He plunged off into the crowd, fumbling his way toward the refreshments.

Justin stood for a minute, an arrested look on his face. Why the little jade! She had no more idea of marrying Reginald than he did, but she had allowed the viscount's father and uncle to think that she meant to do so, purely out of spite. He grinned, in spite of himself, remembering his first encounter with Lady Diana. What a fire-eater! Though out of fairness to the lady, Justin had to admit that he would have been equally incensed if someone had dared to interfere in his affairs the way they had in hers.

The situation called for some delicacy. He could not withdraw the pressure and allow the lady to think she had won. Neither could he push her so far that she accepted Reginald's suit merely to prove a point. From the little he had seen of Diana, Justin could believe her entirely capable of doing such a thing. Perhaps, for once, Alfred in his own bumbling way was right—seduction was the only answer.

Chapter 8

IN the ensuing days, Justin did his best to observe his quarry. Attaching himself to his nephew seemed to be the most effective way to discover Lady Diana's whereabouts, for there was hardly anything that the besotted young man did not know about the pattern of her daily existence. He never tired of expounding on her manifold charms—her grace, her beauty, the elegance of her mind, her intellectual accomplishments ad infinitum—until his uncle thought he was like to be ill of hearing them.

Anyone else would have wondered at this sudden interest on the part of an uncle who had hitherto been bored to distraction by any member of the Earl of Winterbourne's family, but Reginald, never observant at the best of times, was lost in a fog of happiness at the opportunity for catching even the briefest glimpse of his ladylove. Thus it was that he even took to riding in the park, though he was an indifferent rider at best and subject to the whims of his horse, a stolid bay with a gloomy disposition and a predilection for his own stall.

Though he considered himself above such frippery things, Reginald could not help remarking on the magnificence of the animal on which his uncle was mounted one afternoon as they rode together. It pleased him to be seen with such an impressive pair as Justin and Brutus. "Lady Diana is a most elegant horsewoman and is extremely fond of horses, as indeed she is of all animals," he remarked diffidently as they proceeded at a leisurely pace through the park.

They had not gone far before Reginald broke out eagerly, "There she is. I told you she would be here."

Justin was impressed once again at the hold the lady exercised over his nephew, for only someone whose entire being was attuned to his beloved one's presence would have picked out Lady Diana, obscured as she was by the throng around her. She was chatting with a group of young bucks whose eyes for fine horseflesh were only equal to their discrimination in their tailors.

Ferdie's friends, Justin catalogued them mentally; for whatever Ferdie and his coterie had lacked in intelligence, they had more than made up for in their devotion to appearance. How someone of Lady Diana's obvious spirit could have married Ferdie Hatherill was a mystery, for she must have been bored with his inanities within a fortnight. Ferdie had been the best of good fellows—always up for a lark, whether it was a good mill or racing two pigs around Berkeley Square—but one could quickly tire of his constant and mindless pursuit of amusement. Though vastly different from the pompous Reginald, he could be equally as boring in his own way. But at one time he had been wealthy, offering all that Reginald could be expected to offer. Justin's eyes narrowed. It wasn't the first time a clever woman had chosen a simpleton because he was manageable. He urged Brutus forward, eager to listen in on the discussion.

"Why, Reginald, this is a surprise. I had not thought to discover in you a penchant for fresh air and exercise." Lady Diana's smile was warm and welcoming, and she seemed genuinely pleased to discover his nephew engaging in a sporting activity, however mild it was.

Reginald blushed and stammered, "Well, I thought it might be . . .that is to say, you speak so often of the beneficial and stimulating effects of such things on one's intellectual capacities that I determined to start a regular program of healthful pursuits in the hopes that I might overcome the deleterious effects of too much study and . . ." his voice trailed off as he observed the stunned expressions of her companions.

"And I highly approve." The lady came to his rescue. "Not that any of these fellows has ever known the effects of any study at all, much less serious intellectual activity. Why, for Henry here, the perusal of the racing form is totally exhausting, and the idea of reading something as demanding as a newspaper is quite beyond his comprehension," she continued, adroitly deflecting attention from Reginald's painful unease to a cheerful giant who reddened and laughed good-naturedly, remarking as he did so that it was a wonder someone as clever as Lady Diana tolerated such fellows as himself.

"Because, illiterate though you may be, you are a keen judge of horseflesh, which talent you are so very kind as to share with those of us unable to frequent Tattersall's. I am most impressed with Ajax here, and am forever indebted to you for discovering him for me. He is a true gentleman, despite his size and strength, and is always most considerate of a rider who offers him less in the way of horsemanship than he deserves."

This last remark raised a howl of protest from the rest of the group. And it, indeed, was quite obvious to even the most casual observer that the rider was more than a match for the superb animal that she sat with such grace and assurance. "But come," Diana continued, "I am forgetting my manners. Let me make you known to Viscount Chalford and his uncle."

A silent witness to the entire exchange, Justin could not help admiring the lady's skill. Without seeming to expend the slightest effort, she had smoothed over an uncomfortable moment and blended two vastly different groups of people together. In the ordinary course of things, Ferdie's friends would have scorned the viscount for his uninspiring mount, his ponderous speech, and his general appearance as that of a rustic lacking in town bronze, while Reginald would have been equally as scathing in his condemnation of a bunch of useless fribbles who obviously divided their existences between their mounts and their tailors.

Having recently spent a good deal of time in the company of such masters of diplomacy as Talleyrand and Metternich, Justin could appreciate the dexterity with which Lady Diana contrived to make everyone feel reasonably comfortable, and he applauded both the delicacy with which she accomplished her task and the motives behind it all. Another woman might have played one set off against the other into vying for her approval, thus making her the center of attention. Instead, she had done her best to focus everyone's interest somewhere else.

Justin was forced to the conclusion that Lady Diana had acted only out of kindness in doing this—a conclusion that was not in the least congruent with his previous opinion of her.

Sensing herself the object of scrutiny, the lady turned and looked him full in the face, fixing him with those astonishing sapphire eyes that were blue-black in the intensity of their gaze. For the briefest of moments, she stared curiously at him, then raised her chin and returned her attention to her admirers.

The gesture was barely perceptible, but it exuded all the disdain she had expressed for him in their first encounter. St. Clair's jaw tightened, and he gripped the reins so fiercely that Brutus took instant exception and snorted, tossing his head angrily.

Diana shot a quick glance again in his direction, and her lips quivered with amusement. So, she had gotten to him. Good! She had meant to. By what right did Lord Justin St. Clair claim himself judge of her conduct, sitting there raking her with those scornful eyes? What did he know of being at the mercy of creditors, scrimping constantly to stave them off from month to month? If she had been a man, she would have bought a cornetcy or gone to India to make her fortune; and if his high-and-mightiness thought that this entailed snapping up his nephew and his nephew's inheritance, well then let him.

For his part, Justin found himself prey to a curious mixture of emotions. First and foremost was rage, rage at her stubbornness, rage at his powerlessness, rage at being drawn into a situation that was none of his business in the first place. But beyond that was a begrudging admiration for her spirit and something else—call it an odd sort of companionship if you would. Here they were in the midst of a crowd of people, yet it somehow felt as if they were alone, isolated as they were by perceptions to which the rest of them were completely oblivious. There was a certain intimacy in the awareness they both shared of the dynamics at play in the situation—an entire realm of activity that the others were too insensitive, too self-absorbed, or too stupid to recognize.

Lady Diana had been deliberate in her management of the scene. It was a unique experience for both of them—for Diana to have this management recognized and for Justin to discover someone else as clever as handling such things as he was. The lady's quickly suppressed smile was an acknowledgment of all this. Neither one of them had ever encountered a worthy opponent and, even though they were adversaries, this similarity drew them together in an odd sort of way, leaving each one with the feeling that in some indefinable way each had met a kindred spirit.

It was the interchange of a moment. The sense of communication disappeared as quickly as it had appeared, as Diana, leaning toward Reginald and smiling down at him, continued, "I am looking forward to the concert at the Argyll Rooms to which you have invited Aunt Seraphina and me. Pray tell me, what do you know of the performers?"

Justin nearly choked with disgust as Reginald, a beatific expression on his face at being singled out by his goddess, launched into a tangled description of the artists, the music, the composer, and the history of the Royal Philharmonic. The elusive sense of camaraderie was instantly banished as he watched her. She was a coquette of the worst sort, taking advantage of an innocent for her own selfish gain.

Justin averted his eyes from the sickening spectacle. However, in doing so he caught a fleeting glimpse of two things that gave him pause. The first was an impression so slight that it was more a sensation than an observation, but he had the distinct feeling that the jade was again looking to gauge his reaction. She only betrayed herself by the merest flicker of an eyelash, but he had caught the movement out of the corner of his eye as he turned to gaze off over the park. The other was the fatuous expressions of admiration in the faces of Ferdie's friends. To a man they would have declared their horror at being leg-shackled. Marriage was anathema to their free and easy spirits thus a single female could strike as much, if not more, terror in their hearts as a badly cut coat or a spavined horse, but there was not a soul among them who didn't look as besotted as the Viscount Chalford.

If that were the case, then why choose Reginald? Demonstrably less dashing than any of them, less well breeched than Grinstead or Throckmorton, and with fewer expectations than Reginald's friend Denby, who was heir to a dukedom, his nephew was far less a catch than any of them who could have been firmly caught in the parson's mousetrap with only the gentlest of pushes. Egad, by the look on the countenances of the eager group around her, any one of them would have walked into it willingly.

Then why did the harpy not concentrate her efforts where they were likely to be more amply rewarded? Nor did she appear to keep them dangling merely from a coquettish love of conquest. With the exception of her last remark, Diana's con-

duct had not been in the least flirtatious. Justin cast his mind
back. In fact, both here and at the opera her attitude toward
them all, excluding Lord Justin St. Clair of course, had been
that of a tolerant older sister rather than someone desirous of
admiration.

If Lady Diana Hatherill didn't desire marriage—and his
nephew was the first to point this out—then what did she want
from Reginald? And why was she so determined to convince
his family that she did wish it? Was she acting this way purely
out of dislike for being told what to do? Surely no one could
be as proud as all that?

Justin was intrigued in spite of himself. Initially committed
to seeking her out in order to lure the lady away from his
nephew, he now found himself wishing to pursue the acquaintance for his own gratification. He wanted to learn more about
her. Lady Diana Hatherill was both a beautiful and a highly
unusual woman, and she piqued his interest despite her antag-
onism. Justin determined to seek her out when no one else was
around. And this time he vowed not to emerge second best as
he had done from every encounter thus far.

Chapter 9

A FEW casual questions posed to the oblivious Reginald elicited the information that he had invited the two ladies to a concert of the Royal Philharmonic Society the very next evening. Having received so much unaccustomed encouragement from his adored, Reginald, with uncharacteristic boldness, had seized the opportunity of offering his escort before Diana had the chance to resume the reclusive ways of her early widowhood. Much to his surprise and delight, she had accepted.

Unable to believe his good fortune, the viscount kept exclaiming over it all the way home until his uncle, heartily sick of it all, had suggested that a gentleman who was truly in love did not constantly bandy the name of his beloved about in public.

"Oh, but I . . .that is . . .of course you are correct, Uncle Justin. It's just that until now she has so rarely been seen in society, even after the period of mourning was over. And she would never let me accompany her anywhere. Now it seems like a miracle not only to see her, but to be allowed to escort her anywhere."

The miracle of perversity, more like, Justin thought sourly to himself, but he didn't have the heart to point out to his besotted nephew that the lady's change in attitude dated from the very moment that Justin St. Clair had called upon her to dissuade her from pursuing the viscount.

Bored though he claimed himself to be by the subject of Lady Diana Hatherill, Justin could not stop himself from thinking about her after he had left his nephew off. Though he kept telling himself that his thoughts naturally tended to concentrate on something that presented both a mystery and a problem, he could not help picturing her so erect on the huge

gray stallion, the curves of her figure enhanced by the tightly
fitting habit, her beautifully sculpted face emphasized by the
severity of her attire.

Thoroughly disgusted at himself, Justin realized that he too
was going to attend the concert at the Argyll Rooms, though it
would mean having to postpone Suzette's invitation to an intimate dinner party until much later in the evening.

He had hoped to arrive unobserved after Reginald's party
had settled themselves, but fortune was not with him. As luck
would have it, Lady Diana—appreciatively examining the
renowned decorations from Telemachus's search for his father, the ancient bronze fasces supporting the tiers of boxes,
and the unusual chandeliers—caught sight of him the moment
he entered the room. His commanding height and broad shoulders would have made him instantly recognizable anywhere,
but he was especially noticeable in the brilliantly lit theater.

Her eyes widened in surprise. Devotion to serious music
was not a trait she would have ascribed to the Lord Justin St.
Clair, if the picture Reginald had painted of his dashing uncle
were to be believed. Then he must have come expressly to spy
upon her. Diana gritted her teeth. The man's effrontery was
outside of enough!

Closely observing Diana's expression, it was Justin's turn to
be amused. So she suspected him of deviousness, did she?
Good! It was time that he did something to unsettle the lady
for a change. Responding to the challenge in her eyes, he
strode over smiling broadly. "Lady Walden, Lady Diana, you
have no idea the pleasure it gives me to know that my nephew
is making certain you partake of all the musical delights that
London has to offer."

"Sir, I had not thought to see you here." The patent surprise
in Reginald's voice gave his uncle the distinct impression that
he gained very little pleasure from encountering his relative at
that particular moment.

"Why not, lad? If you recall, the last time I came across
your little coterie, it was at the opera. You are not the only one
in the family who is not a barbarian you know."

Reginald flushed and was silent.

"And, pray tell, how did you find *La Clemenza di Tito*?"
Diana inquired, refusing to allow the arrogant interloper to
dominate the scene.

"Oh, it was tolerable, most tolerable, though I believe the character given to Titus was all wrong. '*Quibus rebus sicut in posterum securitati satis cavit, ita ad prasens plurimum contraxit invidiae, ut non temere quis tam adverso rumore magisque invitis omnibus transierit ad principatum.*' "

" 'Although by such conduct he provided for his safety in the future, he incurred such odium at the time that hardly anyone ever came to the throne with so evil a reputation or so much against the desires of all.' Suetonius. However: '*At illi ea fama pro bono cessit conversaque est in maximas laudes neque vitio ullo reperto et contra virtutibus summis.* But this reputation turned out to his advantage and gave place to the highest praise, when no fault was discovered in him, but on the contrary the highest virtues.' If you were hoping to try whether or not Reginald's claims as to my education were true, you chose badly, for naturally I would expect you to choose that text as a test for me," Diana responded in a rather pitying tone.

Justin's eyes gleamed. "I see I have underestimated you, Lady Diana, you are a truly worthy opponent. Perhaps you would defend the liberties Metestasio's libretto takes with history thus: '*Pictoribus atque poetis. Quidlibet audendi semper fuit aequa potestas. Scimus, et hanc veniam petimusque damusque vicissim.*' "

The light of battle in her eyes, Diana retorted, " 'Painters and poets alike have always had license to dare anything. We know that, and we both claim and allow to others in their turn this indulgence.' But Horace also maintained: '*Mediocribus esse poetis non homines, non di, non concessere columnae.*' "

"Touché, my lady." Justin was impressed in spite of himself. "You are correct. 'Not gods, nor men, nor even booksellers have put up with poets' being second-rate.' And in the case of this particular opera, the work is decidedly inferior to the other creations of both the librettist and the composer."

"How very odd, then, that you should waste your time on it. There must be some other reason to explain your presence." The deceptive mildness in Diana's tone was belied by the dangerous glint in her eyes.

"Oh, there was." An answering gleam lit up the gray eyes that held her gaze. "It was Mademoiselle de Charenton."

"Mademoiselle de Charenton?" For a minute Lady Diana was totally bewildered. Then enlightenment dawned. "The beautiful dancer! Yes, I can quite see where *you* would see the attraction." The slight stress she laid on her words hinted that she was under no illusions as to the nature of his interest in the star of the corps de ballet.

"Uncle Justin!" Reginald was shocked. "You should not speak of such things to a gently bred lady."

His uncle was amused. "Why, what things, lad? I was merely admiring the artistry to be seen onstage, and I am sure Lady Diana will agree with me." He directed a quizzing glance in her direction.

"Indubitably. She is a brilliant dancer. I am so glad that others recognize her talent." Diana smiled sweetly at him.

"But you alluded to . . . you . . . oh, very well." Recognizing that his attempts to ameliorate the situation had only made it worse, Reginald subsided into an awkward silence.

"Don't be silly, Reginald," Diana began tartly, "one can not live in society without being aware of such things." Then, realizing that she sounded a trifle severe, she leaned forward smiling. "I am sure you would rather have me be somewhat worldly than stupid."

Reginald was mollified more by the enchantment of his beloved's smile than by her words. "Never could you be accused of such a thing, Lady Diana." Then, completely disregarding Justin's presence, he edged closer. "But you asked me who is to be playing at the concert. Both the Mr. Knyvetts are to appear. In general, they are more noted for their glee singing, but as Mr. Attwood is to conduct, there is certain to be Mozart in the musical offerings."

Ordinarily the viscount, raised to be a most dutiful son and highly respectful to his elders, would never have ignored his uncle so pointedly, but he had not quite liked the way Justin seemed to take over the scene when Lady Diana was around, nor did he care for the way they sparred together—each one so intent on besting the other that neither one seemed to be the least bit aware of anyone else's presence.

This attitude was not lost on Reginald's uncle, who, rather than being offended by it, was highly diverted. Smothering a smile, he turned to Great-Aunt Seraphina to find himself being regarded speculatively by that lady's piercing dark eyes.

"You shouldn't provoke her, you know," she observed composedly. "Unless you're very clever indeed, you are likely to come off the worst in the encounter. While most girls were playing with dolls, she was left with nothing to do but listen to the endless debates between her father and her tutor, or match wits with them herself. Though you seem to suspect otherwise, she does have one of the most well-informed minds it has ever been my pleasure to come across. Thomas, my late husband, always made certain we were constantly surrounded by the best the realm had to offer, so I know whereof I speak. But enough of this. Are you related to Theobald St. Clair?"

Momentarily thrown off balance by the abrupt change in topic, Justin recovered quickly. "He was my great-uncle, ma'am."

She nodded sagely. "A very clever man himself, though I daresay his family doesn't think so, *ruining* himself in trade the way he did."

"No they did not." Justin smiled grimly, remembering the raised eyebrows every time Great-Uncle Theobald's name had come up. "But he held a comparable opinion of your husband."

Seraphina smiled fondly. "Yes, Thomas was quite something out of the ordinary way. He was my closest friend and certainly the most stimulating companion I ever had. We were indeed fortunate to find each other, and I do miss him. I only wish Diana had been able to find someone to offer her something similar. Ferdie was a most amiable boy, but hardly her peer. However, it is difficult for her to find those among the *ton*, her interests being far beyond their petty concerns. We are both of us extremely grateful to Reginald for seeing that we are kept entertained."

Following the direction of the older woman's gaze, Justin caught the tail end of a most vigorous discussion between her niece and his nephew. In truth, nothing could have been less flirtatious than Diana's heated rejoinder, "No, Reginald, I cannot agree with you. I think the Royal Philharmonic is quite right in avoiding programs that feature soloists. So many other musical offerings focus on the artist rather than on the music, and that is because that sort of extravaganza is what most of the members of the *ton* wish for, if they bother to listen at all—which I strongly suspect they do not. I commend Mr. Attwood and the other founders of the Royal Philharmonic Society for recognizing that there are some people with discriminating tastes who appreciate the opportunity to hear fine music skillfully and beautifully executed."

And there was nothing remotely lover-like in his nephew's ponderous reply. "You do have a point, but I cannot think that a few judiciously selected solo pieces performed by the most renowned artists, Clementi, Catalani, or Neate, for example, would be at all amiss."

In truth, the two of them seemed more drawn together by common interests than by any mutual attraction, Justin realized. It was the oddest thing, but somehow he envied his nephew for having discovered someone who could share such things with him—ill-suited as the pair might be in every other respect. Justin returned his attention to Lady Walden to find her regarding him with a wealth of comprehension in those eyes that seemed to miss nothing. "Just so." She nodded meaningfully.

Guiltily aware that she must be privy to his suspicions regarding her niece's relationship with the viscount and his strictures concerning it, he realized that she was, in her own diplomatic way, pointing out to him the erroneous nature of the conclusions he had so hurriedly jumped to. It was a rare thing for Lord Justin St. Clair to find himself at a loss for words, but such was most definitely the case, and he was made decidedly uncomfortable by it. Only the appearance of the musicians and the audience's applause saved him from the embarrassment of having to reply.

Chapter 10

THIS awkward sense of discomfort remained with Justin throughout the performance so that he barely listened to the Boccherini quintet or the wind serenade being offered for the first time to London audiences. In fact, he was still mulling the entire scene over in his mind as he hurried from the theater to Suzette's charming house in Kensington.

Far too experienced a woman of the world to complain at her lover's delay, the dancer welcomed him with as much evidence of delight as if she had not received his note earlier that day warning her of his change in plans.

"I do apologize, sweetheart, but Reginald is making such a cake of himself that he must be watched. How any relative of *mine* could be so wet behind the ears, I cannot fathom, but then, he *is* Alfred's son." It was a relief to relax in Suzette's delightful sitting room before the fire while she took his coat and handed him a glass of port, smiling sympathetically at him.

Taking her cue from Justin's abstracted air, she sat quietly and patiently while he turned over in his mind the variety of thoughts and impressions of the evening. It was not Reginald's situation that was bothering her visitor, Suzette thought to herself. St. Clair was far too different from the rest of his family and far too bored by them to become truly embroiled in their concerns, no matter how much they might try to thrust them upon him.

It was the woman Suzette had seen at the theater, who had such a patent distaste for Reginald's uncle, who was behind this preoccupation, Suzette was sure of it. But Justin's face held a slightly different expression now. Before, when he had alluded to his nephew's situation, there had been annoyance and disgust. Now there was another look in his eyes, one which the dancer could not quite place. Was it uncertainty or confusion? Suzette could not imagine the self-confident Justin thrown by anyone or anything, but he apparently was now.

Justin swirled the port in the glass, sipping it slowly as he stared into the fire. Then, suddenly remembering where he was, he shook his head smiling apologetically at his hostess. "I beg your pardon, I am not being very good company am I?"

Suzette smiled in return. It was impossible to be annoyed with someone who was as aware of his companions as Justin was. In all her experience of men, she had never encountered a one who had given the least thought to her feelings. "You are obviously concerned by the circumstances, and I am a most willing listener should you care to discuss what is troubling you."

He leaned forward to plant a lingering kiss on the inviting mouth. "And why should I waste my breath talking when there are so many things I wish to do with my lips besides make words," he murmured planting a trail of kisses down her neck to her shoulder and following the décolletage of her gown. She shivered with anticipation and gave herself up to the increasing insistence of his caresses as he slid the sleeve off her shoulder and ran his hand gently over the smooth white skin underneath.

"Aaah," she sighed, arching herself toward him and forgetting entirely that she had again failed to get him to confide in her.

Justin too forgot about the entire scene at the concert as he gave himself up to the passion of the moment, immersing himself in the wealth of sensations that swept over them both as he gathered her in his arms and carried her toward the bedroom.

Later, much later as he rode home in the early morning, his thoughts again returned to Lady Diana and the picture of her that Lady Walden had painted.

Perhaps he was mistaken, and friendship was all that she wanted from Reginald. Surely not. Who could possibly refrain from yawning with boredom after more than a few minutes with his prolix nephew? No, that was unfair. Reginald was not the cleverest of men, but he did concern himself with more serious things than most of the people Diana was likely to encounter. Certainly he was a more stimulating escort than Ferdie and his cronies.

And, if the snatches of her conversation that he had over-heard were any indication of the tenor of the lady's mind, then surely she would find the idle gossip, which formed the chief source of entertainment in the fashionable drawing rooms of the ladies of the highest *ton*, tedious in the extreme. She must have been desperate for someone who could share in her inter-ests. No one knew better than Justin how difficult it was to find such people. If that were the case, then he had done her a grave injustice, and it was time he apologized. Resolving to call on her that very afternoon, he drew up in front of his lodg-ings, dismounted, sent his horse to the stable, staggered up-stairs, and tumbled into bed.

When he awoke a good deal later, he was more eager than ever to call in Brook Street. After consuming a huge but be-lated breakfast, fortifying himself with numerous cups of cof-fee, followed by a brisk ride through the park, Justin felt invigorated enough to take on the entire world much less a woman who, despite her widowhood, was no more than a mere chit of a girl.

His intended quarry was in the drawing room comfortably curled up on a divan surrounded by piles of newspapers. Boney was sleeping peacefully on her shoulder enjoying the warmth of the ray of sunshine that washed over both of them. Diana was frowning in concentration as she attempted to sort out the finer points of the debate over income tax that was now occupying the House of Lords, and trying to fathom the effect the variety of possible decisions might have on those persons wishing to invest in the funds. It was all extremely compli-cated, and she was not at all sure she was capable of divining the implications of it all. This sort of speculation seemed the most expedient way to repair her meager finances, but it could be very worrisome.

So deep in thought was she that she didn't hear Finchley's knock, nor was she aware of anyone's presence until the butler coughed discreetly and announced in stentorian tones, "The Lord Justin St. Clair to see you, ma'am."

Aroused unwilling from a pleasant nap, Boney stirred and ruffled his feathers, muttering grumpily, "Insufferable, arro-gant man," the customary sounds his quick ear had picked up in connection with the words *Justin St. Clair.*

Justin grinned. So now it was Diana's turn to blush with

chagrin at the antics of that blasted bird. "Now where do you suppose Bonaparte learned that litany," he wondered aloud.

"Boney is a very clever bird, sir," she replied, a conscious look on her charmingly flushed countenance.

"But not, I think, an independent thinker, eh Boney?" He strolled over to reach out a tentative finger to the feisty gray bird who cocked his head inquiringly, and slowly blinked one eye.

Doing her best to stifle an answering grin as her traitorous pet sidled along her shoulder toward her visitor, Diana continued, "Now that we have succeeded in insulting you, may we know the purpose of your call?"

"Why yes." Justin stroked the iridescent head, which leaned toward him inviting just such attention. "I came to apologize."

"Apologize!" Shaken out of her carefully maintained composure, Diana sat bolt upright, abruptly interrupting Boney's blissful interlude.

"Yes, apologize. You express surprise, but as you do not ask what I am apologizing for, I assume you are still miffed with me."

Diana's eyes darkened. "Miffed is not precisely the word I should choose, furious more like. What right had you, sir, to intrude in my life, to pass judgment on me? What right?"

"None, actually." Justin grinned ruefully. "And that is why I felt I owed you an apology, for I know how I should feel if someone were to force himself into my life and start ordering me about."

There was no resisting his offhand candor. A reluctant smile flickered at the corners of her mouth, but was quickly suppressed. "Yes, you were rather overbearing about it, weren't you?"

"I suppose I was, rather. May I make amends by inviting you and Lady Walden to accompany me to view the collection of Lucien Bonaparte's pictures that will be offered for sale later in the Season? There will also be a public showing just prior to the sale, but Mr. Stanley, knowing that I am particularly fond of the Flemish School, has invited me to view them privately, as there are some very fine pencil sketches by Vandermeer and Jordaens."

This about-face was rather too much for Diana, and she could not help but wonder what was behind it. The combative attitude previously exhibited by her caller had been all too genuine for this new approach to be equally so, and Diana was wary.

She had no intention of being maneuvered into anything by anyone, whether they did so by browbeating her, deceiving her, or charming her. And furthermore, she was not such a green girl that she did not know something of Justin St. Clair's reputation as a man of considerable address. However, she did not wish to be accused of being farouche either. It was something of a dilemma, and she paused for a moment examining her possible responses and their implications.

It was Justin who came to her rescue. Seeing her hesitation, he could not help gloating over her discomfiture. At last he took pity on her, offering her an excuse in the most gentlemanly way. "Of course, you must be prodigiously busy, what with Lady Walden as your guest, and undoubtedly, you still have a great deal to do concerning Lord Hatherill's affairs."

It was completely untrue, but Diana seized upon this gratefully, stammering, "Yes, things are still at sixes and sevens. I only go out on the rarest of occasions. However," she added conscientiously, "it is most kind of you." Though it was not in the least kind, she thought resentfully. One could just tell from the faint glint in his eye that he was thoroughly enjoying the disordered state to which he had reduced her. Now she did not know what to think—a most disconcerting feeling for one who had always been entirely sure of herself and her ability to cope with anything.

"Well then, perhaps another time. Actually, all I truly came to do was to acknowledge that I had, to coin a phrase, been an *insufferable arrogant man*, eh Boney, and to see if we couldn't try to be, if not friends, at least not enemies, or perhaps even civil acquaintances, since my nephew holds you in such high esteem."

The man actually seemed sincere and, after all, the quarrel had not been of her making. Diana inclined her head graciously. "Yes, I believe we could."

Justin took her hand, bowing low over it. "I look forward to improving our acquaintance." A quick penetrating glance, and he was gone leaving her to a welter of confused thoughts.

Which was the real Justin St. Clair: the arrogant uncle bent on preventing his nephew from making a disastrous mésalliance, the clever banterer who could top one Latin quotation with another, or the man she had met just who who seemed to appreciate and sympathize with her? There was no question the man had considerable poise and charm. He had correctly interpreted Boney's remarks with aplomb and had responded with a graceful humor that she could not but admire. And yet . . .and yet, Diana still sensed the unstated competition between the two of them that had led her to believe he enjoyed his ability to throw her and gain the upper hand.

Diana had to admit that she was rather looking forward to their next encounter. Though she told herself, it was merely that she disliked being bested by anyone and that she wished to regain her position of superiority, a small voice at the back of her mind was telling her that she enjoyed sparring with Justin and was invigorated by the challenge he offered.

Shaking her head, she resolutely banished such unsettling thoughts and reapplied herself with vigor to her reading while Boney, thoroughly bored by this tame response to such an interesting and sympathetic visitor, flew over to cling to the curtain and survey the passing scene in the street below.

Justin rode home highly pleased with his conduct. Take that, Lady Diana, he gloated to himself. All the previous times he had tangled with her, she had been in control of the situation and he had come away feeling like an awkward schoolboy. This time he had the upper hand. While it was entirely true that his impulses were genuine—he had called on Diana to apologize because he truly did wish to be friends with someone who interested and intrigued him as much as she did—he had enjoyed throwing her off balance. Her patent confusion at his abrupt change in tactics had made him experience just the slightest sense of superiority.

She had been made uncomfortable by his invitation, and Justin found himself feeling both sorry for her awkwardness and attracted by it. As an articulate woman well able to fend for herself in the world, she challenged him, and he reveled in competing with her. But in the oddest sort of way, her hesitation, which had suddenly made her appear vulnerable, had touched him and drawn him to her in a manner that her unde-

niable beauty and sophistication had not. Justin, too, looked
forward to their next meeting. He did not know in the least
what to expect, but he felt sure, knowing the lady, that it was
bound to be intriguing.

Chapter 11

DESPITE his high expectations, Justin could in no way have visualized where he would next encounter Lady Diana Hatherill. In fact, she was the farthest thing from his mind as he rode up in front of the Stock Exchange, dismounted, and tossed a coin to the waiting boy who grabbed Brutus's reins. He was so immersed in mulling over the possible effects the repeal of the income tax might have on the funds, that he didn't even notice the carriage that pulled up behind him, nor would he have even thought any more of it had not two heavily veiled females emerged and allowed themselves to be handed down by the lackey who had rushed to help them.

Women, at the Stock Exchange? And they were obviously women of the highest *ton* from the look of their clothes, their equipage, and their bearing. In spite of his own pressing affairs, Justin stopped for a moment to gaze curiously at them before entering to conduct his own business.

He was soon so engrossed in the details of a joint stock venture in which he was being invited to participate, that he had entirely forgotten about them by the time he bid good day to Mr. Goldsmith and headed back to collect Brutus.

Much to his surprise, as Justin gained the street he again caught sight of the two women deep in conversation with James Capel himself. Curious, he moved closer as unobtrusively as possible. As he approached, the august gentleman bowed low over their hands and, wishing them both good health and prosperity, bid them adieu. The women thanked him and turned to be helped back into the awaiting carriage. This time, because they had been talking, their veils were lifted, and to Justin's complete astonishment, he recognized Lady Walden and her great-niece.

"Lady Walden, Lady Diana, you here?" he blurted out before he could stop himself. They turned, as taken aback by his presence as he was by theirs.

Diana was the first to recover. "And why should we not be here?" she demanded defiantly.

"Why, no reason, I suppose," he stammered. "It is just that one does not usually think of women in connection with the Stock Exchange."

"And why not, pray tell? Do you think, sir, that women are not capable of entering into such a masculine domain?" Her eyes sparkled dangerously.

"Not at all, Lady Diana, quite the contrary. I was thinking that it takes an extraordinary person to venture alone into such unaccustomed areas as you do." There was not a hint of guile in his voice, nor was there any mistaking the warmth in his tone and the genuine admiration in his eyes.

"Well," she responded in a mollified tone, "financial necessity can give anyone, man or woman, quite an incentive to explore the unknown. After all, great fortunes were never made without great risk."

Despite the bravado of her words, there was such an anxious expression lurking in her eyes that Justin suddenly found himself wanting to help her, to relieve the worries that were behind that look. But all he said was, "It does take a great deal of courage to speculate at a time like this."

"I know," she agreed with a quickly stifled sigh. "What with the abundance of wheat and the lowering of prices, farmers unable to pay bankers and the lack of market for our goods abroad, things look rather grim. I suppose I should be purchasing more shares while they are cheap in the expectation that things will improve, but if they do not, I . . ." Her voice trailed off as the prospect of losing the very little money she had rose up before her.

I must be mad, Diana thought to herself. Instead of saving Buckland, I could be running myself deeper into debt than I am now for the repairs I just had made to the fences. I could lose everything. "Suffice to say, I stand to forfeit all that I had hoped to save by such speculation," she continued briskly, taking herself severely to task for her temporary lack of nerve.

But Justin had noticed her pause and, reading into it various implications, was oddly touched by all that had been left unsaid. "What you say is of course very true, but I believe this resistance to British goods on the Continent is merely a temporary state of affairs. At the moment, Europe needs to recover from years of war and devastation; but that sort of rebuilding will be accomplished very soon and then they will have money to spend on manufactured articles of which ours are vastly superior to any in the world. At the same time, we are developing markets elsewhere in the world beyond the Continent, so I believe your thinking on this matter to be entirely sound," he hastened to reassure her.

"I only hope you are correct," she replied, but the note of doubt remained.

"Lady Diana, I am not indulging in idle conjecture, believe me. I spent a good portion of last year on the Continent discussing economic as well as political questions with those who are most informed about such things. Since my return, I have continued to correspond with those whose clarity of vision and opinions I respect highly. Here at home, I have made it my business to acquaint myself with the engineers and inventors who are working to improve our methods of manufacture and transportation as well as the men in trade and banking. The state of affairs may not seem promising at the moment, but I am certain we are on the verge of more prosperous times."

Justin paused to catch his breath. He had not intended to sound so vehement, but for some unfathomable reason he wanted most desperately to offer her hope and to relieve the anxiety she so clearly felt. Then, too, it was rare that anyone of his acquaintance was even interested in the things that occupied so much of his time and energy, much less understand them. It was a relief to speak of these issues to someone else, as it helped to clarify his own thinking. He glanced down at Diana, and was pleased to see that his words had at least erased the worried frown from her brow.

"Thank you." She smiled up at him. "I don't mean to doubt your word, it's just that I am uneasy at the magnitude of the risk, but I had quite forgot that you had been in Vienna. How very exciting that must have been. Would you, do you think, I mean, I should love to hear more about it sometime. Of course, there is the paltry bit that was in the papers, but in the main, there was so little talk of it here that it is difficult to make out all the points and issues that were being discussed.

And nobody one meets here is least bit interested in such things. Their only concern with foreign affairs was the destruction of Bonaparte, but beyond that, no one stops to consider the other implications of the reconstruction of Europe or the competing concerns of the Allies. It must have required great delicacy and tact to move among so many different people, all of whom were bent on securing their own ends."

"Why, yes, it did demand the utmost diplomacy, which, it may surprise you to learn, I am quite capable of employing." Justin cocked one speculative eyebrow at her.

"It does," she agreed, but the ghost of a smile quivered on her lips, and there was an answering twinkle in her eyes.

The impatient snorting of the horses recalled Justin to his surroundings. "But I am detaining you—most rag-mannered of me to keep you standing here on the street when you must have a thousand things to attend to. Allow me." He held out his hand helping first Lady Walden and then her great-niece into the carriage before closing the door, but he could not refrain from adding, "I am well aware that Lady Walden has numerous acquaintances—friends and admirers of her husband—on whom she may rely to advise her should she need it, but I would be most happy to help you in any way if I may be of the least assistance." Sensitive to Diana's prickly independence he hastened to add, "Not that you are not entirely proficient in making excellently sound decisions yourself, as indeed you seem to be doing. But I am more likely to be in the way of hearing things that can be used to your advantage than you are. I would consider it an honor if you would allow me to do so."

What had come over him, Justin wondered. He sounded almost as verbose as Reginald. Here he was offering to embroil himself in the affairs of the very person from who he was attempting to disentangle his nephew. He must be all about in the head, but he was no proof against the surprise and gratitude that shone unexpectedly in the dark blue eyes looking down at him.

"Why, thank you. It is most kind of you, though there is no need for you to do such a thing," Diana hurriedly qualified her thanks, lest he think her incapable of managing her own affairs.

"Oh, I quite realize that, but it would be my pleasure, believe me." Worse and worse. He sounded like an eager school-boy.

Aunt Seraphina had sat silent through the entire conversation, a highly interested spectator, but now in the interests of the horses, which were becoming restive, she intervened. "That is indeed most kind of you. Thomas always maintained that the most successful businessman was one who listened and observed. The more eyes and ears we have, the better we shall do. Please do come and call on us. All my knowledge of foreign commerce is confined mostly to that in the Indies. We should be delighted to have you visit sometime, but indeed, we must be off." And, that, she thought to herself, should give Reginald a run for his money, as well as company in Brook Street that is worthy of Diana.

"Of course. I apologize for keeping you so long. I look forward to further discussions, and in the meantime I shall make discreet inquiries as to where one can best invest one's capital. Good day." Justin took Brutus's reins from the lad who had been in charge of him and, with a final bow, leapt on the horse's back and headed off down the street, leaving the carriage to follow more sedately in his wake.

There was complete silence all the way to Brook Street as Diana turned over in her mind all the implications of her latest encounter with Justin St. Clair. It had been somewhat of a shock to come upon him involved in a serious endeavor. But even more unexpected and surprising was to have him treat her as an equal who was also pursuing the ends similar to his own. Indeed, it was gratifying.

After his initial surprise at encountering her in such unusual circumstances, St. Clair had accepted her presence there as calmly as he would that of any male acquaintance, and had even offered his support and help. She could think of no one, with the exception of Aunt Seraphina, who would have taken her as seriously. Even Reginald, who professed to admire her for her intelligence, would have considered her appearance at the Stock Exchange highly improper, if not downright scandalous. But St. Clair had not stopped to consider this. In fact, he professed to admire her for such unconventional behavior, even encouraging her in it by offering his assistance.

Justin St. Clair was a man of many facets as she was beginning to discover. Now, instead of wishing he would stop meddling in her affairs, Diana actually found herself hoping he would appear in Brook Street as he had promised.

Knowing her niece's reticent nature, Aunt Seraphina continued to maintain the silence that had fallen the instant St. Clair had taken his leave of them, but from time to time she stole quick but comprehensive glances at her Diana's expressive profile.

Though Diana might not confide in others, her face was a mirror for her thoughts, and Seraphina could read the struggle ensuing in her mind. Here was a man who less than a fortnight ago had implied that she was not fit for his family now eagerly proffering comfort and advice. Which was the real man? Was he deceiving her or had he truly changed his mind about her. Seraphina sensed her great-niece's hesitation, but also her interest.

For the first time in Diana's life, someone whose intellectual capacity matched her own was paying attention to her and appreciating her. Lady Walden could see the effect that that little bit of attention had on her great-niece. There was an intentness, an eagerness about her that had not been there before, and Diana's great aunt congratulated herself for having done her bit to encourage Justin St. Clair's continued presence at Brook Street.

Chapter 12

HAVING quitted the ladies and started off at a lively pace, Justin, also reviewing the previous scene, allowed the reins to slacken as he turned it all over in his mind. His progress along Change Alley, which had begun so briskly, slowed to a crawl. Who would have expected to encounter Lady Diana in such a locale? Did this mean that she was more or less of a fortune hunter than he had originally thought? Was she so intent on repairing her economic situation that she was speculating on the marriage mart as she speculated in the financial markets? Or was she trying, in a most unheard of and courageous way, to support herself without having to resort to the customary way of improving one's capital, which was to contrive an advantageous matrimonial connection.

As he had been so many times before, Justin was entirely perplexed as to the truth of the matter. He could not remember when he had been so at a loss to judge a person or that person's motives, and the lady, it would appear, delighted in confounding him at every turn, never allowing him to guess her true intentions or emotions. Most women, no matter how flirtatious, were entirely transparent in letting one know their wishes and desires, but as soon as Diana was betrayed into revealing one aspect of herself, she was quick to qualify or dispel the impression she had created.

Did this behavior spring from a natural duplicity or from a natural reserve? Was it a mechanism to protect herself and keep others from knowing her too well, and from divining her strengths and weaknesses? Whatever the answer, he was wasting far too much time and energy over it. Lord, he was fast becoming as incapable of wiping Lady Diana Hatherill from his thoughts as was his lovesick nephew, and he didn't even like the chit. Or did he?

Enough of that, St. Clair, he admonished himself sternly. It's high time you sought out more congenial company. And gathering the reins firmly in his hands, he headed Brutus toward the restorative camaraderie of Brooks's.

For her part, plagued by thoughts as unsettling as those that were disturbing St. Clair, Diana, in the ensuing days, did her best to put both the gentleman and his nephew out of her mind. She accepted Tony Washburne's invitations to go riding in the park, attended the exhibition of artists in the British Gallery with Aunt Seraphina, and applied herself to economic matters with zeal, tackling Mr. Robert Wilson's treatise in the *Edinburgh Review* on the high prices of corn, labor, gold bullion, and the depression of the foreign exchange, and poring over several informative pieces on the improvement of agriculture.

Her aunt, meanwhile, was not deceived by this frenzy of activity. To be sure, Diana had always devoted a goodly part of her existence to study of some sort of another, or the perusal of accounts from Buckland as she planned where to put her meager income to the best possible use; but heretofore she had gone about it calmly and methodically, shaping it all into a well-ordered routine. Now there was an intensity about her activities that made Seraphina think her great-niece was avoiding something. It was as though she were keeping herself so occupied that she could not have time to stop and reflect. And Lady Walden could hazard a fair guess as to the nature of the thoughts Diana was trying to push out of her mind.

To test her hypothesis, the older woman had casually alluded to Justin St. Clair upon occasion after their meeting at the Exchange, and had observed with great interest the pensive look that would appear on her niece's face at the mention of this name. Though loath to admit it, Seraphina was thoroughly enjoying her role in bringing these two together. Discreet inquiries made among Thomas's friends in the city revealed Justin to be the sole inheritor of his great-uncle Theobald's fortune and, furthermore, he appeared to be equally as adept at amassing wealth as his renowned relative. The word in the city was that in a very short space of time, through his clever interpretation of political events and their probable influence on trade and finance, Justin had been able to forecast the tides of economic change in order nearly to double what had been left him. During all this, he had exhibited an iron nerve that had allowed him to follow his own instincts, even in opposition to popular sentiment, thus making his investments all the more lucrative.

The more information Seraphina gleaned, the more she was intrigued. While she heartily scorned the idea that a woman needed a man in order to survive, she did long for Diana to know some of the happiness to be found in the sort of companionship she had shared with her own dear Thomas. She was most pleased at the results of her experiment, and was quietly casting about for ways to bring the two together again.

It was with this goal in mind that Lady Walden, looking up from her reading one morning as they were ensconced in comfortable silence in the drawing room, each with her own newspaper, casually mentioned that one of Thomas's oldest and dearest friends, Lord Orpington, had offered to escort them to the Countess of Axbridge's rout. "Now, I know that you have no use for such affairs, my love," she hastened to add, observing the gathering frown on her niece's brow, "but when you consider that you are so rarely seen in public, and then only in the company of Reginald, it would do you good to appear without him. I know how little you care for *on-dits* or those who deal in them, but you would care even less for having it bruited about that you are living in the viscount's pocket."

Seraphina had gauged her niece's reactions to a nicety. After a moment's reflection, Diana sighed. "I suppose you are in the right of it, but it is too tiresome of the *ton* to make one the subject of its gossip, when one has no particular desire to play a great role in it. I leave that to those who wish to cut a dash. Very well, but I would as lief stay at home. 'Tis bound to be a crush, and there is nothing so dull as these affairs that exist largely for those who wish to see and be seen."

Despite her patent reluctance, Diana made a lovely picture as she mounted the stairs, one hand lightly resting on Lord Orpington's arm. Her gown, a blue satin slip under British net, and a magnificent sapphire parure that had belonged to her mother echoed the brilliance of her eyes and emphasized the delicate flush in her cheeks. Lord Orpington, a short spare man with a long clever face and eyes that shone with a keen intelligence, had immediately put her at her ease by declaring, "Seraphina has told me of your interest in the political and commercial affairs of our nation, and I must say I am glad for it. I find it quite necessary, what with my own low taste for trade, to attend affairs such as this in order to reassure the *ton* that I have not turned into a vulgar cit. After all, it is their willingness to entrust me with their financial affairs that has allowed me to accomplish what I have, but it is so very dull to attend these things alone, when one is forced to compliment Lady So-and-So on her charming daughter and marvel that Countess Whatever does not look a day older than she did when I danced with her during her first Season. Now, however, I am able to indulge myself by asking you how you expect the price of bank stock to do, for you are more nearly connected with what is happening in the country and country banks than I, and Seraphina has just assured me that India stock is bound to rise."

Thus, by the time they reached the ballroom, the three of them were so embroiled in such a deep discussion that they barely paid attention to the crush around them. However, little as Lord Orpington's group noticed any of the rest of the guests, there were several of them—Reginald and his uncle as well as Ferdie's coterie—who were most certainly aware of their entrance. The viscount was the first to reach them, bumping into people in his eagerness to be the first to profit from this unforeseen circumstance, and secure a dance with his goddess. Pushing aside with uncharacteristic impatience an awe-inspiring dowager in purple satin, he snatched Diana's hand, bending reverently over it as the injured party muttered darkly to her companion about the sad want of manners in the modern youth.

"Lady Diana," he breathed, "I had not expected to see you here." Then realizing that such a remark might possibly be construed in an unfortunate manner, he stammered, "That is, I know you are begged to attend these affairs, but I had thought the frivolity . . . well, I mean, the serious tone of your mind must preclude . . . I mean, could I have the honor of the next dance?"

Though she found his awkward adoration and his insistence on placing her on a pedestal unnerving, Diana could not help but take pity on him. She hesitated and then agreed. "Why, thank you, Reginald. That is very sweet of you, but I must warn you, I have not danced for so long I am capable of only the most sedate of dances—nothing more dashing than a quadrille."

"Of course not, I should never expect you to indulge in country-dances or, or, the waltz." Reginald shuddered at the thought.

However, as Diana glanced over at the couples now whirling around the floor in that most daring of dances, she thought wistfully of how much she had enjoyed it when Ferdie was alive. Though Lord Hatherill had not possessed much in his cockloft, he had been the most dedicated of social creatures, and as such had been a most graceful and satisfactory partner. But Diana was not about to allow the overly infatuated Reginald the intoxicating experience of waltzing with her. He was adoring enough as it was in his own bumbling fashion. But rescue was imminent as she saw the inseparable trio of Tony, Ralph, and Henry making their way toward her. Their conversation might be far more trivial than the Viscount Chalford's but at least it was enlivening and their presence kept him from becoming too importunate.

Reginald was not the only one instantly aware of Lady Diana's entrance into the ballroom. Justin had been exchanging lighthearted banter with Lady Sybil Feltenham, when for some unaccountable reason his eyes were drawn to the other side of the room just in time to witness Reginald's headlong rush toward Diana. For once, Justin did not blame the lad. Well beyond his nephew's impressionable age, he was forced to admit that there was something truly arresting about the lady that went far beyond her undeniable beauty.

Unlike the rest of the females present, Diana's gaze did not constantly flit over the crowd evaluating this one's gown or that one's jewels. She was totally uninterested in who was partnering whom, focusing instead on the conversation she was enjoying with her aunt and Lord Orpington. The little wrinkle of concentration on her brow as she spoke, first to one and then to the other, made the flirtatious glances and coquettish air of the other women around him seem calculating and frivolous.

With the most feeble of excuses, Justin disentangled himself from the clutches of Lady Sybil and made his way purposefully toward the gathering throng around Lady Diana, who, loath as she was to admit it, had noticed Justin the moment he broke away from the dazzling woman who had been flirting so outrageously with him.

She continued to be highly conscious of him as the tall figure made his progress toward her. The more she was aware of his presence and his obvious destination, the more disconcerted she became. A mere fortnight ago she and this man had been at dagger drawing. Now she was glad to see him and, worse yet, actually hoping that he was coming to see her.

What had come over her? How could she forget her principles so quickly? The man had practically accused her of fortune hunting and now, just because he hadn't been shocked by her efforts to advance her affairs through investment and had even been supportive of them, she was happy to see him.

Control yourself, Diana, he's a diplomat. He knows how to charm even the most demanding of foreign ministers, the most difficult of potentates. An innocent like you is mere child's play for someone like him. Don't administer to his already well-developed arrogance by allowing him to win you over as he has apparently done with so many others. She stole a quick glimpse at the admiring glances and alluring looks cast in his direction as he approached.

By the time Justin reached Lord Orpington's party, Diana had gotten herself well in hand and was able to greet him with a cool graciousness that offered enough contrast to her manner toward Reginald and the others to disconcert Justin in his turn. But with a supreme effort, he quelled his misgivings at her distant air and the obvious lack of welcome on the part of the young men surrounding her. Smiling broadly, he bowed over her hand. "How delighted to see you, Lady Diana. I do hope that you have saved one free dance for me from among your crowd of admirers." He had meant to maintain the same light tone he had used to address Lady Sybil, but somehow he could not keep the edge from his voice.

Highly sensitive as she was to everything concerning Justin St. Clair, Diana picked this up immediately and just as immediately misconstrued it as yet another criticism of her. Well, if he thought her to be that sort of person then she would be. Take that, St. Clair, she muttered fiercely to herself as she sought the proper responses. Tilting her head coquettishly, she allowed the glimmer of a smile to tug at the corner of her mouth. "I expect I might be persuaded to find one free dance for you, sir."

"Good. I shall claim the next waltz, fair lady," he replied matching tone for tone. What was she about? This provocative manner was unlike the previous Dianas he had heretofore encountered—injured and outraged victim of the St. Clair family's suspicions, worried investor, interested listener. So involved was he with trying to interpret this unfamiliar phase that he completely failed to remark his nephew's obvious surprise at her acquiescence.

In fact, Diana was almost as taken aback at her capitulation as Reginald was. What had possessed her to agree to it and in a manner that would have not put the vainest of the Season's incomparables to shame? There was nothing for it now but to accept the hand he offered her, and allow herself to be led onto the dance floor.

Chapter 13

FOR a moment, they were entirely occupied with matching each one's way of moving to the other's while making their way among the other couples, whirling around them to a relatively clear space on the floor. Diana could not help marveling at what a delightful sensation it was to be lost in the music, gliding effortlessly in time to it. St. Clair guided her so deftly that she did not need to think, but could give herself up instead to the wonderful sensation of floating across the room. How she had missed this. Poor Ferdie. Waltzing with him was the closest she had ever felt to her husband, for dancing was the only activity in which he could truly have been said to excel. And Justin was even a more satisfying partner than Ferdie.

Where Ferdie had grace, Justin possessed the agility and strength of a natural athlete. She could feel it in the pressure of his hand in the small of her back leading her, communicating with her. She and Ferdie had been well matched as partners, but somehow she moved as one with Justin St. Clair. What an odd thought.

Pushing it resolutely aside, Diana sought to break the intensity of the silence that enveloped them. "It is a sad crush, is it not? I am told it is one of the events of the Season, and, judging from the brilliance of the guests, I take it to be true. I had quite forgotten what a spectacle these affairs could afford." That was worse. Now she sounded like the veriest chit from the schoolroom.

"You are well amused, I trust, Lady Diana. I am sure that they are far more brilliant now that you have reappeared, my lady," Justin responded smoothly, but inside he was asking himself what ever had prompted to offer Spanish coin to someone like Lady Diana Hatherill. However, it had been automatic, he justified himself. Why should he not? At the moment she was behaving like any other of the *ton*'s dashing matrons. At their first encounter when he had seen the flash of anger in her eyes or when he recalled his impressions of her at their meeting at the Stock Exchange he had thought she was different from all the rest, that she possessed her own particular values that set her apart from the rest of the fashionable throng, but apparently he had been mistaken. Now she seemed like just another coquette eager to win masculine attention, and oddly enough he felt rather deflated by the discovery. Well, he would give her just what she deserved.

So for the rest of the dance he kept up a steady flow of polite chatter, while Diana, firm in her resolve not to let herself take advantage of her own weakness and confusion, responded to his badinage with her own.

To give Lady Diana her due, Justin decided, she was quicker and more clever than most of the women with whom he had enjoyed a mild flirtation that evening or any other, but she was not so unusual as he had at first thought her to be, and his suspicions of her motive in regards to his nephew were once again reanimated.

Later, when he caught sight of Lord Alan Beardsley, some devil bent on extracting an odd sort of revenge made him lead his friend over to her with the suggestion that he solicit Diana's hand for the *boulanger*.

Alan, Lord Beardsley, Marquess of Hillingdon, had looked the picture of misery when Justin ran into him on his way to procure refreshments for Diana and Lady Walden. An unhappy frown crumpled his leonine countenance and drops of perspiration were beading on his brow.

"Alan?" Justin exclaimed. "You here?"

"In the flesh." His lordship sighed gloomily.

"But why? How on earth?"

"Well, you might ask. Needless to say, it is under extreme duress that I appear at . . .at this." He waved a derogatory hand at the glittering assemblage surrounding them.

"What ever could possibly bring such pressure to bear that you would agree to mingling with the yahoos of the *ton*?" Justin wondered. Well acquainted with his friend's reclusive and scholarly tastes, he was indeed surprised to discover him in such a populous place as London, let alone a ball.

"My mother" was the dismal reply. "She promised to leave me alone and allow me to continue to build my observatory at the park in peace if I would attend a few of these . . .these"— Lord Beardsley grasped in vain for words scornful enough to characterize the countess's rout—"affairs with her when I came to town." He finished.

"Silly clunch," Justin retorted unsympathetically. "You should have stayed at home." However, there was a twinkle in his eye.

He and Lord Beardsley had been friends ever since their school days when Justin had defended the younger lad against some of the older boys who were taunting *Moony* Beardsley as they tried to wrest his telescope from him. Alan was a short and awkward boy who was noticeable for his lack of stature and athletic prowess, even among the boys in his own form; but he had hung onto his instrument with such dogged determination that Justin could not help but admire him.

St. Clair had always disliked unkindness of any sort, and he had flung himself into the lad's defense, sending the bullies to rout. So Alan had offered to his defender the only things of value he possessed—to do his schoolwork for him.

It came as a shock to him when Justin had graciously refused, saying that he preferred to do his own. For Alan, already preparing most of the Latin and mathematics exercises for his form and the two above him, this had been a revelation. He had been curious as well as surprised. That such a Trojan as Justin, who had mastered every possible athletic endeavor with ease, not only possessed a mind but used it, was a phenomenon beyond his ordinary experience. Still skeptical, he had grilled Justin in every conceivable way and found him equal to any question he could put forward.

It had been a new experience for both of them. Neither one had ever encountered an intellectual peer among the adults surrounding him. Encouraged by the self-confidence Justin had inspired in him, the young marquess soon caught up to him in his studies despite their three-year age difference, and they had gone off to Cambridge together, where they immediately challenged the entire university; Alan taking on the tutors and Justin every pretty female in the place.

Alan had remained ill at ease among his fellow men, despite Justin's best efforts to initiate him into the more convivial as-pects of university life, until at long last he had begun to relax and enjoy a race meeting here or a mill there. He was forever grateful to his mentor for including him in these adventures and encouraging his acceptance among the students.

He was fully aware that it was through Justin's tutoring that he had become assured enough to allow his understated but rapier wit to shine through his shy appearance, and thus had become appreciated among his acquaintances as an amusing eccentric whose madcap brilliance could be highly entertaining and always educational. But despite Justin's best efforts, women continued to reduce him to a paralysis of fear. From his domineering mother to the local beauties whom she forced him to partner at the local assemblies near Hillingdon Park, he was terrified into silence. His mother would bully and they would simper until poor Alan, unable to hit upon a reasonable topic of conversation, was always eventually forced to turn and flee.

It was not that he disliked woman precisely. He would have given a great deal to possess his friend's easy charm that seemed to endear chambermaids and incomparables alike. But Alan, who had led a lonely childhood with only books and tutors as his companions, had never learned the art of desultory conversation and therefore was ill equipped to converse on any subject lighter than the theories of Pythagoras or Plato's *Republic*. His first essays on such topics had caused young misses to gaze aghast at him and seek solace with anyone, no matter how ugly, poor, old, or feebleminded in order to be able to understand what was being addressed to them. These unfortunate early experiences had given the young Lord Beardsley such a distaste for social intercourse that he had resolutely avoided it at all costs for years; hence his old schoolmate's amazement at coming across him in such foreign surroundings.

"It must have been a very strong attraction indeed that lured you from the safety of Hillingdon Park to the delights of the metropolis."

"It was." Alan sighed at the remembrance of the marchioness's delight at learning her son was forced to make a visit to town.

"That bad, eh?" Justin remarked sympathetically as he caught his friend's involuntary glance to a corner of the room where the Marchioness of Hillingdon was holding court with the other town tabbies.

"Yes." The reply, though simple, held all the eloquence of a desperate man. "I wanted to consult them at Greenwich about some of the instruments I am planning to acquire at Hillingdon. Besides, you know John Herschel has left Cambridge to assist his father."

"He has?" Though Justin's and John's paths had barely crossed, their mutual friendship with Alan had kept Justin aware of the young man's brilliant career at the university. It would have taken a great deal to make him leave its hallowed halls.

"Yes. His father's health is failing, but he insists on keeping up his research, so there was nothing for it but for John to help him. I thought I . . ." Alan's gasp of dismay caused his friend to glance up in time to see the marchioness, like a Spanish galleon in full sail, bearing down upon them.

"Relax, my lad. Let me handle this." St. Clair laid a comforting hand on his friend's shoulder. "How delightful to see you, ma'am," Justin greeted his friend's mother, treating her to the full benefit of his devastating smile. "I admire your skill in luring Alan to the countess's rout, and I am taking advantage of his presence to introduce him to a charming young woman of my acquaintance."

Ignoring Lord Beardsley's horrified gaze and the imploring clutch on his sleeve, he continued, "But I shall return to claim the next quadrille with you if I may. As I remember, you always appeared to your best on the dance floor—such elegance and such queenly bearing. I was quite young at the time, as your husband was still alive, but I do hope you will indulge me."

"Why, how kind. Of course I shouldn't, I am far too old. What must the others think? But thank you, I would quite enjoy that." The lady, taken completely by surprise, stammered like a schoolgirl.

"I am honored. Until then, I expect Lord Wayland here will keep you tolerably amused." Beckoning to a young buck bearing down on them, Justin hailed him. "Hello, Andrew. Thought I might see you here. Be a good fellow and keep Alan's mother company while I take him to meet a young lady I feel certain will interest him."

Lord Wayland, another university acquaintance, struck as incoherent as the marchioness by the picture of Lord Beardsley with a female at a ball, nodded blankly as Justin gave his friend a gentle push in the direction of Lady Diana's little party.

"But, Justin, you know I," Alan began to object then, recalling the truly masterful way in which his former schoolmate had handled his redoubtable mother, fell silent, giving himself up to the inevitable with as much good grace as he could muster. After all, Justin had never steered him wrong before, but there was always a first time, he thought grimly as he followed his friend across the crowded room.

Meanwhile Justin was congratulating himself. He had seen enough of Lady Diana to feel quite certain she would soon have Alan relaxed and conversing as easily as she had charmed the hapless Reginald—and Alan was a far greater catch. Far more intelligent than Viscount Chalford, he had the added charm of having already succeeded to his father's title and fortune, both of which were far more impressive than those that Reginald had to look forward to.

True to his predictions, Lady Diana soon put his friend at ease. On being informed that Lord Beardsley was in town to visit the celebrated William Herschel and his son, she immediately brightened exclaiming, "Are you an astronomer? Then I am quite in luck, for I have a particular question I should like to address to someone well versed in such things. Undoubtedly, you are well acquainted with the *Almagest* are you not, Lord Beardsley?"

Diana's quick assessment of Lord Beardsley's character had not been mistaken. Shocked out of his customary timidity by the lady's apparent knowledge, he replied without even thinking, "Why, yes, but are you?"

"Not well enough, it seems. There are certain concepts that I still find perplexing and, knowledgeable as Lady Walden and Viscount Chalford are in their own particular realms, they have not the least interest or inclination for matters scientific."

"Are *you* an astronomer then?" Alan gazed in patent amazement at this astounding young woman.

"Oh no, not in the least," Diana hastened to reassure him. Actually, I was reading Ptolemy's *Harmonica*, which I found to be so fascinating that I turned to his other more famous work, which was even more intriguing, but rather rough going for me I am afraid. I am unable to grasp his theory of the equant, but I feel sure that with a little explanation on the part of someone who understands it, it would become clearer to me."

Lord Beardsley stood openmouthed. He very rarely expected such words to issue from the mouths of his fellow men, much less a female. In fact, so interested was he by the phenomenon that he quite forgot his customary shyness when faced with a member of the opposite sex. "Well, it is not all that complicated really if one stops to consider . . ." he began.

"Alan, why do you not explain all this to Lady Diana during the quadrille. Your mama keeps looking over here, which reminds me of my promise to lead her in this next set. I must take my leave of you." And with that Justin was off leaving his friend to stare helplessly after him.

"She does look as though she wishes us to dance," Diana commented, correctly interpreting the marchioness's rather pointed looks in their direction.

Alan nodded glumly.

"Well, as she seems to be one of *those* sorts of mothers, perhaps we had better do so. Tony Washburne has just such a mama. She is forever keeping her eye on him, but once he has danced with me and one or two other unexceptionable women, she usually quite forgets about him and disappears into the card room."

"She does?" The concept of thus handling an interfering parent was obviously a new and striking one to his lordship.

"Oh yes," Diana blithely assured him, "and as he doesn't really consider me a female and as I can usually find him at least one other person who doesn't simper at him, we deal extremely well together. I am not a bad dancer, and I can see that you are quite light on your feet. We should manage very well I should think, and then your mother will ignore you, I promise."

The idea that he, Lord Beardsley, who had always been the last boy to be chosen for a team at games, should be thought of as anything but clumsy was so novel that at first it was impossible for him to grasp. But the more Alan considered it, the more he realized that it was self-consciousness more than anything else that had made him awkward. After arriving at this discovery, he actually began to relax and enjoy discussing with Diana the purpose of his trip to London, the Herschels and their work, and his own particular interests in the field.

Thus it was that Justin, catching sight of his friend as he and the Marchioness of Hillingdon completed a figure, was astonished to see him talking and dancing as easily as anyone else in the room. As chief architect of the entire situation, he should have been inordinately pleased, but somehow he was unaccountably annoyed that Diana had been so successful at making Lord Beardsley relax.

After conducting Alan's mother to the card room and assuring himself of her comfort, Justin made his way back to the group where Alan was earnestly explaining to a genuinely interested Diana how Ptolemy had improved upon Hipparchus's original star charts while Lady Walden and Lord Orpington were deep in a discussion of the East India Company.

In fact, Reginald was the only one who paid the least attention to his uncle's approach. "Hello, sir." He seized upon Justin eagerly and was about to launch into one of his usual extended discourses when a silvery voice fluted, "Justin St Clair, how perfectly charming to see you here."

Justin turned to find himself confronted with a vision "Hello, Blanche," he greeted her with tones that failed to echo the lady's enthusiasm.

Secure in her position as the reigning toast of the clubs Lady Blanche Howard was oblivious to the gentleman's lack of interest, launching instead into a running commentary of who had set her cap at whom and which one of the Season's crop of hopefuls was most likely to be sought after. "But I must say there are far more young ladies than gentlemen here and there is positively no one besides you and Lord Livermore who has the least amount of dash." The beauty pouted prettily at him.

"Blanche, you must overcome this blind partiality on your part. What about Viscount Rexhame? No one who has recently fought two duels can be said to be lacking in *dash*," Justin began helpfully.

"What, Colin? He's a mere baby—wet behind the ears. need someone who is a man of the world." Laying a small white hand on his arm, she raised adoring blue eyes to his face.

Any other man would have been reduced to abject slavery—transfixed by her melting look, the perfect rosebud mouth parted slightly, and a delicate blush tinging the perfect complexion—any other man but Lord Justin St. Clair that is. Accustomed to being sought after by women of all nations and all ranks, he remained unmoved in the face of such loveliness. In fact, misliking altogether the young lady's proprietary air, he hastily disengaged his arm. "You flatter me, Blanche, but I rather fancy that is Castlereagh beckoning to me, and one ignores such a summons at one's peril."

He truly had remarked the foreign secretary glancing in his direction, and had caught the statesman's eye in order to have an excuse to escape. Just to give credence to his words, Justin did stop to exchange a few desultory remarks with the gentleman, pausing just long enough for the briefest of exchanges before he quit the ballroom in disgust.

Why had he returned to England? He should have stayed on the Continent. At least there the women were only out for amusement instead of one's hand in holy matrimony, and at least there they were honest about it.

Lady Blanche Howard did not care a fig for Lord Justin St. Clair. All she cared for was to capture his wealth to add to her already considerable fortune, his impeccable lineage to lend respectability to her family's recently acquired title, and the cachet of having won one of the *ton*'s sought after bachelors.

Justin snorted in disgust and directed his coachman to Suzette's. She at least had a perfectly healthy appreciation for his appetites and maintained the relationship on the most practical of levels, so that it was mutually beneficial to both of them with no false protestations of undying affections to confuse the issue.

Chapter 14

IT was with the utmost sigh of relief that Justin climbed the stairs to the opera dancer's house and handed his hat and cape to Mademoiselle de Charenton herself. For all that theirs was a financial arrangement, Suzette greeted him with far more real appreciation in her eyes and far less covetousness than Lady Blanche had.

"Suzette, my dear, you look utterly ravishing." Justin's eyes slid appreciatively over the diaphanous gown that revealed more than it covered. He planted a lingering kiss on her generous lips and allowed her to lead him to a satin-covered divan before a welcoming blaze, and gratefully accepted the glass of brandy she handed him. How blessedly quiet and serene it was here, the crackle of the fire the only sound, the soft candlelight washing over silken hangings. Justin sighed and ran a hand over his brow. Why did he bother with charades such as the Countess of Axbridge's rout? He always came away feeling as though he were nothing so much as a Thoroughbred on parade at Tattersall's, and his encounters this evening had done nothing to lessen this sensation. Lady Diana's behavior had only made it all worse. He had been beginning to believe that she at least was a woman who was above such things. Almost she had convinced him of her uniqueness with her obvious knowledge, quick mind, and her determination to prove herself in what had always been a strictly masculine domain. But she had proven tonight that she was no better than any other member of her sex or the *ton*, for that matter.

"Ah, *mon chéri*, you must not frown so." Suzette came to sit next to him, her eyes full of concern.

"I beg your pardon, my dear. How rag-mannered of me to ignore the most beautiful woman in all of London." He raised his glass to her before gulping it down.

"Flatterer. The countess's rout must have been a terrible squeeze to make such an eligible bachelor depart after such a brief stay and looking so *ennuyé*. Relax, *mon brave*." She traced the line of his jaw with one dainty finger before reaching up to pull his head down to meet her eager lips. Justin sighed and gave himself up to her caresses.

The candles were guttering and the fire had sunk into embers before, exhausted, he finally emerged from their passionate embrace as they lay on the soft carpet in front of the hearth and stared up at the cherubim holding the garlands of roses across the corners of the ceiling. One hand absently stroked the flame-colored hair that fanned out across his chest, and a smile of pure satisfaction hovered about his mouth. Suzette stirred sleepily and then propped herself up on one elbow to gaze down at him.

"Feeling better now, *chéri*," she murmured softly.

"Much better." He pulled her to him. "You are a most delightful antidote to the social rigors of the *ton*, and offer a delicious contrast to all those women bent on being hailed as incomparables."

The dancer sighed with satisfaction and lay her head back against his chest. Certainly Justin St. Clair provided his own *delicious contrast* to any lover she had had before, and she certainly had had her pick of the best that England and Europe could offer. "Ah, *mon pauvre*, you are one who is hopelessly romantic, *non*?" Her tone was teasing as she tugged a dark lock of hair that had fallen over his forehead, but the emerald eyes looking deep into his were serious.

"I?" He sat up in mock horror. "I, the man who is dubbed a perennial bachelor, the scourge of husband-hunting damsels, romantic? How could you possibly arrive at such a cork-brained conclusion?"

"Because you are so *ennuyé* by those marriage-mad young ladies. You are *dégoûté*, which means that somehow they do not measure up to some ideal that you have. Therefore, you must hold some romantic but unattainable notion of what a woman must be." She eyed him closely as he stared intently into the fire. "I am correct, *non*?"

Justin remained silent for some time, his gazed fixed on the glowing embers. At last he turned to her, his expression more somber than the dancer had ever seen. "You are a wise woman, Suzette, a wise woman."

"I know," she gave a little shrug, "which is why I do not pursue such hopeless dreams. Me, I prefer to fix my mind on those things which are attainable."

"But do you not long for true love, mademoiselle; a love so strong that it binds you to another in a union of the minds and souls, so strong that it transcends all other petty concerns?"

The dancer laughed. "You are a fool, my friend. Such things do not exist, and I am grateful that I was made aware of this at such a young age. I learned that one can not truly rely on anyone but oneself to take care of one, and I am stronger for it. Whenever I encounter someone as wonderful as you, it is a surprise of the most delightful, *non*? And it is a good deal better to see things this way than to be constantly disappointed in others." She gave an expressive Gallic shrug.

"But come, let us forget such weighty matters and enjoy ourselves while we may." She crooked a smile at him, as he pulled her down again on top of her and reveled in his strength and passion.

Later, as he rode home in the early morning fog, Justin could not help reflecting on his mistress's startling observation. For years, he had enjoyed beautiful women whenever he had found them, and they, if he had not become a complacent coxcomb, had thoroughly enjoyed him as well. But he had never given any thought to falling in love. However, it appeared, given his recent passionate outbursts, that perhaps all along he had been seeking, if not love, then something very special, and apparently he had not been finding it.

Why else would Lady Blanche's determined attentions have affected him so? Any other man he knew would have flirted right along with the incomparable and taken pleasure in feasting his eyes on her beautiful features and elegant figure, while relishing the envious glances of the young bucks jealous of him for capturing the admiration of the celebrated beauty. He must be all about in the head. It was not like him to be so nice about a liaison with an attractive female, and here he was actually avoiding it.

Nevertheless, his distaste for the social machinations of the *ton*, particularly those females bent on matrimonial advancement, lingered with him to such a degree that he eschewed the haunts of the *ton* where he might fall prey to such schemes, resorting instead to the more honest companionship and bonhomie to be found at Brooks's, Gentleman Jackson's, and Tattersall's. He even took to avoiding rides in the park at the fashionable hour, choosing instead to enjoy the peace and serenity of early morning gallops when his fellow horsemen in the park were far more intent on their mounts than on the effect they were having on those around them.

Among the military men exercising their horses regularly at daybreak and a handful of serious sportsmen, he would often catch sight of a lone woman who usually avoided the others to such a degree that it took some time for Justin to recognize Lady Diana Hatherill. Although, once he had done so, it occurred to him that he should have known her immediately, even at a distance, by her magnificent animal and graceful seat.

She was the last person on earth, with the possible exception of Lady Blanche, whom he wished to encounter, representing as she had at the Countess of Axbridge's, all that was deceptive in human nature. But he could not stop himself from admiring the picture she made every morning as she cantered across the dew-washed grass, oblivious to everything but the freshness of the day and the exhilaration of the exercise.

It was clear from the way she often leaned forward to stroke Ajax's neck, from the way his ears twitched as she appeared to address remarks to him, and from the way he responded, that the horse and his mistress enjoyed a rare degree of communication and companionship. It was also evident, from the distance the lady kept between herself and the groom, not to mention the other riders, that she wished to shun all human contact, a situation that Justin could not but find intriguing.

How had someone who seemed to revel in the solitude of the park in the early morning dealt with the gregarious Ferdie, who considered himself alone and isolated if he were stuck with only his regular trio by his side? Once again he wondered how such a match had come about. Not that the lady did not appear to be on the best of terms with her husband's friends, but it was becoming increasingly clear to Justin how very little Lady Diana and Ferdie must have had in common.

Why even she and Reginald were more alike. Had she married Ferdie with the same end in mind that Lady Blanche had.

After all, it hadn't been until after Ferdie's death and the extent of his debts had been discovered—though those who had spent much time with him at the gaming tables had begun to have their suspicions—that she had begun to try to earn her own way in the world. For all Lady Diana had known when she married him, Ferdie had been a wealthy personable young man with a great deal to offer the daughter of the wellborn but impoverished Marquess of Buckland.

For some inexplicable reason, Justin found himself resisting the notion that Diana had married solely to improve her worldly situation, but why he should reject this idea so, given the evidence of his own eyes, particularly at the countess's rout, was more than he could fathom. Annoyed with himself for such preoccupation, he sought to forget it all by immersing himself in business affairs, but here, too, he found his mind wandering back to Diana and her surprising presence at the Stock Exchange.

Hating himself for doing so, but in the grip of a terrible compulsion, he had mentioned the lady to Mr. James Capel, whom he had encountered one morning upon entering the exchange. A wary look had appeared in the gentleman's eye at the mention of Lady Diana, but Justin, long accustomed to eliciting valuable information from unwilling sources, was able to reassure him enough that the gentleman soon waxed enthusiastic about his unusual client.

"Yes, to be sure, she is a remarkably astute young lady indeed. Most well-informed and with the iron nerve that allows her to take the risks that are likely to offer a good return. Of course, she has been well schooled by Lady Walden, but she is quick to learn and possesses an almost masculine grasp of figures. If I could have a son gifted with such abilities, I should count myself truly fortunate." Then, alarmed that the warmth of his admiration had betrayed him into confiding too much, he caught himself quickly, "But it is getting late, and I have a most pressing appointment a few moments hence." With that brief apology, Mr. Capel hurried quickly away before he could be lured into further indiscretions.

Justin had remained thoughtful. It was a mystery, indeed, but the only way to arrive at the truth behind Lady Diana was to seek her out. He had promised to discover for her all that he could about unusual and profitable opportunities in which to invest, and he set himself to do just that, haunting the nearby coffeehouses in the hopes of picking up a useful tip. He was a well-known and respected figure among those who frequented the Exchange, and it was not long before he had accumulated enough information to justify a call in Brook Street, though he was surprised at the trepidation with which he looked forward to the visit.

At their last meeting, the understanding and trust that had previously seemed to be developing between them had somehow evaporated to be replaced by an uneasy half-flirtatious, half-antagonistic repartee that had kept them at a guarded distance. Now he was uncertain as to how to change all that, but his curiosity was far too strong to let it daunt him, and a fortnight after their encounter at the Countess of Axbridge's, he presented himself at Brook Street where he was conducted immediately to the drawing room.

Much to his disappointment, Lady Walden was its only occupant. "Do sit down," she invited him. "I apologize for the slight deception. Lady Diana has gone off with Lord Beardsley, and I did wish to have a word with you myself, so I allowed you to think that she was at home."

"Alan? Here?" Justin did not even attempt to keep the astonishment from his voice.

"Oh yes. He has been quite a frequent visitor—a bit shy perhaps, but quite a brilliant fellow. And I am delighted that he has taken to visiting Diana. Reginald is all very well, of course, but he cannot offer her the intellectual challenge that Lord Beardsley does." Lady Walden paused to observe the expression on her visitor's face. She had hoped to shake him, and she had. She could see that her great-niece's easy intercourse with his old school friend had made Justin stop to reflect on the sort of person that Diana must be. And such reflection could only redound to her niece's credit, for only her particular mixture of charm and intelligence could lure someone such as the Marquess of Hillingdon out of his reclusive ways.

Chapter 15

IT had in fact been quite a surprise to Diana when Finchley had come to announce his lordship's presence the morning following the Countess of Axbridge's rout. Even Alan was astounded to discover himself calling on any woman, much less a woman whose acquaintance he had made only briefly the night before, but she had appeared to be so genuinely interested in the subject of astronomy and so desirous of learning more that, enthusiast that he was in that particular realm of science, he had felt compelled to bring her his very own copy of Ferguson's *Astronomy*.

It wasn't until Finchley had admitted him that the enormity of the entire enterprise struck him. The Marquess of Hillingdon had never willingly conversed with a woman before in his entire life and now here he was actually seeking one out. By the time he and the butler reached the top of the stairs, Alan was frantically casting about for a means of escape, but before he could conjure up anything besides ignominious flight, Finchley had opened the doors, announcing in stentorian tones, "The Marquess of Hillingdon."

Somehow the inadvertent, "Oh, my goodness!" and the frantic rustling of papers that he overheard did a great deal to put the visitor more at ease. Heretofore he had been under the apprehension that women lay in wait in their drawing rooms, transformed by toilettes that had been arranged to a level of sublime and arcane artistry, preparing themselves for the advent of hapless males such as he. Certainly the only female of his acquaintance, the Marchioness of Hillingdon, did precisely that. The notion that he had actually caught a female unawares was oddly comforting.

He was even more reassured as he stepped into the room, for its floor was awash with newspapers, journals, and books of every description. In fact, at the moment it so much resembled the floor of his own library that he was more intrigued than intimidated by its occupant.

"How nice of you to visit," Diana greeted him with a friendly smile. "I would offer you a chair, but it will take a moment." She made haste to sweep the latest edition of the *Times* off a comfortable *bergère*.

At last Alan had the courage to look at her directly. She was just as unaffected and friendly as he remembered, and far less frightening, attired as she was in a simple morning dress of lemon-colored cambric muslin with a most becoming ruffled high collar of the same material. Clinging to her shoulder was a magnificent African gray parrot.

"*Psittacus erithacus*, I believe," he observed. Too intrigued by her companion to be self-conscious, Alan leaned forward to get a closer look.

"Hello, hello." Agreeably flattered at being addressed so respectfully, Boney inched forward to get a closer look himself. "Delighted to meet you," he chanted in the best imitation of Diana's voice.

"And a most clever one at that," Alan continued as he cautiously extended a hand. With a rare show of condescension, Boney hopped onto it.

"Do you know parrots?" Diana asked eagerly. "It does seem to me that he is very clever, even for a parrot, but I am rather partial I must confess."

"I am only slightly acquainted with their history," Alan responded modestly, "but I believe that though they are endowed with the ability to imitate, they do so only when they are so disposed and never upon command or when one wishes them to."

"Oh, Boney is more than delighted to talk." Diana laughed ruefully. "But he does so only when he has judged a person to be worthy of the effort. You are to be commended at having won him over so quickly. In general, he deliberates at length before deciding to accept someone into the circle of human beings whose existence he acknowledges."

"I am indeed flattered, and I do have the highest regard for the species. They are extremely intelligent and gregarious as this fellow here so patently is." Boney winked and thrust out his chest at such obvious words of praise. "They have been interacting with humans since antiquity, but perhaps you are familiar with Pliny's discussion on their speech and suggestions for training them."

Diana admitted that she was not.

"Ah, I shall have to find the passage and show it to you. But speaking of books, I have taken the liberty of bringing you my copy of Ferguson's *Astronomy*." Alan paused as he was struck by misgivings. "I beg your pardon. I suppose it is quite presumptuous of me, but last night you posed such questions as to make me think . . .well, indeed it is a fascinating study and . . ." he trailed off in an agony of uncertainty.

"How very kind of you." Diana was touched as much by his respect for her interest in the subject as by his undisguised enthusiasm for it. "The study of the heavens involves so much of the history of mankind—explorations, philosophical debates, religious controversies, mathematics—that one cannot but be fascinated, though not a little daunted by its magnitude."

"That is why I selected Ferguson. Herschel himself was introduced to the science by this very book. He usually takes it and Smith's *Harmonics* with him when he retires to bed every evening, so you can see it is sure to inspire."

Diana laughed. "I fear I shall disappoint you, for I feel quite certain that not only will I fail to grasp a great deal of the work itself, but I shall never become a great astronomer."

"Oh, do not say that, Lady Diana. Why anyone with an inquiring mind may do so if he or she but set her mind to it. After all, Herschel began life as a musician and did not truly become an astronomer until he was a good deal more advanced in years than you are. Nor should you let your sex interfere with such aspirations, for, after all, Herschel's sister Caroline is a highly regarded astronomer in her own right. She even commands an annual pension for her contributions to the science."

"I can see you will have me a stargazer yet." Diana could not but be flattered by his belief in her intellectual capacities, and found it rather touching that he should be so eager to encourage her. "But come, sir, tell me more. How did you yourself become a student of the stars. You must be quite a distinguished scholar yourself if you move in such exalted company."

The marquess blushed vividly. "At the outset I was inter-

ested only in the mathematics of it for the most part, but I
made the acquaintance of John Herschel when I was in my last
year at Cambridge. I was introduced to him by two friends of
mine, Charles Babbage and George Peacock, both of whom
share my passion for mathematics. We became friends, meeting often to discuss anything and everything. One holiday,
knowing my reluctance to return home, my interest in optics,
and my wish to acquire a better telescope, John invited me to
visit him at Slough where his father had his observatory. It
was the most astounding and enlightening experience I have
ever had to see an entire household devoted to the study of the
heavens and the pursuit of knowledge. I have done my poor
best to emulate them ever since. Perhaps you would like to
visit them. I should be delighted to take you down, for my sole
purpose in coming to town was to visit them in order to learn
how to go about setting up my own observatory."

"You are most kind. I believe I should enjoy that," Diana
thanked him. It was something of a novelty to discover someone so entirely given over to one interest that all else was of
secondary importance. After spending what little time she had
in the *ton*, she found the marquess a refreshing antidote to all
the petty and frivolous concerns of most of its members.

However, something was puzzling her. Thinking back to
their first encounter, she recalled that it was Justin St. Clair
who had introduced them. Had he done so out of a spirit of
mischief, hoping to provide a distraction from Reginald? Very
likely, she thought furiously to herself. The mystery of it all
was that a Corinthian and a rake such as Justin St. Clair should
have any acquaintance with, much less friendship for, the
misogynic Lord Beardsley. In spite of herself, Diana could not
help alluding to this odd state of affairs.

"Oh, Justin," a singularly appealing smile lit up the marquess's features, "he's not as much a here-and-thereian as he
would have one think. In fact, he is quite extraordinarily
clever, though he would take great exception to my telling
anyone so."

"He is?" Diana exclaimed in astonishment. Though, the
more she considered it, recalling their exchange at the concert
and chance meeting at the exchange, the less she was surprised
by it.

"Oh yes. But in school the fellows make your life so miserable if they suspect you of being the least bit interested in your studies, you know. Justin was also so athletically inclined that he could make friends with everyone, even those who were sporting-mad, and he was so careful to hide any of his intellectual interests that no one had the least suspicion he was a true scholar. I do not know when he studied because every time anyone saw him, he was up to some sort of lark, but he always managed to excel, though he was rebellious enough that he was constantly at odds with the masters."

"A holy terror, in fact," Diana agreed nodding. This was far more in keeping with the Justin St. Clair she knew.

"Yes." Alan grinned reminiscently. "But it was all in fun. He was never unkind the way the others were." The grin faded into a frown. "And he risked a good deal to become my friend." Without the least intending to, the marquess launched into a description of the day the two of them had met while Diana and Boney sat silent listening intently.

They shook their heads sympathetically at the appropriate moments and exclaimed in disgust at the cruelty of schoolboys. Observing the varied expressions that crossed the narrator's face as the story was told, Diana began to form a very different picture of Justin St. Clair. Yes, he was toplofty and interfering, but always in the interests of what he thought was right and moral. Yes he was arrogant, but only to depress pretensions in others. The characteristics she had first ascribed to a roué bent on dissipation were nothing more than natural results of an adventurous spirit and an energetic mind stifled and bored by the enforced participation in the empty routine of the beau monde. She sighed to herself. How well she understood the rebelliousness that this prospect could engender.

"So you see," Lord Beardsley concluded, "it is actually Justin to whom I owe my continued interest in astronomy. If he had not rescued me and my telescope from certain destruction, I might never have carried on as I have. But," he glanced in horror at the clock, "I have taken up far too much of your time."

"Not at all" was the warm reply.

"Not at all," Boney echoed.

"My interest has been quite piqued by all that you have told me. It is so rare that one comes across someone who converses intelligently that I quite delight in every opportunity that is of fered to me. Besides, as I mentioned before, though I am quite capable of pursuing knowledge on my own in most subjects, I am woefully ignorant in those areas of mathematics and natural sciences in which you excel. It is most refreshing to meet a person who sees the world through different eyes."

"Perhaps you would like to accompany me to Greenwich tomorrow?" Alan could not have told from whence or how the invitation sprang to his lips, but having issued it, he hastened to reassure her. "The observatory is quite worthy of a visit and they have recently completed an addition to house even more scientific instruments. Most people cannot appreciate such things, but the craftsmanship is excellent and the clocks are truly magnificent. There is so much to see even if one is not an astronomer or a navigator, and the architecture is superior as well. It would be a most pleasant drive and I would be very honored if you would accompany me." He paused to draw an anxious breath.

Diana laughed. "Enough, enough. I am quite convinced, and I am most flattered by the invitation. I should be delighted to join you."

"You are? You would?" Alan could not believe his ears. "Why, then I shall call for you at half after eleven. But now I must bid both of you good day." And before he could stop to reconsider his rash actions or lose his nerve, he bowed hastily to Diana and Boney and bolted from the room.

"Qwak, Qwak," Boney clucked in approval at such an appreciative visitor.

"Yes, indeed, he was very nice, was he not Boney?" Diana agreed. "But shy, very shy, poor man."

Chapter 16

SHY was not the first adjective that Justin would have chosen to describe his friend when he encountered him outside of Hatchard's several days later. Jubilant was something more like the way Lord Beardsley responded to his casual, "Why, hello, Alan. You are looking in prime twig for someone forced to pass his days in the frivolous metropolis." He bent to retrieve a volume that had slipped from the pile of books the marquess was clutching. "You must be keeping yourself well amused."

"Oh, tolerably." Alan responded in such an uncharacteristically offhand way that his friend bent a penetrating gaze on him.

"Hipparchus?" Justin turned over the volume, which he still retained in his hand. "But Alan, surely you know this by heart now."

A vivid blush stained his lordship's freckled countenance, and he shifted uncomfortably from one foot to another. "Well, I do, but this is for Lady Diana."

"Lady Diana?" Justin exclaimed in astonishment. Then the old lady had not been having him on, not that he disbelieved her, for Lady Walden was too awake on all suits to treat Justin St. Clair as a flat, but the idea of Alan calling on a woman had been almost too incredible.

"Yes. Lady Diana Hatherill. You introduced me to her at the Countess of Axbridge's rout," Alan retorted not a little defensively.

"And so I did, dear fellow," Justin responded hastily in as conciliatory a manner as possible. "So I did. And I am delighted that you have thought fit to continue the acquaintance. It's only that you are such a misanthrope in general that it is something of a shock."

"I wouldn't say I was a misanthrope. I like good company as well as the next man, it's just that it is so devilish hard to come by." Lord Beardsley defended himself.

"Now, there you have it. I am in complete agreement with you, and I am delighted to have been the means of introducing you to one of those rare creatures who fulfills your rigorous qualifications." The sardonic edge to his tone was completely lost on Alan.

"She is a most agreeable person. It is easy to like her, and I find that I quite enjoy her company," his friend replied simply.

"You do?" Justin tried, not entirely successfully, to hide the note of disbelief in his voice.

"Yes I do. She makes me feel comfortable. She doesn't use any of those tricks to impress that so many others do. She converses most sensibly on any number of topics, and she can interest herself in anything. I find that a very attractive quality in anyone. I took her down to Greenwich with me, and she declared herself most grateful, for very few people think to offer her amusement that stimulates her mind." Alan spoke with modest pride.

Justin looked at him blankly.

"Well, why shouldn't I take a lady to Greenwich? I should have taken you after all if you had been around, and Lady Diana is just as clever as you are."

Oh, overweening pride, you are trampled into the dust, Justin exclaimed bitterly to himself. However his reply was one of airy unconcern. "Why indeed? And did she enjoy herself? Or perhaps, more important, were you able to enjoy yourself?" Justin simply could not picture his old schoolmate allowing another human being let alone a female, to tag along with him to his mecca.

"Yes I did. You know, Justin, it was very nice having someone to talk to on the journey there, someone rational that is. And she behaved in the most unexceptionable manner when we arrived, not putting herself forward, observing everything in a most intelligent manner and asking questions that were entirely to the point—illuminating even. I have not spent time as pleasantly with many a clever man, but excuse me, or I shall be late in calling on her." Lord Beardsley retrieved his books, nodded to his friend, and climbed into the curricle that had been waiting patiently for him. The lad holding the horses handed him the reins, and he headed off into the press of traffic, leaving Justin to stare off down Piccadilly after him.

Ah, St. Clair, now you are in the basket, he muttered. Not only is Reginald head over heels, but even Alan is in a fair way to being bewitched. No, that was not being precisely fair to the marquess. Alan might not have spent much time on the town, but he was not precisely green either, being far too intelligent to be taken in by a pretty face or a coming manner. If Alan liked and trusted Lady Diana, why then, she was someone worthy of it, and Justin St. Clair, difficult as it was to fathom, might just possibly have been incorrect in his reading of the lady's character.

Certainly during his visit in Brook Street a few days earlier Lady Walden had done her best to prove to him that her niece was someone who should command his respect. Having dealt summarily with the slight deception she had practiced on her visitor, she had gotten right down to the matter at hand. "Sit down, St. Clair," she had reiterated, pointing to a chair with an air that brooked no refusal. "I am glad that we have this opportunity to speak privately, for I have a favor to ask of you."

"Your servant, ma'am." Justin bowed before disposing his well-knit frame in the chair indicated.

"You may get away with that with your opera dancers or your foreign coquettes, sirrah, but you should know better than to accede to my wishes without first discovering what they are," she chided severely, but her eyes danced.

"Why ma'am, it is precisely because you are not one of my *opera dancers* or *foreign coquettes* that I offer my services without reservation. You are far more likely to make a practical suggestion than exact an extravagant demand."

"Touché! I quite see why you are such a favorite with my sex, but it will do you little good with me, for I've both a bone to pick and a favor to ask, and as I am a great believer in getting to the unpleasant business first, I shall start with my quarrel with you."

"Very well ma'am," Justin replied meekly, wondering just what precisely this surprising lady had in store for him.

"To begin with, you must stop hovering over Diana."

"Hovering?" Justin sat bolt upright. "Hovering? I do not . . ."

"Calm down, man. To someone as independent as Diana, it

looks like hovering, the way you constantly appear the moment Reginald escorts us anywhere. And if Reginald weren't such a milksop, he . . .well, never mind that. You mislike my words, but you *do* hover and Diana is an adult, as is your nephew, I might add. No, don't poker up at me. I don't for a moment believe that you are doing this of your own accord." Again Justin made as if to speak, but Aunt Seraphina cut him short. "Let me say my piece, and then I shall allow you to say yours.

"As I was saying, I detect the fell hand of the Earl of Winterbourne. You, for all your faults, are not a busybody, and if Alfred continues to press you, you may tell him for me that I shall never make that son of his my heir—more fool he for thinking it. The only way Reginald could in any way approach what I shall leave behind is by marrying Diana, though I shall will all of it to her in her own right. He could do worse than to marry her. She has more than enough brains for the pair of them."

Lady Walden paused for a moment, never taking her eyes off her visitor who sat transfixed, unable to respond in any way. "And now that I have ridden roughshod over you, I shall have the unmitigated gall to ask for your help."

"I am all ears," Justin retorted dryly, but there was a glint of humor in his eyes.

"I am sure you are. But in truth, I would be exceedingly grateful if you could share any information you might glean down at the 'Change. Diana simply will not accept assistance of any kind from me, with the exception of advice that is, and she is struggling so hard to keep her head above water. Geoffrey, brilliant as he was, simply had no head for business. To be perfectly frank, he never had a head for anything, but antiquity."

A reminiscent expression clouded the alert dark eyes. "Poor Diana. He hardly paid the least attention to his daughter until she was old enough to read Greek and Latin and speak about those things *he* wished to discuss. She has been looking after Buckland practically from the moment she could do sums, and a difficult time she has had of it, too. Geoffrey had been making mice-feet of the estate since he inherited it. It was a wonder it wasn't all to pieces. Then when Ferdie came along, I had hoped . . .well, you know what Ferdie was, a charming spendthrift with not enough sense to keep out of the River Tick. And now she's trying to salvage a small pittance left her by both men and won't accept help from anyone."

Lady Walden allowed herself a sigh of exasperation. "Diana is as proud as the devil and stubborn as a cart horse. However, she has profited handsomely from the little knowledge I have been able to share with her concerning the workings of the financial markets. But my experience is limited by what Thomas knew, which was mostly trade and that was mostly in India. You, sir, are a man of affairs familiar with the goings-on on the Continent. You move among men who are in the thick of it. All I ask is that you make good on your offer to share with her any insights you might glean. She's a good girl, but she won't brook interference or assistance from anyone as I well know. However, I am sure you can manage to help her in a way she can accept. Thank you for listening to an old woman. And now I am sure you are longing to be gone." With that she had rung the bell, and Finchley had shown him out.

First Lady Walden and now Alan. Neither of them was anybody's fool and both of them believed in Lady Diana. Whose fool was he for doubting her? Justin resolved to banish his suspicions for the moment and accept the lady at her word.

Breaking out of his reverie, he began to saunter toward Gentleman Jackson's, as it was abundantly apparent he was in need of much vigorous exercise to clear the fog from his brain.

Justin had not proceeded more than a few steps before he was accosted by his nephew. "Uncle Justin!" The surprise in Reginald's voice at discovering his relative on the doorstep of Hatchard's was not particularly flattering.

"Hello, Reginald." A sudden though struck Justin. Perhaps instead of *hovering* over Diana and his nephew, he should throw them together to watch what would happen if he did not put Diana on her guard. Perhaps if she didn't feel challenged or threatened by Justin, the lady would reveal her true motives. With this laudable intention, he extended an invitation for Reginald and Diana to join him in viewing the *Judgment of Brutus*, now being displayed at the Egyptian Hall along with mosaic floors from Rome, the Louvre, and Malmaison.

Reginald blushed with pleasure at this unlooked for condescension on the part of his fashionable uncle. Despite his father's frequent and vociferous animadversions on the numerous defects of Justin's character, chief among them being a lack of proper reverence toward the Earl of Winterbourne and all he stood for, Reginald secretly admired his dashing relative. It was with real regret that he declined the offer. "I am going into the country for a few days," he apologized.

"Well, then, some other time perhaps," his uncle replied casually. "No doubt your father will be pleased to welcome you home and see you safely away from all the temptations of the town." Justin had merely been offering the usual expected remarks, but he was astounded to see the blush that suffused his nephew's face and a conscious look that Reginald did his best to banish. It was almost as if the lad had something to hide.

"Yes, I suppose he would do so except that, I'm going . . . that is, I don't expect to see father as I am going to visit a . . . a friend." Reginald shut his mouth with a snap, as though betrayed into revealing more than he wished to.

Justin fixed his nephew with a piercing gaze while Reginald shifted uncomfortably from one foot to another. No doubt about it, there was something havey-cavey here, though it was very unlike the viscount to concoct a Banbury story. The Earls of Winterbourne and their heirs might be pompous windbags, but they were a truthful lot. Nor did they possess either the originality or the stomach to do anything deceitful, shocking, outrageous, or even mildly amusing.

Reginald ran a nervous finger around the inside of his neck cloth, as though it were choking him. "Thank you anyway, sir. Now, if you will excuse me, I have an appointment with Mr. Mawe in the Strand. He has an outstanding collection of mineral specimens, which he has cataloged and is desirous of showing me. Good day, Uncle Justin." And he hurried off down the street as quickly as he could without losing his dignity, leaving Justin again to stare blankly down Piccadilly. Damn! Once more he was forced to collect himself, as he muttered angrily under his breath, "I am beginning to look as though my wits have gone wandering. If I'm not gaping after one person, I'm gawking after another. I can't get to Gentlemen Jackson's too soon. At least there if I am tipped a doubler, it will be by a worthy opponent."

Chapter 17

B UT there was a nagging uneasiness that lurked at the back of Justin's mind all the time he was sparring. Even a bout with the champion himself could not distract him entirely from reflections on his nephew's uncharacteristic and puzzling demeanor. Reginald was the very soul of rectitude, to the point of sanctimoniousness. He couldn't help it, such was the destiny of all the Earls of Winterbourne, but it most certainly did appear that he was up to something. An ugly and highly unwelcome suspicion began to form in Justin's mind, and he could not help but have his misgivings as to Lady Diana's whereabouts.

Justin tried unsuccessfully to put the entire episode from his thoughts by returning home to pore over newspapers and correspondence. Finally, flinging down a surprisingly lengthy letter from Charles Stewart, which only made him long for Vienna and the days of the Congress, he sauntered off to Brooks's in search of diversion. He had toyed briefly with the idea of calling on Suzette, but he knew, devoted artist that she was, she would most likely be practicing with her dancing master. Besides, as a woman, she was bound to remind him of Lady Diana, which was counter to the whole purpose of his visit to Brooks's.

"Justin," a jovial voice called out the moment he entered the gaming room.

"Hello Sally," he greeted Lord Humphrey Salcombe who was lingering by the faro table relishing the deep play of other more hardy or foolhardy souls than himself.

"Haven't seen you this age, old fellow. Been rusticating?" Sally cocked a waggish eyebrow.

"Rusticating, Justin. You're all about in the head," the Honorable Nigel Clutterbuck scoffed. "He's been lying low with a particularly lovely ladybird, eh, Justin?" He winked lasciviously before returning to the game in front of him. Leave it to St. Clair to win the most delicious woman to appear onstage for many a Season. It was positively and most certainly unfair the way beautiful women seemed to fall at his feet. There was no denying the charm of his clever wit, the glint of humor deep in the gray eyes that missed nothing, the lazy smile, and the languid grace, but there was plenty of well-enough-looking fellows on the town, many of whom had far more to offer in terms of wealth and title.

"If that's what they're saying in the clubs, then it must be so, eh, Nigel?" If anything, Justin appeared to be bored to the extreme by a subject that had everyone else at the table agog to hear the latest detail.

Nigel shook his head smiling. He was a cool customer was Justin St. Clair, casually dismissing his conquest of La Charenton as though all of the male population in London hadn't been courting her for months with singular lack of success. St. Clair merely had to appear on the scene, and she was his. Life was certainly inequitable at times.

Justin strolled around the room looking for play deep enough and opponents challenging enough to test his skill and to distract him, but after a brief hand of whist and winning a tidy sum at faro, he gave it up as a bad job and returned home for a few hours before dressing for Lady Upton's ball.

To be sure, Justin had no real interest in attending the ball. In fact, he had nearly tossed the gilt-edged invitation into the fire after his bout of disgust over the Countess of Axbridge's rout, but he felt certain that it was a large enough and an important enough affair that Lady Diana was certain to attend it. He took his time getting ready, debating with himself all the while as to his real reasons for doing such a thing. He had a distinct abhorrence of such crushes and why the whereabouts of another member of the *ton*, and a female of doubtful motives at that, should preoccupy him so much that he subjected himself to it, he could not say. Even worse, he preferred not to hazard a guess as to the meaning of his obsession with it all.

He must be slipping, he thought to himself as he mounted the red-carpeted stairway leading to the brilliantly lit doorway of Lady Upton's magnificent residence. In his youth, he would never have allowed Alfred to saddle him with his silly old womanish worries, let alone embroil him in them. He should have washed his hands of Reginald's entanglement at the outset. After all, if the lad weren't allowed to make mistakes, how could he possibly learn from them? He must be dicked in the nob to have given in to his brother's overwrought fears for his son and heir. It was boredom that had done it Justin decided as he handed his cape to a hovering footman. After the challenge and excitement of Vienna, where conversations decided the fate of nations, London, with the same old faces, the same old *on-dits*, the same scheming mamas and their marriage-mad daughters, had been deucedly flat. Alfred, bless his hidebound soul, had offered an intrigue of sorts to occupy his mind, and, desperate for diversion, he had eagerly grasped at the opportunity.

And it had been amusing. Lady Diana had been a far more worthy opponent than he had expected. She was a clever, even a witty antagonist who revealed unexpected depths that, he was forced to admit, had piqued his interest; but this was going too far. Justin St. Clair would not have endured one fashionable ball even for a woman to whom he was madly attracted, and now here he was attending a second. He paused on the threshold of the ballroom ablaze with light from the huge crystal chandeliers and the reflections off silks, satins, and the jewels draped around the necks of young and old, glittering in elegant coiffures and encircling plump wrists.

There was Sally Jersey holding court as usual, chattering and flirting with a bevy of admirers. Over in a corner, Mrs. Drummond-Burrell was haughtily observing the scene while making her usual pronouncements to the town tabbies who hung fawningly on her every word. And in between them was a sea of eager faces—young misses hoping to catch the eye of an eligible parti, town beaux surveying the latest crop of beauties, anxious mamas thrusting their daughters into the perfect position to be noticed. But nowhere did he catch a glimpse of the coolly elegant figure of Lady Diana Hatherill.

He knew her well enough to be certain that she would stand out among the crowd as she had at the opera, the Argyll Rooms, and the Countess of Axbridge's rout. Perhaps it was her taste for simple but arresting costume that made everyone else seem fussy and overdressed, perhaps it was her self-possession or the proud air with which she carried herself, but she was always easy to pick out in any gathering. And she was most definitely not part of this one.

He turned to go, but before he could make any headway toward the door, a voice cooed in his ear, "Justin, you naughty man, you shall not escape this time without dancing with me."

Blanche! He was well and truly caught, and he did at least owe her a dance from the last time he had cut her. Sighing inwardly, he summoned a civil smile to his face and turned to extend a hand. "But of course, Lady Blanche. I should never treat a neighbor so shabbily." In fact, Lady Blanche had not been a neighbor when he had lived at Winterbourne, but that had never kept the lady from presuming on her close geographical connection to the rest of the family to establish a closer relationship with one of London's most eligible bachelors.

Blanche had pouted mightily when her papa, a newly created peer, had elected to leave the metropolis in order to acquire respectability with some acreage in the country. Ruralizing did not agree with a young woman accustomed to attracting an enviable following among the town bucks wherever she went until she discovered the identity of the younger brother to the pompous, verbose earl and his equally dull wife, whose land marched next to her father's.

Her appreciation for the charms of country life had increased with every opportunity she had to encounter Justin St. Clair. Not one to be swayed by a handsome face alone, she had taken careful note of his elegant equipage, impressive stable, and exquisitely cut jackets, and she had immediately written him down as an acquaintance worthy of cultivation. Discreet inquiries as to the size of his income and his reputation in the *ton* had only furthered her desire to form a closer connection, and she had done her best to cross his path whenever possible.

If her parents took any notice of their darling's sudden interest in making the rounds of the neighborhood, calling on people she had previously stigmatized as a set of country bumpkins, or a passion for the local hunt that she had often described as a gang of greasy farmers, they made no mention of it, merely being thankful for the peace from her complaints and her sighings for London.

As for Justin, at first he had been only too delighted to feast his eyes on a face of dazzling beauty, a ravishing figure, and a well-turned ankle. A little flirtation was a delightful antidote to his brother's endless monologues on the folly of the Prince Regent, the wastefulness of the government, and the shocking morals of the *ton* in general, but he was not about to offer anything more. He had seen the acquisitive light in the eyes of women bent on catching him in the parson's mousetrap often enough not to recognize the gleam in Blanche's eye, and he played a very careful game—never allowing them to be caught alone where he could be forced into disastrous intimacy, and avoiding all talk that related even in the slightest to his future.

He had been even more evasive in the very public eye of the *ton* and did his best, without being brutal, to dampen the playfully possessive air she adopted toward him. It was the fear that he had been rather too abrupt before for which he was now paying the price by dancing with her. But he did wish she would stop chattering and just let him enjoy in peace the ripe expanse of bosom revealed by her décolletage or the tantalizing outline of her thigh against the thin silk of her gown.

Nodding at the appropriate moments and rewarding her with and occasional, "Most fascinating, no really?" which he inserted so adroitly that the lady never even noticed the slightly glazed look in his eyes or suspected for a moment that he had so successfully focused his attention elsewhere that her conversation was reduced to a soporific buzzing at the back of his mind, he was able to keep his mind on what truly concerned him—the location of Lady Diana. It was only when the dance ended that he nearly gave himself away by neglecting to stop with the music.

"Justin, you were not attending." A gathering frown wrinkled the smooth white forehead, and the enchanting corners of the full rosy lips turned down ever so slightly.

"But Blanche, how could I, when I was concentrating so much on the delightful picture you present?" he protested quizzing her.

"Naughty man," she laughed, tapping him with her fan and smiling with satisfaction. There, let Belinda Attwater eat her heart out over that. She might be a duke's daughter and an incomparable at that, but she had not captured a single partner as worthy of note as Justin St. Clair. Blanche tossed her head in a way most calculated to do justice to her exquisite profile, making sure that at least several pairs of envious eyes were fixed on her and her partner.

It was fortunate for her pride, monumental though it was, that she was not privy to her quarry's thoughts, for all through the dance Justin had been casting about for a believable excuse to call at a certain house in Brook Street the next morning. Taking to heart Lady Walden's remarks, he had been reviewing every possible scrap of information he had overheard in Capel Court and the coffeehouses around the Stock Exchange, trying to dredge up something of note to bring to Lady Diana's attention, if she were at home that was—a state of affairs he very much doubted after his brief conversation with Reginald.

Aha! At last he had it—the waterworks. Knowing that Diana was familiar with agriculture and that Lady Walden would be well apprised of the state of the East India Company stocks, he felt certain that she would be concentrating her investments in those areas. Now, what was it he had heard about the waterworks? Oh yes, Jeremy Southbridge had alluded to some way of eliminating the fierce competition between the companies that was responsible for keeping share prices so low. It was something to bear in mind and which would surely add diversity to Lady Diana's finances. Justin smiled and nodded with satisfaction. That was the ticket. He could now drop by Brook Street with impunity.

Gazing up at him, Blanche sighed with satisfaction. "I am so glad that you think Cleopatra is an appropriate costume for Lady Topham's masquerade. I had worried lest it be rather too daring, but if you approve, then it is certain to be a success." Blanche smiled coyly up at him.

Justin gave a barely perceptible start as he frantically strove to bring his mind back to the present. "Oh, er, that is, I am glad you are reassured." Lord, what had he agreed to? The masquerade, that was it. "I regret that I shall be unable to appreciate the results of your choice of character and costume, as I fear I shall be away from town." When was the silly masquerade anyway? He couldn't recall it, small wonder considering the stack of invitations gathering dust on his mantel where he had carelessly tossed them. However, he must remember to avoid it at all costs.

"It is too bad of you, Justin, for I intend to be the belle of the ball." Blanche pouted prettily, biting her lower lip in a way that had been known to drive lesser men mad with desire.

I'll wager you do, he muttered grimly to himself. "In that case, you will hardly miss my support. But now, if you'll excuse me, I really must go—early morning tomorrow." And with that, he was off leaving her seething with frustration.

Why was it that despite his address and his air of easy flirtation, she never felt certain of Justin's admiration. Blanche liked a man whose sophisticated tastes could do her justice, but St. Clair was just a little too practiced. Her eyes narrowed. We shall see, she nodded slowly to herself. When I am done, the high and mighty Justin St. Clair will be begging to dance with me. And she resolved to consult with her dressmaker the very next day about increasing the décolletage on the white satin ball gown with silver net. Then we shall see St. Clair, the beauty smiled slyly to herself. Then we shall see.

Chapter 18

ACTING on his inspiration, Justin planned to present himself at Brook the next morning as soon as he had pumped Jeremy for all the information he could share concerning waterworks companies and the rumor of possible agreements among them to share the market in order to raise their rates.

He finally ran Jeremy to earth at Garraway's, where he was enjoying a solitary pot of coffee. His friend's bony ugly face lit up at the sight of Justin. "Hello, Justin, don't tell me you've come to consult me for advice! You must have lost all your fortune at play if you are making use of something other than your own clever nose to smell out a bargain."

"Now Jeremy, I am not so toplofty that I can't acknowledge the value of someone else's opinions, or at least your opinions." Justin pulled up a chair while Jeremy called for more coffee.

Jeremy Southbridge, another acquaintance from university days, smiled. "Flattery will get you nowhere, St. Clair. I have heard of the enormous profits you've made. Others may call you a lucky devil, but I know better. You can't live next to a fellow for years without becoming accustomed to his ways. For all your love of cutting up a lark, you're a serious sort and when you wish to learn something, there's no one quicker than you."

"Come off it, Jerry," Justin scoffed. He was glad to see that his old friend had at last found success. Wherever Justin went, he heard Jeremy quoted and his name invoked to give credence to a venture. Son of a poor but scholarly clergyman, Jeremy had been sent to university to follow in his father's footsteps, but his independent spirit had rebelled against this fate. Strengthened largely by Justin's faith in his enormous abilities and his encouragement, he had eschewed the church for the city, where his quick grasp of affairs and his encyclopedic memory combined with a perfect wizardry with figures had soon made him a force to be reckoned with.

But he had never forgotten how night after night Justin had listened sympathetically to him as he questioned his faith and wrestled with his conscience. Now it was with real pleasure and the hope that he could at last return Justin's favors that he sat and considered intently all the questions his friend put to him.

"Yes, if she has placed her finances as you say, investment in waterworks shares might be highly advantageous. Mind you, the shares will remain as low as they are now for quite some time, but it is only a matter of time before they climb enough to make her a wealthy woman."

"Thank you, Jerry. She hasn't a great deal to invest, but she has an excellent grasp of such things, and I know she will appreciate your counsel." Justin rose and shook his friend's hand.

"She must be a rare creature, indeed. There are very few men I know, present company excepted, who can be said to understand these things," his friend replied with a rueful grimace.

"Thank you. That is high praise. Yes, she is a rare creature," he responded wryly, thinking of his various *contretemps* with the lady in question and trying to envision the next one. After a few more desultory remarks and reminiscences, Justin quitted his friend and headed around to Brook Street where, just as he had expected, Finchley informed him that Lady Diana was not at home.

"Very well then, could you tell her that St. Clair called and will call again tomorrow?"

"I am afraid, sir, that Lady Diana has been called out of town, and we are not certain precisely when to look for her return." There was real regret in the butler's voice, for he still cherished hopes that this particular gentleman was interested in his mistress.

"Oh." Justin adopted an air of studied casualness. "Then I suppose I had best speak to Lady Walden."

"She is out at the moment as well, but I shall tell her you called. I am sure she will be happy to receive you another day." With some difficulty Finchley covered his disappointment. If the gentleman's business could be conducted with either of the ladies of the house, then it would not appear that his interest was the least bit amatory. He sighed inwardly. Then, in a rare departure from his usual dignified demeanor, he confided, "But we don't expect Lady Diana to be away for long. She has just gone down to Buckland to see to a few repairs."

"Has she now," Justin replied.

Despite years of sizing up callers at a glance, Finchley was not at all certain what to make of the glint in this particular caller's eyes or the arrested expression on his face, and he could not for the life of him decide whether he had done his mistress a good turn or a bad one by divulging her whereabouts.

Thanking the butler, Justin hurried back to Mount Street to collect his curricle and the few things he would need for a journey. Previous inquiries had revealed that the Marquess of Buckland's estate was little more than an hour's drive from the metropolis, but one never knew what he would find. It was best to be prepared for anything, though St. Clair, usually so far ahead of his fellow creatures that he had little trouble predicting their vagaries, was hard put to hazard a guess as to what he might discover when he arrived.

Either Diana was a devilish deep 'un or she was entirely innocent. Bold and independent as she was, he could not quite believe that she would have the brass to convince Reginald to run off to her family estate in order to trap him into marriage. But neither did he believe that she, clever businesswoman that she was, would not have appointed as her agent at Buckland someone perfectly capable of handling any emergency. Perhaps Buckland was merely a ruse, and even now they were on their way to Gretna Green. Shaking his head with frustration, Justin climbed into his curricle. Whatever the situation, time would reveal all.

In truth, both of these possibilities were entirely off the mark. Diana had less idea of and less interest in the Viscount Chalford's whereabouts than his uncle did, and her estates were quite adequately looked after by the Tottingtons, who had to all intents and purposes been running the place during her father's time.

No, it was purely and simply a need for escape that had sent her fleeing to Buckland like a rabbit to its hole. The events of the recent weeks had upset her equilibrium more than she cared to admit, even to herself, and the idea of being in the country with nothing more complicated than dogs, horses, and sheep for her companions was a most soothing prospect.

So, having put about the story that she needed to oversee repairs, she packed a few belongings and Boney, and made good her escape, leaving Lady Walden and Finchley, neither of whom believed her excuse for a moment, to make of her actions what they would.

She had taken Ajax with her, and a few long rides in the blossoming countryside had gone a long way to making her feel very much more the thing. It felt good to chat with the villagers and see how Farmer Onslow's new crops were greening Buckland's long idle fields that he was renting and making it look prosperous again.

The little money she had been able to reap from her investments had been put to good use mending fences and repairing some of the crumbling brickwork on the house itself. All in all, Diana derived a good deal of satisfaction from making the place look better than it ever had and knowing that it was her energy and intelligence that had made it possible.

The Tottingtons had greeted her with gratifying enthusiasm, happy to have her back where she belonged after such a long time, and eager to discuss the improvements that had been made. "Why you could live here right comfortably now, my lady. Thanks to the work that's been done, not a single chimney smokes nor are there nearly as many drafts," the housekeeper volunteered proudly. "It would be good to have the family back."

The older woman sounded wistful, and Diana thought back to the many hours she had spent with both of the Tottingtons learning about the house and estate and its neighboring village. Everything she knew of a practical nature she owed to them, and it did her heart good to sit once again in the enormous kitchen discussing the simple daily chores that made up their existence. After the rarified atmosphere of the *ton* where reputations were made or broken by a look here, a comment there, it was most reassuring to be in an atmosphere where one's work and energy showed immediate and concrete results.

Concerning herself with the question of new curtains for the morning room or conversing with Farmer Onslow about the weather and the crops, Diana was soon able to put Reginald and his uncle clean out of her mind, and it wasn't until one day in the library when her eye chanced to fall on a volume of Suetonius that, recalling her verbal battle at the Argyll Rooms with Justin, she realized how much he had cut up her peace.

Their acquaintance had forced her through a gamut of emotions she had never known herself to possess, from rage at his misreading of her character, to admiration of his quick wit and his knowledge of affairs, to curiosity at the many and contradictory facets of his personality. And now, having successfully avoided it for some time, she was thinking about him again. Diana shook her head briskly and sought to put him back out of her mind where he belonged.

Returning the volume she had pulled down from the shelf, she quickly gathered up her skirts and hurried out into the welcoming sunshine of the garden where the sounds of yapping and scuffling informed her that the recently born puppies of the Tottingtons' terrier were romping merrily, offering just the distraction she needed.

There were four of them—balls of white fluff and limitless energy with bright eyes and black noses. She stepped out into the garden where a minute's search unearthed a stick just the right size. Diana tossed it a few feet from where two of them were wrestling. Little white ears pricked up eagerly, and in a moment they all converged on the stick growling and pushing each other in their eagerness to be the first to grab it.

Diana laughed and strolled over to pick it up, whereupon they all sat down abruptly, eyes fixed expectantly on her, pink tongues panting in anticipation. She hurled the stick as far as she could to the end of the garden and tore along with them as they tumbled over one another in their haste.

Delighted to have a real human entering in their games, they raced alongside her, barking happily. At last, discovering that they were more interested in playing with her than in chasing the stick, Diana left off throwing it and began to run around the garden laughing heartily when she changed direction and caused them all to pile up at her feet before they could recover themselves.

Breathless with excitement they ran. Diana couldn't remember when she had felt so free and happy—certainly not when she had been a child. She had never truly romped when she was young because she had never had anyone to romp with. To be sure, she had had her fair share of torn dresses and skinned knees from climbing trees and falling off her pony, but these had all been solitary activities, and they never had been as exuberant as this.

Nor had she had any pets before Boney. Of course she had had a series of ponies, but she had longed for a dog. However, her father, certain that any dog would head straight for the library and the piles of books and papers scattered around, had expressly forbidden it. Ferdie, exquisite that he was, had been equally convinced of the destructive characteristics of canines, though he envisioned his gleaming Hessians and biscuit-colored pantaloons as the primary targets rather than the library.

But now there was no one to stop her, and she gave herself up to the glories of playing with them, giggling helplessly as she tripped over her skirts and fell while they climbed all over her, licking her face and wagging their tails furiously. Catching her breath at last, she pushed a few strands of hair from her eyes, dumped them out of her lap, rose and dashed to the other end of the garden, the puppies in hot pursuit.

It was at this precise moment that Justin, tired of waiting for Mrs. Tottington to locate the mistress of the house and intrigued by the sounds of unusual commotion, strolled into the garden.

Diana rounded the corner at the lower end and, with a burst of speed, sprinted toward the house, oblivious to the presence of a visitor. Meanwhile, Justin stood looking around in an effort to locate the source of all the commotion. He identified it just as Diana and the puppies turned another corner and raced full tilt toward him.

In the split second before they mowed him down, Diana happened to glance up. She came to a screeching halt, her hand flew up to her mouth in dismay, and the puppies tumbled wiggling and yelping at her feet. Diana was the first to recover. "Oh dear!" A blush suffused her already flushed cheeks, and a rueful twinkle sparkled in the dark blue eyes.

Chapter 19

FOR his part, Justin stood rooted to the ground, too nonplussed to speak and overwhelmed by a confusing variety of emotions. First and foremost was surprise. Cynic that he was, he truly had not expected to find her at Buckland and alone. And if she were alone, where on earth was Reginald, he couldn't help wondering, though his nephew's whereabouts appeared to be quite the furthest thing from Diana's mind at the moment. Surprise was quickly succeeded by an unwelcome feeling of guilt that he had so badly misjudged and mistrusted her when she had apparently been honest and straightforward with him all along. And last, but certainly not least, was shock at discovering an entirely different person from the harpy of his brother's imagination and the woman of the world of his own.

He could see clearly now that in truth, Lady Diana Hatherill, for all her cleverness and sophistication, was not much more than a schoolgirl. With her hair tumbled down her back and her blue eyes wide with astonishment, she looked to be barely fifteen. This sudden and radically changed perception of her was throwing Justin completely. Instead of forestalling the wily machinations of a temptress, he was here spying on an innocent girl enjoying her home in the country. Justin felt like the worst sort of cad.

At the same time he was overcome by the strangest rush of tenderness as he looked down at her standing there in her simple morning dress of faded blue muslin. She was far too young to be burdened with running an estate, maintaining an establishment in town, and making her own way in the world. For a brief moment, he had the maddest desire to lift all these burdens from her shoulders so she could continue to laugh and play as she was now.

From the little information Lady Walden had shared with him, Justin imagined that Diana had had very little chance in her life for the sort of frolicking she had so obviously been indulging in, and he was enchanted by what he had seen of it. No other woman he could think of would have taken such delight in something as simple and ingenuous as frisking with a litter of puppies. And yet, she was as sophisticated as the most worldly female of his acquaintance. Her tastes were as elegant as that of the most fashionable ladies of the *ton*, and her mind far more cultivated and refined than most—a truly unique and intriguing mixture of many facets that Justin was rapidly finding irresistible.

These were the sensations of an instant, and then he, too, was flushing with embarrassment as he sought frantically for a plausible and acceptable excuse for his abrupt intrusion into what was obviously a very private world. "I beg your pardon, but I was on my way to visit a friend and found myself in the vicinity."

The blue eyes regarded him solemnly, a hint of wariness replacing the sparkle that had been there.

"I thought I might stop by, as Lady Walden asked me to share any news I might glean on the exchange that could be of use to you, and, not knowing when you might be returning to town, I thought I might drop in and impart it to you." Damnation! He sounded as awkward and pompous as the Earl of Winterbourne at his most prolix. And she wasn't helping him in the least, standing there observing him silently while he struggled for an explanation and not making the least push to make it easy for him. Why, if he weren't mistaken, Justin thought he could detect just a hint of amusement in her eyes, as though she were enjoying his discomfiture.

In fact, Diana was. Now that she had rallied from the initial shock at being discovered in such an undignified situation by the last person in the world she expected or wished to see, she had been overpowered with curiosity. What possible motive could Justin St. Clair have for calling on her, especially when she was nowhere near his precious nephew? That he seemed to be almost as taken aback as she by their encounter was indeed perplexing. What had he expected? Despite his previous apology, Diana suspected that he still mistrusted her, and she was not at all certain as to how to interpret his sudden appearance at Buckland. But then her sense of humor had gotten the best of her.

Really, the expression on his face had been too funny when she and the puppies had just barely avoided running him down. And now to hear the coolly superior Justin St. Clair stumbling over his words like some schoolboy caught in a compromising situation was indeed most satisfying.

Twitching her now-bedraggled skirt from the sharp teeth of one of the puppies and ignoring the curls twining around her face and cascading down her back, Diana broke the uncomfortable silence. "How kind of you to call. Won't you come in and partake of some refreshment?" She inclined her head graciously, gathered up her skirts, and picked her way elegantly toward the house, acting for all the world as though she were wearing her most fashionable London attire and did not have a large smudge of dirt on her nose.

In no more than a twinkling of the eye, she had metamorphosed from a playful young girl to a self-possessed woman. Justin could not help admiring the instant and unembarrassed transition, but he was quite sorry to see the girl disappear. There had been an innocent charm about her exuberance and delight in life that was irresistible and all too rarely encountered in the exalted circles of the *ton* where boredom was the only emotion one confessed to. He sighed and followed his hostess down the flagged path leading to the French doors of the drawing room.

At Buckland the precariousness of her pecuniary circumstances was more evident than at Brook Street. The carpets, though of magnificent quality, were worn, and the rich material of the draperies was threadbare, though once again, as it was at Brook Street, everything was in excellent taste and exquisitely clean.

Several account books were strewn on the floor, and a copy of *Lowe on Discount and Interest* lay open on a chair. Justin raised an appreciative eyebrow. The lady's tastes in reading were heavy indeed! What a curious and intriguing mixture she was. He found himself looking forward to discussing Jeremy's suggestions with her, though he could tell from the skeptical look in her eyes as he had offered the reason for his visit that she hadn't believed him for a moment. It was a novel experience dealing with someone who was awake on every suit.

Though he welcomed the challenge, Justin was forced to admit it was the slightest bit unsettling.

Diana rang the bell and Mrs. Tottington, who had already divined her mistress's wishes and only stopped to allow enough time so that Diana would not know she had been hovering shamelessly at the door listening with all her might, appeared bearing a tray of sherry, ratafia, biscuits, and orgeat.

Smiling at the housekeeper's ill-concealed interest, Diana thanked her and offered Justin his choice before adding thoughtfully, "Though I daresay you must be thirsty after your ride and are longing for a pint of home brewed. Mrs. Tottington, I believe, is accounted the producer of one of the best ales in the county." She smiled again as that lady blushed with pleasure.

"If her brewing is anything like her housekeeping I am sure it is beyond compare, but this selection is more than ample, I assure you," Justin replied, winning yet another female heart with his customary ease and address.

Blushing and disclaiming in delighted embarrassment, Mrs. Tottington edged out of the room, though she would have given anything to stay. She was just about to pull the door to behind her when there was a squawk, and Boney sailed into the room to light on his mistress's shoulder. Carefully she closed the door and hurried back to the kitchen.

"I tell you, Daisy, he is that handsome and such an air of distinction," the ecstatic housekeeper confided later to the scullery maid hired temporarily from a local farm to help out during the mistress's visit. "You could have knocked me over with a feather when he came driving up asking for the mistress. I do hope . . ." She sighed. "Poor lamb, she deserves a fine gentleman such as he, but she vows she will never let another man bring worry into her life. And it's no good telling her that not everyone is as helpless as that young wastrel she was married to nor as absentminded or as lacking in sense as her father." Mrs. Tottington shook her head and applied herself vigorously to the pastry she was rolling out, while Daisy nodded in solemn agreement and returned to chopping onions.

Unaware that she was the topic of such speculation, Diana greeted her pet. "Hello there, Boney." She stroked his head as he nuzzled her cheek. "You remember Justin St. Clair."

"Insufferable, arrogant man," Boney muttered in disgust tucking his head under his wing and promptly falling asleep.

"I can see he never forgets a face or an epithet." Justin grinned.

It was Diana's turn to look uncomfortable. "No," she responded ruefully. "You'll have to forgive him. He has been thoroughly enjoying commanding my undivided attention here in the country, and he is just put out at having to share it with anyone. He is a rather jealous creature, I'm afraid, but as he has often been my only companion, I feel compelled to indulge him."

Her tone was light, but there was a wistful note that did not escape Justin's keen ears, and once again he felt a swell of—was it tenderness or compassion—as he pictured the lonely life she must have led.

Diana sank gracefully into a comfortable chair, gesturing toward one opposite as she did so. "But you mentioned news that you wished to impart." Again there was an ironic raising of delicately arched brows and a dry note in her voice that suggested she was not fooled for an instant by the ostensible reason for his visit.

Nor was she. Diana knew the surrounding countryside well enough to be aware that there was no one in the immediate vicinity who would be hosting Justin St. Clair, especially at this time of year. Neither did she believe that he had just heard economic news of such import that he felt compelled to inform her of it immediately. Then why had he appeared? It must have something to do with Reginald, but she could not fathom what.

She had been blessedly relieved when that young man had confided rather sheepishly that he was attending a study party with Denby and the Duke of Bellingrath's son at Bellingrath's country seat, for it meant that without having to resort to out-and-out cruelty, she was freed of his adoring presence, which, flattering though it was, had increasingly begun to wear on her nerves.

"Why yes, I happened to encounter a particular friend of mine in the exchange the other day," Justin began. Then he paused. No, he could not lie to her. He would tell her the real reason behind his unexpected call. She would be furious, with every justification, but that could not be helped. For some strange and inexplicable reason, he wished to be totally honest with her, no matter what it cost him. Somehow it was the vision of her in the garden and the realization of just how young and vulnerable she truly was, and guileless as well, that had forced this decision upon him.

This picture of her made him feel like a world-weary cynic who could no longer appreciate the simple truth when he saw it, who attributed devious methods to everyone merely because he had been too long among those who were that way. But, more importantly, Justin wished very much to be friends with her, and one could not be friends without complete openness with each other. She had been open with him, and he felt the veriest cad for not treating her in a similar manner.

The more he knew of Lady Diana Hatherill, the more he wished to know. She had begun by proving to be a uniquely worthy opponent, had continued to impress him by demonstrating that she was possessed of a cultivated mind and keen intelligence, and had finished up by revealing herself as an enchanting girl-woman. He was captivated and there was no help for it, Justin decided. If he were to learn more about her, he would have to reveal more about himself no matter how unpleasant such a revelation might be.

Chapter 20

HE coughed uncomfortably. "Actually I . . . in truth that is . . .no, that is not precisely why I came here." He paused as his characteristically ready wit deserted him entirely. "That is, I did see Jeremy, and he did offer most interesting advice, but I really came here because . . ." How difficult it was to admit it with those blue eyes regarding him so cautiously. "I came here because Reginald told me he was going into the country, and you had disappeared, and I thought, I thought . . ." he broke off helplessly, fuming at himself for his lack of address.

There was a squawk of protest as Diana leapt up from her chair. "You thought I had cozened your precious nephew into running off with me," she hissed. "You, you . . ." words failed her as she took a furious turn around the room in a futile attempt to control her temper. She stopped directly in front of him, eyes flashing. "I ought to call you out!"

Justin was momentarily diverted by the thought. "Pistols or swords?" He almost wished she would call him out, for he was virtually certain that this surprising woman was probably adept at both, and it would allow him some form of atonement for his unchivalrous behavior.

"Your choice," she snapped. "But never mind, I shouldn't waste my time fighting with someone as despicable as you are." She resumed her angry perambulations.

"Very wise," he agreed with her. "I shouldn't either. They're not likely to fight fair you know."

"Precisely. You have not been fair from the start, while I . . ."

"No, no," he interrupted soothingly. "I was completely honest with you at the outset. I told you, rather baldly as I recall, what my motives were, what I thought of you. It is only lately that I can be accused of having been less than candid with you. But I do not think you have been entirely forthcoming yourself."

"What?" Diana came to a dead halt in front of her adversary while Boney flapped desperately in an attempt to maintain his balance. "I have never lied to you the way you have lied to me."

"No, *hoaxed* was more the word I had in mind."

She stared at him, eyes widening in disbelief.

"Come now, do you really mean to tell me that you would have allowed my nephew to become such a regular fixture in Brook Street if it hadn't been for my opposition?"

A delicate flush crept across her cheeks.

"Just so," he could not help retorting with a certain smug satisfaction.

"And why should I not when you and your brother, pompous fools that you are, kept worrying that I should ruin him. *I* ruin *him*, ha! The Bucklands were managing estates here far before any upstart St. Clairs appeared. *I* ruin *him*! At least I might give him a little character. If you think I wish to be saddled with Reginald or any other man, you are fair and far off. Men are nothing but babes with no more idea how to look after themselves than . . . Oh it's beyond all bearing. Of course I don't want Reginald. But why I should give such a precious pair as you and the Earl of Winterbourne the satisfaction . . ."

"No," he held up a hand. "Granted, I have been all kinds of a fool, and a boor besides. Undoubtedly I deserve any insult you can hurl at my head, but please don't put me in the same class as Alfred."

"Very well then, you are worse than he is because at least he, odiously condescending though he was, said his piece and left me alone. You, however, have dogged my footsteps, spied on me . . ." Diana was too furious to continue, but her faithful companion took over, beating his wings and squawking.

"Well, I shall have to be satisfied with that I suppose," Justin conceded. "Being worse than Alfred is preferable to being likened to him."

"Yes, no doubt it is all very amusing to the great Justin St. Clair, but I . . . Oh, you . . ." Diana broke off.

"Insufferable arrogant," Boney suggested helpfully.

"Yes! And infuriating, too. I should have you thrown out," she fumed.

"Please do not, for I should like very much for us to become friends and that will not happen if you show me the door, though I richly deserve it, I admit. But bear in mind that I volunteered all this with the certain knowledge that it was to my discredit, and I did so in the hopes of making you trust me. I should find it difficult myself to forgive someone who had intruded so brashly into my life, for I detest meddlers of all sorts. But I am willing to acknowledge that I was entirely in the wrong. And I do sincerely wish to become better acquainted. I admire your spirit. You have a character and an independence that is too rarely encountered in this world. Your mind is particularly well-informed, and . . ." Damn! In his desperate effort to convince her, he sounded as eager and verbose as Reginald ever had.

He did sound as though he were trying to flummery her, but a quick glance informed Justin that his words had given the lady pause. Some of the fury had drained from her eyes, she was breathing more calmly, and her posture was more relaxed. Smiling ruefully he continued. "I am going about this all wrong, I know, but believe me, I am entirely sincere. I wouldn't mind if you did marry Reginald, should be delighted, in fact. But you would be bored with him in a fortnight, and the idea of Alfred as a father-in-law doesn't bear thinking of. Trust me on that one. I freely admit that you have given Reginald as much dash as anyone could—something his father and uncle so noticeably failed to do. Why, in his courtship of you, he has even stood up to his father, which makes me quite begin to like the lad." Justin stole another cautious glance at Diana.

Her lip quivered. It was infuriating, but she could not help it. There was something irresistible in the man's outrageousness. He truly did appear to be sincerely sorry for his behavior despite his flippant attitude. Besides, she did enjoy crossing swords with him, and if she were to throw him out now, he was like to go out of her life forever, and she would not entirely wish for that. One thing that could be said for certain about Justin St. Clair was that he had greatly enlivened her existence.

Quickly taking advantage of her hesitation, Justin pressed

home his argument. "And I quite honestly have financial matters to discuss with you. You will find I can be quite helpful when I am not trying to thrust a spoke in someone's wheel," he pleaded.

"I suppose, since you have had the nobility to reveal your nefarious plot, the least I can do is to respond with a certain degree of magnanimity," Diana conceded doubtfully.

"Not nefarious," he implored his gray eyes twinkling, "merely misguided."

"Very well, misguided, then." She shook her head. "Small wonder you have the women of Europe at your beck and call and the diplomats eating out of your hand. I must say, though it galls me to do so, that you do have considerable address. I can rarely be talked 'round, but as you say, you do have some advice to share with me, so perhaps it is worth my while to allow you to stay."

Justin grinned. "My misspent youth did teach me one thing, and that was how to calm down someone who was in a towering rage. Lord knows I induced enough of them." He looked at her keenly. "No, don't poker up at me. You see before you, someone who is most sincerely repentant. And, yes, I do have something of significance to pass along to you."

Diana sighed resignedly. "I must be all about in the head to let you cozen me so, but one must make sacrifices in the interest of gaining knowledge I suppose." She took some heart from his slightly crestfallen expression, glad to think that she wasn't as easily won over as he had hoped. "And what, precisely did you friend tell you that was of such burning importance?"

So she still didn't trust him? Justin supposed that he had to agree with her. And after all, he wouldn't really have wanted her to give in without the least demur. "My friend, a capital fellow with finances, Jeremy Southbridge counseled me to buy shares in waterworks companies."

"Waterworks? But they are competing so fiercely against one another by cutting their rates that scarcely a one of them is making any profit all," Diana protested.

"Just so." Justin couldn't help feeling inordinately proud of her for being so well-informed, though he could no more have said why he should care than he could explain the growing protective feeling that made him wish to help her in any and every way he could. "But Jeremy assures me that the situation has become so acute that there is a movement afoot to divide up the market, so there will be less of that."

"And they will be free to set their rates in their own particular districts," she remarked thoughtfully. "Yes, I see what you mean. It would certainly give me an investment in a slightly different area. And though everything seems to be doing universally poorly at the moment, at least this would be something that is not tied to agricultural prices or the consols." Diana gestured toward the fields visible through the drawing room windows. "Farmer Onslow, who rents my fields, was complaining bitterly about the price of wheat. He expects to get so little for his crops this year that it is hardly worth his while to rent the land at Buckland. And the market for wool is not any better, so even if he or I could afford sheep, it would do us no good." A tiny sigh escaped her and a worried frown wrinkled the smooth white forehead.

Diana was silent a moment pondering it all, then, with a brisk shake of her head, she went on. "However, there's nothing for it, but to continue as we are and hope that with peace in Europe and a chance for recovery on the Continent, we shall soon have a market over there again. After all, things were in worse straits when Papa died, and I haven't had to sell anything yet. I shall continue to put the meager profits I make into whatever investment looks promising so that I can use the interest to make the necessary repairs around here." A sweep of the hand, accompanied by another sigh hinted at the extent of the work that needed to be done.

"You have set yourself quite a task. Maintaining an estate of any size, much less the magnitude of Buckland, is no small burden. I was always eternally grateful to Alfred for being born first and relieving me of it," Justin replied sympathetically.

Diana nodded. "There is so much to do that at times I do not know where to begin. Papa neglected everything dreadfully— fields, fences, tenants' cottages, the house itself—everything, that is except the library." No matter how she tried, Diana was unable to keep the acid note from her voice.

First the marquess and then Ferdie, both of them irresponsible and spendthrift in his own way, Justin thought to himself. He must have been dicked in the nob to think that she wanted to add Reginald to the list of helpless men who had required such looking after. Once again he was seized by the oddest wish to relieve her of all her burdens, to make up for the deficiencies of all the others, but with someone as capable and independent as Diana, that was no small task.

"I see you have begun by repairing the fences and cottages—very wise, in my humble opinion, for that is likely to provide the quickest return on your investment. I should be most curious to see what else you have done."

Diana scrutinized him cautiously, but there was not the slightest hint of guile in his expression. "You would? There is not a great deal to see, but we could take a ride around the estate. Ferdie's horse, Faro, is here and longing for exercise. I try to give him a run now and then, but Ajax becomes unconscionably jealous. It won't take a minute to put on my habit." And with that she was gone, Boney still clinging gamely to her shoulder.

Hearing her mistress disappear upstairs, Mrs. Tottington, who had been keeping a weather eye on the drawing room and its occupants, came bustling in, ostensibly to retrieve the tray, but her face wore the determined expression of someone with a mission. "I don't care if he is a nob," she had declared to Daisy, "he would not be here if he weren't interested in my lady, and I intend to see that he doesn't leave Buckland without being more so." She had flounced off very much on her dignity.

"It's a right good thing to have company here," she confided to Justin as she picked up the glasses. "My poor lady has spent too much of her life alone for one as pretty and gay as she is, no thanks to that father of hers. His lordship was a brilliant enough gentleman when it came to books, but he was a fool where his daughter's well-being was concerned. Why she's been taking care of this place since she was eleven, no thanks to him, and her husband was no better—a gamester if there ever was one," she paused to draw only the slightest of breaths and make sure that her words had had their desired effect before continuing. "You must excuse me, sir, for running on so, but it does put me in a pucker to think of all the work she has done with no thanks from anyone." There, she had said it. With a gusty sigh, Mrs. Tottington departed leaving Justin to make what he liked of the interruption.

Her intrusion had accomplished all that she had hoped, and Justin was in a thoughtful mood when Diana appeared looking most businesslike in a slate gray habit, her hair ruthlessly pulled back under her hat, but the severity of her attire only emphasized the slender figure, delicate features, and enormous blue eyes.

Still preoccupied with the housekeeper's words, Justin followed her silently to the stables where Ajax and a magnificent bay were awaiting them. "Poor Ferdie. Faro was the result of the only bit of luck he ever seemed to have in all his years of gaming," she remarked sadly, "and I haven't the heart to get rid of him. But he has done little else but remain at Buckland eating his head off. He will be delighted to a have a rider on his back who is worthy of him."

Chapter 21

INDEED, both horse and rider were pleased. It was a perfect spring day when the air smelt fresh with the promise of growing things, and everywhere the eye could see were the brilliant greens of new growth. It had been some time since Justin had ruralized, and somewhat to his surprise he realized, he had missed it. The lush countryside was both peaceful and soothing after the bustle of world capitals, and bird song was a delightful contrast to the rumble of carriages and the shouts of hawkers, chairmen and all the rest of the noisy populace that inhabited those places.

They rode along companionably while Diana pointed out the improvements she had been able to effect. There was pride in her voice as she spoke of new roofs on cottages, fields fenced in, brickwork re-pointed, but Justin, astute as he was, also sensed the frustration over the previous disorder and decay that her father's lack of interest had precipitated. He felt the strain of the constant scrimping and saving that had been forced on her by the marquess's inattention to pecuniary details.

Suddenly aware of how much she had been chattering, Diana fell abruptly silent. Her companion glanced quizzically at her, and she laughed apologetically. "Do forgive me for running on so. It's just that I have never ridden around Buckland with anyone and, it is such a rare luxury to be able to discuss it all with someone other than Ajax."

Justin was unprepared for the flattering effect those simple words had on him. He felt oddly privileged that she felt comfortable enough with him, trusted him enough to share her private world with him. At the same time he was touched by the loneliness he heard in her voice. He pictured her as both Lady

Walden and Mrs. Tottington had described her, a solitary little girl with far too many responsibilities for one her age.

Tentatively he began to question her, careful lest she feel he was prying, but her initial wariness had disappeared, and encouraged by the presence of a sympathetic listener, she shared the details of a barren childhood—the long hours spent poring over books in an effort to command her father's attention and win his approval, the struggles to grasp enough of the principles of accounting, agriculture, and housekeeping to run the estate.

It was a pathetic little recital, and Justin could not help wishing for some way in which he could make it all up to her. He could not refrain from thinking that if it had been he instead of Ferdie Hatherill, he would have showered her with attention and lavished her with every possible comfort instead of spending his life at sporting events and gaming tables. No wonder she was such a self-sufficient thing. She had grown up raising herself, all the while doing her best to look after those who should have been caring for her.

Justin cursed himself for being a blind fool. If he had taken the time to ask questions and listen at the beginning of their acquaintance, he would have known that the last thing Lady Diana wanted or needed in her life was another male burden and Reginald, babe that he was, would have been nothing more than that for someone as capable as Diana no matter what he stood to inherit.

"I am afraid I lack the experience to appreciate all that you have accomplished," he apologized as she described the recent drainage of some farmland. "Alfred has spared me those concerns so that I have been able to waste my life gallivanting about the Continent."

It was Diana's turn to be arrested by the tone in his voice, and she was surprised at the bitterness in it. She had always considered the worldly, slightly cynical Justin St. Clair to be unaffected by such sentimental emotions as regret or concern over other people's impressions of him, but the way he spoke left no doubt that someone, probably the bombastic Alfred, had leveled these charges at him more than once. "I should not call being an architect of a lasting peace in Europe precisely wasting one's time." She sprang to her companion's defense.

"Perhaps not, but to the Earls of Winterbourne, anything but the circumscribed life of a conscientious landowner is not only improper but highly suspect. It's a wonder Alfred has anything to do with me for he certainly had no commerce with Great-Uncle Theobald until the last when he tried to secure his fortune for Reginald and his sisters. But I suppose what one studiously ignores in a distant relative, one can not overlook in a brother, painful though it must be to be associated with someone associated, however distantly, with trade and politics." Justin's wry expression and the half-humorous, half-sarcastic note in his voice made light of it all, but Diana sensed that at one time he had been hurt by this active disapproval.

"Do you owe your tremendous success more to your Great-Uncle Theobald or to your own spirit of rebellion?" Diana spoke in a rallying tone, but there was a sympathy and an understanding in her eyes that warmed him.

"Ah, that is a question." He laughed. "Or perhaps it was boredom. Looking after his affairs gave me something to do. I fear I found life sadly flat without university or school authorities to flout."

"Why did you not join the army? Surely there were choice spirits there would have been up for any sort of a lark."

"Yes," he agreed slowly. "But the actual business of throwing oneself in the cannon's mouth is rather straightforward you know. It's either your life or somebody else's—not a great deal of challenge, other than the physical, or complexity in that." Again he shrugged it off with deprecatory humor, but considering it all, Diana realized that he often must have found himself as at odds with the *ton*'s conventional mode of existence as she had. How odd. And for all these years she had been thinking that if only she had been a man, her life would have been more suited to her tastes.

"No," he replied as she voiced this thought, "those who are army mad think of little else and such a hail-fellow-well-met attitude can begin to pall after awhile."

"I am sure we are lucky you finally threw in your lot with Sir Charles Stewart. Though less bloody than Ciudad Rodrigo or Waterloo, the maneuverings at Vienna can have been no less dangerous in their own way and certainly just as decisive as any battle. How thrilling it must be to have had a hand in history."

"No one has put it quite like that to me before, but believe me, at the time it felt more like endless, childish wrangling than history," he responded smiling reminiscently.

By this time they had reached the house, and Diana noticed in some surprise how far the sun had progressed in the sky. "I had no notion it had gotten so late," she apologized. It really was time for him to be returning to London if he wished to make it before dark, but somehow she was loath to see him go, and unwilling as she was to admit it to herself, she couldn't think when she had enjoyed a conversation more. "We keep country hours here, so I confess that I shall be having dinner soon. I would ask you to join me, but that would mean you would have to make your journey in the dark, and of course . . ." she broke off detesting herself for sounding so eager to have him stay.

"However, it is a full moon and promises to be a clear evening," Justin hastened to respond before she could think it over any further and change her mind. "I should be delighted to accept your invitation." He jumped lightly off Faro and turned to help her dismount, smiling up at her as he did so.

Though ordinarily she would have scorned any such assistance, Diana silently allowed him to help her down without protest. There was something so natural and easy about it. However, there was nothing natural about the breathlessness that suddenly assailed her when she looked up at him. Though the smile still lingered, the gray eyes were suddenly intent, almost questioning, and she was uncomfortably aware of the strength in the hands encircling her waist. She hastily dismissed the momentary weakness in her knees and the flutter in her stomach as having been caused by her sudden and rapid descent. She had never felt that way before and found it most disconcerting.

For his part, Justin, too, had been taken aback at the effect that proximity to Lady Diana had on him. It was the oddest thing, but as he had looked deep into the sapphire eyes that were regarding him with such seriousness, he had wanted to wrap his arms around the slender waist he was holding and cover her with kisses—tracing the delicate lips with his and then sliding down into the enticing hollow at the base of her long white neck hidden by a froth of lace. It was the vision of an instant, but it was enough to make his heart pound and his breath come in gasps. Such an intense reaction was not like

him. Why he had been far more intimate with far more enticing women without ever having experienced these symptoms,
and he was infinitely relieved by the immediate appearance of
a lad from the stables who came to take their horses.

"I must apologize further," his hostess began as she led him
to the house, "but in addition to keeping country hours, I have
my dinner served in the morning room because it is quite the
pleasantest place in the house."

"A freethinker to the last," Justin teased.

"Freethinker?" Diana was taken aback.

"Not so much a freethinker as an independent thinker," he
amended. "I like that in a person." He sank into the chair she
indicated and gratefully accepted the glass of port she offered.
"You do not take the world's opinion or convention for guidance, but tackle problems on your own, seeking solutions that
are right for you in the most creative way."

"I shouldn't call myself creative in the least," she replied,
ringing the bell before disposing herself in an opposite chair.
"I merely respond to the circumstances."

"Yes, madam?" Mrs. Tottington materialized in the doorway.

Justin smiled to himself. Only someone who had been
standing within earshot could have appeared with such dis-
patch. Though ancient, Buckland was not particularly large as
houses went, but it would have taken her considerably more
time to reach them had she been in the kitchen or the housekeeper's room.

"Our visitor will stay to dinner. I trust that does not discom-
mode anyone," her mistress replied.

"Oh, excellent, I mean, not in the least, my lady. Very good,
my lady." The housekeeper did not even try to hide the excitement in her voice or the eagerness with which she fled from
the room to prepare a dinner worthy of the gentleman from
London.

Diana glanced up ruefully to find her guest regarding her
with sympathetic amusement. "I should call your *mere response to circumstances* highly original," he continued
smoothly picking up the thread of their conversation. "The expected thing for a woman in your position to do would be to
cast about for a wealthy husband. After all, witness my reaction to your friendship to my nephew, and I am not one given

to the common way of thinking." He held up an admonitory hand. "Don't fly up in the boughs. Lowering as it is to admit my lack of perspicacity, I was guilty of nothing more than a conventional interpretation of the situation. You, on the other hand, had no such schemes in your mind, but set about to take care of yourself by investing what little you had—a solution so unusual that the preponderance of the *ton* has no conception of it. Consider their unreserved scorn for trade, which is a far more dependable means of repairing lost fortunes than the more traditional resort of the gaming table. No, I find you most creative, and courageous, too."

"Why, why, thank you," Diana stammered, suddenly shy before the warmth of his tone and the admiration in his eyes. Then recovering quickly she continued, "But you have followed an unconventional path yourself. Aunt Seraphina has several times spoken of your great-uncle Theobald as a man of affairs."

"Yes he was. He saw early on that if England is to remain a powerful nation, it must develop its industry as well as its army and navy. Industry needs capital. He was a brilliant man, and the idea of living out his days in the accustomed fashion of a titled gentleman of independent means was infinitely boring to him. Much to the horror of the rest of the family, he began to interest himself in banking and finance. He always told me that the play and the company in Brooks's, White's, and Boodle's was far less deep or risky and far less congenial than that which was experienced every day in the city, and far less productive. He was a fascinating man, was Theobald. Alfred loathed him. He offended every single one of my brother's conventional sensibilities." Justin smiled bitterly and Diana suddenly pictured him as a questioning, eager, restless lad, always at odds with the stolid Alfred and, undoubtedly with most of the rest of society.

"He must have been exceedingly grateful to have a great-nephew with your interests and aptitude."

"Oh, he was, as much because it annoyed Alfred as anything. 'Progress was never made by the maintenance of things as they are,' he used to remind me. My family makes a religion out of keeping things as they are."

"How very odd then that you should rush to your brother's side and your nephew's defense when you were informed that he had fallen into the clutches of a harpy," Diana remarked with a challenging gleam in her eye.

Justin shrugged. "I was bored," he responded simply.

"Of all the . . ." Diana began furiously.

He grinned. "And you were the most worthy adversary I'd had in years, and far more interesting and intelligent than anyone else in London."

"More than Mademoiselle de Charenton?" Diana could not refrain from inquiring skeptically.

He burst out laughing. "I said *interesting*, and you are far more interesting, I assure you. Talented though she is, Mademoiselle de Charenton offers a feast for the eyes only. You offer a good deal more."

Diana could not help wondering precisely what it was she did offer, but somehow, glancing up into the eyes dancing with amusement, she did not have the temerity to ask.

Justin took pity on her. "You have an elegance of mind that I find far more intriguing, though that is not to say that I find your person any less elegant. And one can see," he surveyed the books crowding the shelves, "from whence it came. Tell me, did your father teach you himself?"

Thus by fits and starts, they found themselves sharing reminiscences of childhoods that were strangely similar in that neither one had met with any real understanding on the part of the adults around them or companionship from their peers.

From there, conversation drifted to politics and Justin's role in the recent events in Vienna, and then on to the future of the Continent and the economic and political implications of the changes occurring so rapidly. They became so immersed in their conversation that the time passed unnoticed until Boney, a rather disgruntled observer who had been moving restlessly on his perch for some time, flapped over to his mistress's shoulder intoning sepulchrally, "Bedtime, Boney. Bedtime, Boney."

"Good heavens," Diana clapped a hand over her mouth and peered at the mantel clock, "so it is." She turned to Justin. "I'm dreadfully sorry it is so late. I have been chattering on like a regular jaw-me-dead."

Justin smiled. "Now where did you learn a turn of a phrase like that? Not from your father, I'll warrant. But I have been doing more than my share of the talking." He rose to go, "And

I can't remember when I've enjoyed a discussion more. But I shall impose on your seclusion no longer. The moon has risen enough for me to see very well, and I must be on my way."

"I apologize for Boney's inhospitable remark," she continued walking over to the bird's cage and unfolding the cover. "But he is rather particular about his bedtime, especially when he is not the center of attention. I'm afraid I have catered too much to his wishes, and how he had become something of a tyrant. My only excuse is that he has been my constant companion."

There wasn't a trace of regret in her tone, but once again, Justin was struck by the loneliness of her life and his own urgent wish to do something about it in a way that her husband and father had so lamentably neglected to do. "However, he is a far more clever companion than most of us are blessed with," he remarked sardonically as he headed for the door where Tottington, having been informed by his wife of the advent of a most intriguing visitor, was hovering in the hope of having his own chance to catch sight of and evaluate this paragon. In the main, his wife's opinion could be relied upon, but where the welfare of her mistress was concerned, she was apt to lose her customarily objective perspective.

"I'll just send 'round for your carriage then, sir." He came forth from the gloom of the cavernous hall to get a better look. Bessie was right, the gentleman was a true out-and-outer, top-of-the-trees by the look of him, and possessed of a good deal more in the brain box than that useless husband of hers had been.

In no time, the curricle was at the door, and, bidding adieu to his hostess, Justin climbed in. He turned to give a final salute, and then he was off, carrying with him the picture of her standing in the ancient doorway, light from a *torchère* flooding around her emphasizing the delicate curves of her face, the more voluptuous ones of her slender figure, and catching the gleams of her dusky curls.

Chapter 22

IN fact, the image of her remained strongly in his mind the entire journey. The evening was as beautiful as the day had been—mild with only the slightest of breezes stirring, and the moon washing over the landscape to make it as bright as day though softer and almost magical.

How wrong he had been about her, and how very glad he was to have been able to right that wrong. He could not remember spending so congenial an evening with anyone, not with fellow students at Cambridge, not with Stewart and his cronies in Vienna, and certainly nowhere else. The conversation had been both restful and stimulating—restful because he had never felt so accepted, so at ease with anyone, and stimulating because her quick mind easily grasped all that he had said, seized on the most important points, and then expanded upon them with questions or opinions of her own and leading them both on to new perspectives on the subject at hand.

Talking with Diana had made Justin realize just how devoid of meaning most social intercourse was, and he was conscious again of the distaste for the *ton* he had experienced at the Countess of Axbridge's rout. But this time it was not unmixed with hope, for at last he seemed to have discovered a woman who was not bent on snapping him up in holy matrimony. In fact, he had been surprised and amused at the vehemence with which she had denounced the institution when he had suggested it as the normal way in which women repaired their fortunes.

"Marriage?" The blue eyes had opened wide in astonishment. "Why on earth should I wish to burden myself with another helpless male. It is far more amusing and infinitely more comfortable to pursue my livelihood on my own."

A brave woman was Lady Diana Hatherill—unafraid to take

on the world and its attendant problems alone. Actually, she appeared to look upon her meager finances and the large expenses facing her less as problems and more as interesting puzzles. She had almost made light of the roof that was in desperate need of repairs or the risks she faced investing at a moment when British trade and agriculture were in a decline. It was not so much that she was unaware of the gravity of it all—he had seen the worry at the back of her eyes—as she was anxious to demonstrate herself perfectly capable of dealing with such things on her own and not the least in need of any assistance.

It was a novel situation for Justin not to be asked for help. Why, even Alfred, wealthy and blindly secure in the supreme rightness of his own opinions, had come running to his younger brother when confronted with the least little ripple in the bland smoothness of his prosaic existence. And there were scores of others, such as Alan, whom he had rescued at one time or another. Somehow he had always been cleverer at extricating himself from difficulties and stronger than anyone around him, and they had naturally turned to him for guidance. Now here was a woman, a girl actually, he reminded himself as he recalled the romp in the garden, who had let him know in no uncertain terms that she needed no assistance or interference from anyone. And what did he wish to do but help her? It was ironic to say the least.

All of a sudden, Justin could think of nothing in the world that he would like to do more than erase the tiny wrinkle of worry from her brow and make the air of worried preoccupation disappear. He wanted to eliminate every possible concern from Diana's life so she would always be as happy and carefree as she had been with the puppies in the garden.

He could hardly believe it himself that he, Justin St. Clair, who had only been able to find adventure and amusement stimulating enough to occupy him in the political intrigue of one of Europe's most historic moments, should now wish for nothing more than the opportunity to make a woman's life easier. What had come over him? I must be in my dotage, he muttered to himself as he feathered a particularly sharp turn in the road.

But Justin could not banish the image of Diana and the puppies from his mind, and he spent a good deal of his journey trying to figure out what he could do to bring that joyous look back into her face. "Aha!" he finally exclaimed to the world at large. " 'Tis not highly original, but it might be effective all the same, and even she, stiff-rump that she is, could not refuse it. I shall give her a puppy." And with a congratulatory smile, he cracked his whip over the leader's heads feeling more pleased with himself and life than he had since his return from Vienna.

Meanwhile, preparing for bed, Lady Diana was also in a reflective mood. Who would have thought she could have spent an entire afternoon and evening in the company of Justin St. Clair without ripping at him? In fact, somewhat to her dismay, she had quite enjoyed herself—a lowering thought especially as she had been so determined to have nothing to do with him. However, when she came to know him, he was not truly as arrogant and irreverent as it first appeared. She supposed that being possessed of an intelligent and inquiring mind amid a family of dullards had led him to expect very little from mankind in general—an expectation that would have all too frequently been further borne out by contact with the majority of the members of the *ton*.

There was no doubt he was a clever man. Why, he had never once looked at her blankly as nearly everyone, with the exception of Aunt Seraphina, was inclined to do. And he had been an intent and most sympathetic listener, grasping immediately all that she was trying to accomplish without even once suggesting, as so many had, that such things were far beyond the scope of the female mind. He had entered so wholeheartedly into her schemes and her worries that for the first time she felt she had a friend, Aunt Seraphina again excepted, of course.

Diana stretched luxuriously in front of the fire and then climbed into bed. Yes, all in all, it had been a most pleasant day indeed. It had been thoroughly delightful, though highly unusual, to share thoughts with someone else as she made the rounds of the estate and ate her evening meal. Hitherto she had avoided companionship except on the rarest of occasions because for the most part other people only interfered with whatever task she had set herself or, worse still, they inhibited her thinking. Oddly enough, having St. Clair along had expanded it. Discussing things with him had helped her to see other as-pects that had previously escaped her. It was a novel experience. Her father, on the rare occasion when he exerted himself, was a brilliant conversationalist, but the topics that he could be convinced to discuss were limited to classical antiquity. Any other question, no matter how pressing, had been beneath his notice. And Ferdie confined his very limited powers to fashion, the turf, and gaming—not necessarily in that order. While it was true that Reginald shared some of her interests, he was more prone to pontification than true discussion; but in any case, his observations were never what one would deem enlightening.

All of a sudden the solitude that she had sought so desperately at Buckland seemed far less enticing than it had when she had left Brook Street, and the days ahead appeared rather empty. In actuality, there was not all that much left to do that could not be accomplished by leaving instructions with the Tottingtons, who were more than capable of executing them precisely as she wished. Perhaps she would return to Brook Street in a day or so. After all, it would not be polite to leave Aunt Seraphina there alone much longer.

However, an unpleasant little voice in Diana's head would intrude, warning her that it was not for nothing that Justin St. Clair had a reputation among the ladies. Undoubtedly, a diplomat such as he was a master at telling each and every one exactly the words they wished to hear. Diana did her best to silence the uncomfortable voice, for she did not wish to believe such things of him. Surely no one could be so duplicitous and not betray it somehow? And whenever he spoke, he had always looked directly at her, the gray eyes steady and calm, twinkling occasionally when he roasted her, but always clear and honest. There had not been the slightest indication in his manner that he was offering her Spanish coin. Yes he was glib, and there was often an ironic note that crept into his voice, but surely he was in earnest when he spoke. There had been an intentness in his gaze as he listened to her story, followed by a warmth of approval that surely could not have been feigned.

Don't be such a goose, Diana, she admonished herself severely as she rolled over and thumped the pillow into what she hoped was a shape more conducive to sleep. It is merely that you want to believe him. What experience do you have of men such as he? Just because you could run rings around Ferdie and Reginald does not necessarily mean that you are up to snuff where a man like St. Clair is involved. Why if Princess Bagration had a tendre for him, he is undoubtedly a master in the art of dalliance, for no one as worldly as she would take just anyone for a lover. Just because it doesn't feel like a flirtation to you, doesn't mean it isn't. He has merely adapted his style to suit yours because he wishes to distract you from Reginald. Therein lies his skill—he is able to give each woman what she wants and thus make her think that she holds some particular charm for him.

She fluffed the pillow again and lay staring blindly at the ceiling, hoping desperately that for once her natural wariness was misplaced. She had enjoyed herself so very much today, riding along in such a companionable fashion, exchanging opinions on everything from crop rotation to the probable length of time it would take before there was again a market on the Continent for British goods.

Then there was the way he had looked at her as he helped her down from Ajax. Diana didn't want to think of that. Somehow the feelings it recalled were too unsettling. She tried to push the memory from her mind, but she could not forget the strength of his hands at her waist and the vision of the powerful shoulders as he swung her from the saddle as though she were a featherweight, or the warmth of his hands through the fabric of her habit as he stood gazing down at her. Their firmness had felt oddly comforting, almost caressing, and there had been an arrested expression at the back of his eyes as if he were seeing her for the first time.

For a moment Diana had experienced a feeling of closeness as she had never felt before. It was as though they were the only two people in the world. The sensation lasted only a moment, but it had left her as shaky and breathless as though she had run a great distance. She had felt the blood rush to her face, her heart beat uncomfortably, and she could not seem to get enough air. How strange. She had never had such a thing happen before, and she was quite sure she did not wish to again. It had been most unnerving to discover that someone could have such an effect on her. Why, she was no better than couples she had seen stealing kisses on country lanes or in darkened rooms at routs and balls. Heretofore she had proudly considered herself above such things—after all, Ferdie had never had such an effect on her, and he had certainly been an attractive gentleman for all his other faults. This was entirely too disturbing, and to think it had been inspired by St. Clair, who was no doubt accustomed to evoking such responses with every woman, was a lowering idea indeed.

On second thought, perhaps she should not return to town. Best to remain at Buckland a few days and recover her equanimity. No, that would never do. That was to give in to this sudden and, she hoped momentary, weakness. She would return to Brook Street, her objectivity restored and discover for herself whether or not St. Clair was being aboveboard with her or simply playing a very deep game. After all, Aunt Seraphina appeared to like him and to trust his judgment, and certainly she was nobody's fool.

Diana sighed. Life had been so much simpler and calmer before Justin St. Clair had come into her life. How she wished he would go away again. No she did not. While it was true that her existence had been more serene, it had also been rather routine—empty even. In any event, there had not been a dull moment since he had appeared. Courage, Diana, she rallied herself. And somewhat comforted, she at last fell into a restless sleep.

Chapter 23

ACTING immediately on his inspiration, Justin began scouring London for the perfect puppy the very next day. He set the inimitable Preston to making inquiries and was highly pleased when his henchman was able to report in the space of a few days that he had discovered what he believed to be just the thing at the Sun in Barnes, where the landlord's terrier had given birth to a litter of puppies several weeks before. "But you must go and see for yourself, sir, as they are all of them to be recommended, and as this is to be a present, you would naturally wish to choose it yourself."

Justin shot his servant a suspicious look, but Preston's customarily impassive countenance was even more wooden than usual. "Very well. As always, you are in the right of it. If you will be so good as to get my hat and gloves, I shall be on my way," he replied, resigned to an expedition that was likely to prove tedious in the extreme.

Had he glanced in the looking glass in front of him, he would have seen what his ordinarily sharp eyes had failed to detect before—the knowing look and sly smile that betrayed themselves on Preston's face the minute he turned away from his master. He's catched at last, the faithful retainer exulted to himself. Diamonds and kickshaws are one thing, but puppies? Puppies for a lady are a different matter altogether. This is serious enough to bear some watching.

Preston was not alone in this opinion. A good deal later, Lord Beardsley, strolling along Piccadilly on yet another foray to Hatchard's, was astonished to look up and see his friend skillfully maneuvering his curricle through the press of traffic with a small white dog sitting obediently by his side. He waited until Justin was forced to halt behind a knot of carriages before hailing his friend. "Competing with Poodle Byng are you, Justin?" Alan could not suppress the grin on his face.

"Nothing of the sort, my lad. This dog represents a most arduous expedition and the successful completion of a serious quest on behalf of a lady."

"Never tell me that opera dancers have begun to prefer dogs to diamonds?" Even Alan, lost as he often was in the obscuring fogs of physics and astronomy, had heard of Suzette de Charenton.

"Not opera dancers, you nodcock, Lady Diana," Justin exclaimed in disgust at his friend's unusual obtuseness, forgetting entirely that just because that particular lady was rapidly becoming an obsession with him did not mean she was equally obtrusive into the thoughts of others.

"Oh. I thought it was the birds she was so taken with," Alan responded blankly, his mind wholly occupied with the vision of the *ton's* most accomplished lover, whose generosity toward his mistresses was legendary, making a present to a woman of a puppy. Alan looked thoughtful.

"She is," his friend responded impatiently, "but she also wants a puppy."

"She does? Did she ask you for one? She certainly hasn't mentioned such a thing to me."

"Of course not!" For reasons he could not fathom, Justin was unaccountably annoyed—annoyed that Alan should question his judgment, annoyed that Alan should question Justin's familiarity with the lady, and thoroughly annoyed that for some unknown reason Alan seemed to expect he should be as privy to the lady's wishes and desires as Justin was. "But she does," Justin continued, failing entirely to mask the belligerence of his tone.

"Oh, then I expect you're in the right of it."

The studied casualness of Lord Beardsley's voice was not lost on Justin, but the penetrating glance he directed at his old schoolmate failed to enlighten him. His lordship's stolid countenance remained as impassive as ever, giving no clue as to what he might be thinking.

Before Justin could probe further, a break appeared in the snarl of carriages, his horses strained at their bits, eager to take advantage of the situation, and Justin was forced to oblige them by moving along.

Alan, however, remained as though rooted to the pavement. Not usually perceptive where human beings were concerned, he had been struck by the change in his friend's demeanor. It was difficult to pinpoint, especially for someone who was inclined to make the heavens rather than his fellows the subject of his observations, but it seemed to him that the sardonic expression that customarily inhabited St. Clair's features was not so pronounced this time.

The cynical note was absent from his voice, and the slightly contemptuous look in his eyes had been replaced by something else. What was it? Alan racked his brains. When Justin had mentioned Lady Diana's name, there had been a warmth in his tone that Lord Beardsley had never heard before. This was something indeed, for St. Clair rarely mentioned his fellow creatures with any degree of approval. Yet, he had sounded admiring, almost reverent, if the truth were told, when he spoke of her. And the look he had given Alan when he had had the temerity to speak of the lady's tastes, why, it had been downright fierce. It was almost as though Justin were daring him to say anything that was not entirely adulatory of the lady.

As if I would, as if I could, Alan muttered to himself indignantly as he remembered back to the surprise with which Justin had greeted the news that he had escorted Lady Diana to Greenwich, and the faintly condescending air with which he had listened to Alan's own appreciative description of Diana's manifold and unique charm. Something must have happened to change all this.

Suddenly the marquess, who had never evinced the least interest in the thoughts and feelings of his fellow human beings, was consumed with curiosity about Justin's. Was it possible that he had developed a tendre for her?

That was quite unlike the Justin St. Clair he knew. Alan had been privy to his friend's youthful escapades from the serving wench at a favorite tavern near the university to the wife of one of the masters, and even he, removed as he had been from it all, had heard of St. Clair's exploits among the more dashing matrons of the *ton*; but he had never known him to evince the least interest in any of these women. When taxed with his many conquests by envious comrades, Justin would merely respond with a deprecatory shrug and some offhand reply that showed all too clearly the pursuit of beautiful women was nothing but a game to him—a delightful one to be sure, but a game nevertheless whose chief attraction was the challenge of the chase.

"You delight in the mysteries and intricacies of your theorems and axioms. I prefer to confine myself to the study of the vagrancies of feminine behavior—a far more difficult subject to fathom than mathematics, but infinitely more rewarding," he had often confided to Lord Beardsley with a rakish grin.

However, today there was something different. Could it possibly be true that Justin St. Clair was catched at last? Ambling along toward Hatchard's, Alan wasn't sure how he felt about all of this, but he set about in his best scientific manner to analyze the situation.

One the one hand, there was Lady Diana—beautiful, intelligent, independent. She would be the perfect companion for a man who insisted on accomplishing something productive with his clever mind instead of wasting it by devoting it entirely to the frivolous pursuits of the fashionable world; a man, moreover, who possessed a limited circle of close friends simply because he would not suffer fools to waste his time. On the other, there was Justin, who had never been constant to a woman in his life and was known to select only the most sophisticated, dashing women as his mistresses, and had also been heard to declare that love was a figment of most people's overheated imaginations or a useful device for poets.

Alan did not want Diana to be hurt. He liked her too much. She was too honest and genuine a person to be drawn into a liaison with someone incapable of love or constancy. Certainly Justin had never demonstrated that he was capable of either of those things. But perhaps with the right person, he would be. There was no doubt that he could experience life's softer emotions; after all, it had been nothing but sympathy and kindness on his part that had brought about his friendship with Lord Beardsley. Once Justin liked and respected a person, he would do anything for him as Alan well knew. It was merely that there were very few people whom Justin St. Clair could respect.

Lady Diana was certainly someone possessed of all the qualities that his friend usually admired, but Alan had detected some sort of friction between them. It had been the impression of a moment to someone not ordinarily cognizant of such

things, but there had been a flash in the dark blue eyes and a
hint of defiance in the musical voice every time Diana had
mentioned Justin's name. And now that he considered it, he
remembered the decided lift to her chin and the quick glances
to Justin's direction when she had been speaking to him at the
Countess of Axbridge's rout. It was almost as though she were
challenging St. Clair—a welcome change from the fawning attitude of most women who, from the little Alan had seen, appeared to be lining up to cast themselves at his friend's feet.

And Justin too had evinced the same sort of symptoms.
There had certainly been some devilry in his expression when
he had introduced Alan to Lady Diana, and he had certainly
been testy enough when her name had come up just a few minutes ago.

Alan smiled to himself. Having examined all facets of the
phenomenon and conducted a rigorous analysis, he decided
that a person could reasonably conclude that a match between
Lady Diana Hatherill and Lord Justin St. Clair might be a very
good thing for both of them. Certainly each of them would
provide the other with stimulating company, something they
both enjoyed but, as Alan knew from painful experience, was
so very difficult to find in the *ton*—or anywhere else, for that
matter.

Though not at all given to reflection on matters of the
human condition, Lord Beardsley was happy in the thought
that perhaps Justin had found someone to care about; for it
seemed such a pity that someone as sensitive as the schoolboy
who had saved Alan from such misery had never found that
sensitivity in others or had ever had his ready sympathy returned—hence his cynical outlook on life. From his own experiences with her, Alan felt confident that Lady Diana was
entirely capable of rectifying the situation.

While Alan remained wrapped in his cogitations with
pedestrians on Piccadilly surging around him, Justin presented
himself at Brook Street and, puppy in hand, asked after the
lady of the house.

"Madam is in the drawing room, sir. If you'll just follow
me." Finchley welcomed him with as much dignity and
aplomb as if his caller were not vainly clutching a wriggling
ball of fur. But the butler did unbend enough to permit himself

a small sly smile as he ushered St. Clair toward the drawing room.

"Lord Justin St. Clair to see you, madam," he intoned majestically, opening the double doors. Boney, taking his daily exercise by circling the room, paused in mid-flight to let out a horrified "Scraaack!" at the sight of the visitors, one of them in particular. Dismayed, he plopped down on the arm of a nearby *bergère* then, having satisfied himself that his first horrified impression had been correct, took himself off to cling with offended dignity to one of the curtains. He turned his back to the room's occupants and sought to forget the unsettling developments by concentrating on the passing scene in the street below.

His mistress, however, was more forthcoming. "Good morning, sir. And who is this you have brought with you to call on me?" She rose to greet them. Though her words were addressed to Justin, her welcoming smile and extended hand were for the bright-eyed bundle under his arm, which at this moment was surveying the room, particularly that part occupied by the injured Boney, with lively curiosity.

Though he had known how it would be, Justin could not help but feel the slightest twinge of annoyance that the gift's deliverer should receive so much less attention than the gift itself. In fact, Justin thought acidly to himself, he might just as well not have been there. "You seemed to be having such fun at Buckland that I thought you might like one of your own." In spite of the number of times he had practiced this little speech en route from Barnes, he still could not quite manage the offhand tone he had tried for. He needn't have worried as the gift's recipient, entirely occupied with having her hands vigorously licked, barely heard his words.

It took a moment before Diana absorbed their import, but when she did, the delight on her face was more than enough to make him forget his touch of irritation, the harassing trip to Barnes and the even more harassing drive back with a passenger who insisted on climbing down at the most awkward moments. In fact, he forgot everything but the sparkle in her eyes, the delicate flush that suffused her cheeks, and the entrancing way her lips parted in delighted disbelief. "For me?" she whispered, hardly daring to ask.

Justin could only nod.

"Oh, oh, how lovely! I can't remember the last time some-one gave me a present," she exclaimed, entirely forgetting poor Reginald's laboriously chosen offerings.

"The landlord at the Sun assures me that he is sired by the best ratter around, and is in a fair way to proving his heritage."

"I expect you are," Diana replied, taking the square little jaw between her hands and looking into the bright eyes. She relieved Justin of his burden, laughing as it licked her face. "But there are precious few rats around here. You are like to find life in London sadly flat I am afraid, but we shall do our best to keep you amused. We can walk in the park, though doubtless you will find it just as dull as Ajax does." Diana set the little dog down.

"And Ajax's mistress," Justin interjected.

"And Ajax's mistress," she agreed. "But you, my fine fel-low, will make life infinitely less dull for me. I can see that the curtain tassels are already on their way to being dismantled and strewn around the drawing room." She bent down, snap-ping her fingers to distract him from the quarry and could not help laughing as he came bounding back toward her, a ball of fluff, full of exuberant energy and expectation.

Seeing her this happy and excited was all the reward that Justin had looked for, but when Diana turned to him, her face suddenly serious, eyes bright with unshed tears, to stammer, "I can't thank you enough for bringing . . . for you, your kindness . . .for thinking of me . . ." he was unprepared for the rush of emotion that overwhelmed him.

It was a jumble of feelings that he could not quite identify, but first and foremost was the thrill of having been able to do something—such a little thing really—that brought joy into her life and made her look, for a moment at least, as young and carefree as she had at Buckland. Along with that came the feeling that in doing this he had become in some way special to her. After all, Lady Diana Hatherill was a lady who tried hard to convey the impression that she needed nothing, but he had been able to see beneath that cool, collected exterior and gratify a wish that even she herself had not been aware of.

Those magnificent eyes of hers were telling him all these things, even if her voice could not, and Justin could not re-member a time in his life when he had felt so pleased with himself or with something he had done. He wanted the moment to last forever, but an insistent canine tug on Diana's skirt distracted her and broke the spell.

"Does he have a name?" she asked.

"I don't believe so. I was rather hoping you would give him one as well as a home."

Diana thought for a moment. "I shall call him Wellington. I already have a Bonaparte who is master of all he surveys. I feel that this little fellow will rather change all that, and besides, he certainly looks to be a tenacious sort." By now the puppy had seized a discarded copy of the *Edinburgh Review* and, growling ferociously, was tugging it around the room, swinging his head from side to side in a valiant attempt to deliver it a death blow.

"Wellington it is then," Justin agreed solemnly. "And I leave him in your care knowing that he will lead the best possible life a dog could lead. However, I confess to having another motive in coming here, which is to invite you and Lady Walden for the second time to join me in viewing the pictures from Lucien Bonaparte's collection that Mr. Stanley has for sale. You were rather too busy when I asked before, but perhaps now that you have had some time at Buckland to oversee your affairs, you are more at liberty than you were previously."

Damn the man, Diana muttered to herself. There was no mistaking the gleam in his gray eyes or the quizzically lifted eyebrow. He had known that the first time she had refused him out of a churlish desire to give him a set-down. And now, having wormed his way into her good graces, he was determined to press his advantage. Well, she would not allow him to get the best of her. "Yes, I have sorted everything out. It was rather in a muddle, but now I have dealt with it and can do things with a clear conscience," Diana lied badly. And who was worse? He knew she was lying—a quick glance up at him was enough to assure her of that.

He smiled back at her, and the provocative look was replaced with one of friendly sympathy. How easily the man read her thoughts—a state of affairs that was both alarming and comforting at the same time. "I'm glad. Thank you. I do look forward to having you join me and hearing your opinion of the pictures." The teasing note was entirely gone now, and there was no doubt of the genuine eagerness in his tone. "But now I had best leave you two alone to make friends."

Justin bowed and was gone before Diana even had a chance to thank him again for his extraordinary kindness. What a strange combination he was, by turns cynical and teasing, and yet full of understanding and sympathy. For a moment there, she could even have sworn she detected tenderness in his expression as he had watched her with Wellington.

Wellington! Diana looked hastily around, fearful that her momentary distraction would have contributed to the destruction of her drawing room, or at least to the curtains. However, her present was sitting quietly by the window, head cocked, eyes bright with inquiry as he studied Boney, who continued to stare fixedly out at the scene below.

"Come along Wellington," Diana called. "We shall introduce you to the rest of the household." The little dog's ears pricked up, and he bounced happily over to his new mistress, ready for the next exciting discovery his suddenly eventful life had to offer.

Chapter 24

AND somehow, with the arrival of Wellington, Diana's life seemed more eventful, too. A less cantankerous companion than Boney, he was always overjoyed to see her and endlessly interested in everything and anything she did, whether it was consulting with Cook on the menu, listening to Finchley's weekly report on the household, walking in the park, or doing errands in Bond Street. Every time she caught him looking at her, his eyes bright with curiosity and expectation, Diana thought of Justin and was warmed again by his thoughtfulness.

The felicitousness of these reflections was evidenced in the pleasure with which she greeted him a few days later when he came to escort the ladies to Mr. Stanley's rooms in St. James, and Justin was surprised at the effect her welcoming smile had on him. Hitherto, Diana had received him with wariness, if not downright hostility, but now there was a lilt in her voice and an eagerness in her look that made him feel as though she were glad to see him and was looking forward to being with him.

It was such a simple thing, but somehow Justin found it more appealing than all the seductive glances that had ever been cast his way. With something of a start, he realized that for the first time he could remember a woman was happy to see him because she enjoyed his company and not because he was a skilled lover, a wealthy protector, or a conquest to flaunt before the *ton*. It was wonderful to feel that someone he had come to admire and respect for her own unique qualities liked him for the same reason.

All this was the revelation of a minute as he helped the ladies into the carriage, but Lady Walden, who had been observing him intently, quickly concealed a knowing smile. Even when her niece and St. Clair had been at daggers' drawing, she had sensed how it would be. Years of traveling with her husband and meeting people from a wide variety of backgrounds had made her wise in the ways of the world, and she knew that two people who could provoke each other to such a degree had more in common than they recognized, and that sooner or later they were bound to realize it.

It had not escaped her either that even though each professed to be disgusted by the conduct of the other, they never failed to gravitate toward one another no matter how large the crowd that separated them. As much as she was gratified by her own perspicacity, Aunt Seraphina was even more delighted to see the glimmerings of contentment and happiness that had lately manifested itself in Diana's animated expression, renewed energy and zest for everything. The arrival of a new puppy, no matter how delightful, could not solely account for this. However, watching Diana and Justin together at this moment, Seraphina knew she had to look no farther to divine the true cause of the change in her niece.

"I understand we are to thank you for the introduction of a charming new member to our ménage, and a good thing it is, too. We were fast on our way to becoming more sedate than the town tabbies, and stood in desperate need of a little livening up," Lady Walden commented as Justin climbed in behind the ladies.

"Now, that is a bouncer if ever I heard one." He laughed. "Never have I seen two ladies in less danger of becoming town tabbies than you two. Why, if I call and discover you at home—not jauntering off to the country, the Stock Exchange, or some fearfully blue event of high cultural significance—I consider myself extremely fortunate. I live in constant expectation that Lady Walden will convince Lady Diana to repair her fortunes by becoming a nabob, and I shall arrive in Brook Street one day only to discover you have both taken off for India. Oh Lord," he broke off as the ladies exchanged glances, "now I have done it. You will be off tomorrow. I shall have to set a watch on all the ports in order to keep the only two intelligent women I know in England."

"Not likely." Lady Walden chuckled. "Much as I would enjoy adventuring again, I fear I am not what I once was and should only burden my companion on such a trip, dearly as I would love to go."

"So should I," her great-niece echoed wistfully.

"Having introduced such a radical notion, I am almost tempted to offer my escort, but for the moment, I shall have to confine it to St. James Street—sadly flat I know, but I shall do my best to enliven it as much as I can," he apologized.

And indeed Justin did enliven it. Having accepted his invitation as much out of curiosity and—she hated to admit it—a desire to see St. Clair again, Diana found herself agreeably surprised by his familiarity with the painters exhibited. He spoke most knowledgeably of the artists of the Flemish school that were being offered for consideration. Certainly Mr. Stanley, who welcomed them with utmost cordiality, seemed to hold his patron in high esteem. It was an aspect of Justin that Diana had never seen, and it intrigued her to think that a notorious rake, a man of affairs and one who obviously excelled in athletic pursuits could also possess such an appreciation for the aesthetic, such a degree of refinement and discrimination in fine arts.

Diana was noticeably silent observing his reactions to certain paintings—as he peered closely at the execution and the brush strokes and then stepped back to experience the full effect of the composition—It was an entirely unexpected aspect of his character and she enjoyed watching his appreciation of it all.

Ever sensitive to Diana's presence, Justin soon became aware of her scrutiny and turned to her with a smile. "I am not a complete barbarian you know."

She blushed vividly. "Indeed, I never said you were. I . . ."

"You may be pardoned for holding such an opinion of me, as I am always at pains to keep the world from guessing any serious interests I might have," he replied sardonically. "For it is the quickest way to destroy one's pleasure in something—letting the world in on it to cheapen it with inane comments and senseless chatter. When I was with Stewart, I had the opportunity to indulge my taste for such masterpieces to the top of my bent as we traveled from country to country stopping at one palace after the next. In the midst of such intense negotiations, I found it most soothing to wander off and spend time alone with the art of our hosts. I was always certain to find solitude, as the rest of them were far too busy dividing up Europe and sharing the spoils to waste their time in the contemplation of beauty."

"How wonderful it must have been to see so many places, to learn so many new things." Diana sighed.

"Yes it was. I miss waking up in the morning knowing that I shall be going to bed in some place entirely new the next day." However, as he spoke, Justin realized that he was enjoying it all far more now that he was sharing it with her than he had before. How much more exciting it would have been if he had had Diana with him, her eyes shining with interest and enthusiasm as they were now, and how much more life would have to offer now if she were sharing all of it with him.

The fleeting expression on Justin's face was not lost on Lady Walden, who, never one to miss an opportunity, chimed in, "Indeed, it is highly invigorating to be constantly experiencing new places, different scenery, and foreign customs, but it is not half so instructive and not nearly as comfortable if one is doing it alone. Thomas could always point out things I had missed, and I did the same for him. We discussed our impressions endlessly as we made our journeys, which whiled away some exceedingly tedious moments, I can assure you. But I must ask Mr. Stanley if this is a Ghirlandajo, as I suspect it is." Having deftly planted this seed, she made haste to leave the two of them alone as she went over to speak to their host.

"Do you collect any particular artists yourself?" Diana wondered.

"I admit to a highly unfashionable preference for the Flemish masters. Their ability to capture light and use it to its fullest extent, their close attention to detail, and their interest in the observation and recording of the elements of everyday life appeals to me far more than the grandiose subjects and vast canvases of most of the others. I should like to possess a few very special favorites of mine, but I have never stopped anywhere long enough to call home," Justin replied, surprising himself as he heard the hint of wistfulness in his tone.

He had always thought that his peregrination sprang from a boredom with the *ton*, a disgust for the sort of narrow life that Alfred and so many others led, but now he seemed to detect a note of regret in his own voice. Perhaps he truly did wish for the comfort of such an existence but feared being caught in the trap of mundane details that would surely make him as lacking in vitality and insight as his brother was. Or perhaps he had thrown himself into a life full of challenge and adventure in order to hide his loneliness from himself. His had been a solitary existence in spite of the scores of women who had participated in it. However, none of them, no one in fact, had actually shared it. And whenever he had stopped long enough to consider it, Justin had instantly become aware of such a corroding sense of emptiness that he had kept moving, amusing himself with one outrageous exploit after another.

He looked down to discover the blue eyes regarding him with such a wealth of comprehension and sympathy that it was his turn to be stunned. In an odd way, he suddenly felt as if he *had* come home. For the first time in his life, someone seemed to understand and to take on his feelings. He was overcome with a sense of peacefulness and comfort that he had never known before.

"It must be difficult not having some place to retreat to where you can restore your spirits and forget the follies of the rest of the world." Diana's reply was simple, but somehow it made Justin aware of a very special bond between them. Until now no one had ever taken the trouble to know him except in the most superficial sense, but she was making the effort to look below the surface, to discover the real Justin St. Clair. He found himself overcome with gratitude, and something much more, at her concern.

A discreet cough brought Justin to his senses, and he realized that Mr. Stanley was waiting expectantly for him to comment on the collection in general or some paintings in particular. "I beg your pardon, Stanley. You have a rare offering here, and I appreciate your generosity in showing it to us privately. I am quite intrigued by that Jordaens over there, but I am afraid I shall require more time for consideration if I am to spend the rest of my life with it."

Mr. Stanley beamed. "Very good, sir. I quite understand. You have made a wise choice. One must not purchase any work of art unless one is totally *bouleversé*. I shall hold it separately awaiting your instructions." Still beaming, he ushered them off the premises and set the painting aside to keep it until his patron should decide.

As they emerged into the warm sunlight, their host re-

marked, "As it is such a fine day, I hope I might be able to entice you into a drive around the park before I return you to
Brook Street. I realize," he nodded toward Diana, "that it is
rather tame sport for such an intrepid horsewoman, but . . ."

"Oh, I do not care, and it is so deliciously sunny. In fact, I
quite enjoy being driven because I am at leisure to take everything in, instead of worrying about keeping Ajax in check,"
she replied hastily.

In truth, it was one of those beautiful spring days when the
earth seemed full of possibility, from the buds bursting on the
trees to the daffodils springing up everywhere, and she rather
disliked the idea of returning indoors.

They rolled along in contented silence, relishing the fineness of the day and observing the splendid horseflesh and
equipages crowding the park. However, they had barely a
chance to make any headway in the park before they were accosted. First it was Tony Washburne who trotted up, a welcome smile on his ruddy countenance, booming, "Lady Diana,
devilish good to see you again. Beautiful day, eh what?" and
seemed content to ride silently alongside the carriage for a
while, smiling affably until he was hailed by an eager group of
young bucks.

The next to command their attention was Lady Blanche
Howard, whose costume of an open robe in the chemisette
style with blue ribbons on the sleeve and a white lace cornette
headdress also trimmed with blue ribbons, made everything
and everyone around her seem clumsy and dirty in comparison
to her blond loveliness. The beauty, despite the coquettish
glances cast in Justin's direction, was considerably less
pleased to see his companions than Tony had been.

However, except for one quick disdainful glance in Diana's
direction, she hid her dismay under a barrage of inconsequential chatter. Did St. Clair know that the Montmorencys were in
town? She believed Ralph, Lord Montmorency, had been a
friend of Justin's at university. And she felt certain he would
be attending Lady Topham's masquerade. Had he selected a
suitable costume? For her part, she believed she had at last settled on Cleopatra.

Unwilling observers of this concerted attention, Diana and
Lady Walden could not help exchanging glances of amuse-

ment. The gentleman looked to be so very bored and the lady so very eager.

At length, Justin was able to break in and stem the seemingly inexhaustible flow of inanities. "I would not worry so Blanche, if I were you. You will no doubt appear so lovely in whatever costume you choose that everyone will recognize it as you, and never even stop to wonder what character you are portraying." Damn! He had thought the blasted masquerade over, and that he had successfully avoided it.

"But have you met Lady Walden and Lady Diana Hatherill? Please allow me to make them known to you. Lady Blanche Howard is a friend of the *family*." He turned to his companions, neither of whom had missed the slight emphasis he had placed of the word *family* or the rueful expression in his eyes.

Forced to acknowledge the presence of the other women, Blanche lost all interest in the conversation and, hurriedly summoning over an eager swain who had been hovering nearby in the hopes of attracting her attention, instructed her coachman to drive on.

"Actually, I am only acquainted with Lady Blanche as a neighbor down at Winterbourne, but she claims it does a great deal of good for her reputation as an incomparable to be seen with me," Justin hastened to explain. Then, realizing the infelicitousness of this remark, he fell uncomfortably silent as he became aware of just how much an *insufferable arrogant* man he must appear.

A small stifled sound made him glance at Diana to see her looking over at him, eyes dancing merrily. "Of course, I do not agree with her, nor do I understand why . . ." he became hopelessly tangled in his disclaimers. Just precisely why was he so anxious that she be assured that Blanche meant nothing to him? Justin could not remember when he had ever been at such a loss for words, surely not since Cook had caught him stealing a plum tart she had left cooling in the window.

Fortunately for his self-esteem, Lady Walden took immediate charge of the situation. "Diana tells me that you are encouraging her to put some of her capital into the waterworks. She assures me that you expect them to show more profit in the near future."

"Yes." Justin seized the opportunity gratefully. "Jeremy insists that though the price of shares is quite low at the moment, it is sure to rise when the territories are divided so that the companies are not forced to cut their rates so drastically in order to compete with each other."

"Hmm." The sharp dark eyes were thoughtful. "A clever piece of thinking, and it does offer a way to broaden one's field of investment. Tell me, where does your friend come by his information?"

And with the conversation safely diverted to the far less dangerous topics of finance and investment, they enjoyed a most stimulating discussion for the rest of their tour around the park. So engrossed were all three that they were completely unconscious of the notice that was being taken of them by many of the park's fashionable denizens.

To be sure, there was nothing so unusual about a gentleman's taking two ladies for a drive, but when the gentleman was Lord Justin St. Clair, whom the *ton* was accustomed to seeing alone, magnificently mounted and stopping to talk with only the most dashing matrons of the beau monde, and when one of the women was a highly respectable woman well on in years and the other an extremely pretty but reclusive young widow, well, then, it was something indeed! More than one discreet glance carefully hidden behind a parasol was cast in their direction, and more than one knowing look was shared among the fair occupants of several carriages.

Chapter 25

THE fashionable world that had first been treated to the sight of Justin St. Clair tamely driving through the park with two unexceptional females was not left to speculate long as to the probability of his appearing in such unusual company for a second time. The very next evening, he could be seen seating them in a box at the Theatre Royal where they appeared to be thoroughly enjoying Miss O'Neill's interpretation of the Lady Teazle in *School for Scandal*. And what was more, St. Clair, who ordinarily divided his time between staring speculatively at the actresses or subjecting the audience to ironic scrutiny was doing neither, being engaged instead in a most earnest discussion with both of his companions. He even went so far as to laugh heartily now and then. In truth, the unusual state of affairs in the box was almost as diverting, if not more so than the action onstage to many in the audience. Afterward in select salons throughout the town, there was far more discussion concerning St. Clair and the ladies than there was of Mr. Sheridan's play.

This remarkable phenomenon showed no signs of abating, though neither did it appear to be developing into anything more intriguing. The celebrated bachelor's attentions, which never revealed anything but interest of the most platonic sort, were equally divided between the two ladies. He was as solicitous of Lady Walden as he was of her niece, and he apparently found the conversation of either lady as amusing as that of the other.

It was a great puzzle, indeed, but as nothing further seemed to come of it, the *ton* turned its fickle attention to more promising topics such as the Princess Charlotte's impending marriage or the possibility that Lady Clothilde Danforth was about to contract a hopeless mésalliance; so hopeless in fact that it was rumored that the young lady found herself in a most interesting condition.

However, talk did not die down before it had reached the ears of Euterpe, Lady Sarandon, who, wishing to be the first with the *on-dit*, penned a coyly speculative letter to her poor friend Amelia—eternally immured in the country at Winterbourne—inquiring if perhaps her scapegrace brother-in-law had been catched at last. Amelia taxed her husband with this information at dinner that evening, and Alfred, forced to withdraw his concentration from a formidable slab of roast beef, exhibited a rather disappointingly benign reaction to such startling news, merely muttering, "Eh, what's that, Lady Winterbourne? Euterpe shouldn't spread such stories. Justin leg-shackled? He's too much a here-and-thereian ever to settle down. Anyone trying to predict Justin's future is likely to catch cold at that." As if to punctuate his point, the earl stabbed viciously at a boiled potato, applying himself with gusto to the task immediately at hand.

Good! He congratulated himself for having consulted Justin on this affair. For once in his life, his brother actually was proving to be of use to someone besides himself. Now all that Alfred had to do was to talk some sense into his son's head, get him to abandon his ridiculous notion of setting himself up as some sort of whining pedant, and point out to him the necessity of his returning to Winterbourne to take up his proper role as receptacle of his father's wisdom, as well as the treasured inheritance that was to be passed along to him, and all would be well.

The Earl of Winterbourne was provided with the opportunity to embark upon this laudable program at a much earlier date than expected, as the Viscount Chalford who, with the exception of his unfilial interest in scholarship, truly was a dutiful son and devoted brother, stopped off at Winterbourne en route to London from his study party at the Duke of Bellingrath's enormous estate.

With a certain amount of forethought, unusual in someone as oblivious as Reginald, he had had the wit to invite Denby and Cedric, second son to the duke, to stop at Winterbourne with him. For surely his father, faced with the scions of such ancient and noble families would curb his objections to his son's wasting his time in his scholarly pursuits.

Reginald had accurately gauged his parent, and the earl was mollified by the sight of his exalted connections. However, he had not been able to keep himself from offering one piece of fatherly advice as his son was about to depart. "You're a fine lad, Reggie," he began, impressively laying a heavy paternal hand on his son's shoulder. " 'Tis better by far to be spending time with these fine fellows than at the feet of a siren and a fortune hunter."

Emboldened by the proximity of his friends and week of pursuing his own interests, Reginald replied with uncharacteristic firmness, "If you mean Lady Diana, sir, she is not a fortune hunter. As Lady Walden's great-niece, she is heiress to considerable fortune of her own, so has no need of any others."

An angry flush suffused the earl's already florid countenance. "Oh, come now lad, this is the purest speculation, why . . ."

"I heard it from Lady Walden myself," the viscount responded resolutely. "Good-bye Papa. Good-bye Mama. Be a good girl, Sarah, and remember to read the Plato I marked for you." Reginald turned to wave to the others standing inside the doorway before climbing into the Bellingrath carriage, which immediately began to proceed down the gravel drive leaving his father to gaze blankly after them and wonder if perhaps he had not been too clever for his own good. The situation certainly needed taking in hand. Much as he disliked the thought, he might be forced to post up to town and set things to rights. Leaving a fortune to a woman; who had ever heard of such a preposterous notion?

During the blissful days spent in the country, his mind roving from Catullus to Tacitus, Virgil to Pliny the Younger, Reginald had hardly given a thought to his goddess, but having had her recalled to mind by his father's infelicitous remark, he was eager to see her again. He barely stopped at his lodgings long enough to refresh himself after the journey before hurrying to present himself at Brook Street.

As he approached that temple of all his hopes and dreams, he was struck by what looked suspiciously like his Uncle Justin's curricle being led around to the back. Uncomfortably aware of the slight friction that seemed to exist between his beloved and his uncle, Reginald at first misdoubted his sight, but there was no mistaking the splendid horseflesh and elegant equipage of someone as noted for his rigs as Justin St. Clair.

Puzzled, Reginald followed Finchley to the drawing room where a remarkably domestic scene met his eyes. Seated next to each other on the settee poring over some important looking documents were his uncle and his ladylove. A ball of white fuzz slumbered peacefully between them, its head resting in the lady's lap while over in a corner by the fire Lady Walden was perusing the *Times* and, off by the window, Boney clung to the curtains.

"The Viscount Chalford, my lady," Finchley announced.

"Well hello, Reginald. Did you have a pleasant journey?" Diana rose to greet him, disturbing the ball of fuzz that uncurled itself into the recognizable shape of a puppy before turning around to plump it's chin on Justin's knee and resume his nap. "And have you completely had your fill of scholarship? We have nothing to offer you here that is more uplifting than idle chatter."

"Oh no, Lady Diana. Your conversation is always enlightening." Reginald blushed vividly.

"Been on a study party have you, lad?" Justin looked up from the papers he was perusing long enough to smile quizzically at his nephew.

"Well I, well, yes, Uncle Justin, I have." It all came out in a rush. "You see, Denby's a first-rate scholar, and he and I were, well we, well Cedric . . ."

"Good lad. It sounds far more intriguing than anything London has had to offer this age, and it is a shame to put a good mind to waste in the empty amusements of the *ton* or the rustic pursuits of a country gentleman." Justin returned to his papers.

"It is? I mean, you don't mind?" Reginald could hardly believe his ears.

Justin laid down the papers again. "Of course I don't mind. I consider all those things to be a dreadful bore myself. It is just that I find the problems plaguing the European powers and the intricacies of trade to be far more riveting than Homer or Virgil—but to each his own."

Reginald stared at his uncle, but there was not a hint of the usual biting irony in his tone, no satirical gleam in his eye. He merely sat there stroking Wellington's ears while the puppy snored blissfully.

"There, I knew your uncle would understand." Diana smiled at him as she rang for refreshments. "An I am sure Aunt Seraphina does, too. Now, do tell us all about it."

And Reginald proceeded to do so, waxing eloquent on Denby's brilliance, Cedric's diligence, and the joys of having a fine library all to oneself. So full was he of the glories of it all that he barely noticed the others. But later, as he strolled toward his lodgings, it occurred to him that he had never before felt so at ease with his brilliant sardonic uncle.

He had always admired Justin's intellectual prowess, but his uncle's wit had always been so biting, his remarks so caustic that Reginald had been awed into silence in his presence. Somehow now he seemed—Reginald sought for just the words to describe him—softer and more friendly, that was it. He couldn't think when he'd seen his uncle act just that way. Nor had he ever seen him pay much attention to the opinions of others. However, he had been respectfully silent when Lady Diana and Lady Walden spoke. And several times Reginald had intercepted glances between his uncle and Lady Diana, which, even to the most obtuse observer, hinted that they were on excellent terms.

What had occurred? Certainly before he had gone into the country, they had not rubbed along at all well. Reginald was not precisely certain whether or not he was pleased with the turn of events. To be sure, he wished for the two people he most admired in the world to be friends, but . . . but there had been something else—a warmth and intimacy call it—that was not normally present among casual acquaintances. He shook his head. It was all rather puzzling.

However, over the next several days, it became increasingly clear to the Viscount Chalford that Lord Justin St. Clair and Lady Diana Hatherill had buried whatever differences they had once had and were quite enjoying each other's company. Reginald caught glimpses of them riding in the park and attending the opera. He even saw them entering the exhibit at Somerset House where the picture of the Prince Leopold was on display. Of course, Lady Walden was always a member of these parties and was equally engaged in all the conversations, but a careful observer, such as the viscount had now become, was still left with an impression that some special sort of communication existed between his adored Diana and his uncle.

To be sure, Reginald, even in his wildest dreams, had never expected to win the hand, or even the attention of such a goddess as Lady Diana. At most, he had only hoped to be allowed to worship her from afar. He had been ecstatic when she had allowed him to call on her or to escort her to the theater, but if the truth were known, he had not been precisely certain of how to proceed next and for some time had been uncomfortably aware that as her most devoted admirer he ought to do something, but what? The idea of being anything more than a suppliant to such an exalted being terrified him. In fact, he could not imagine how his uncle could converse with her so casually and so easily.

To be perfectly honest, Reginald had felt somewhat relieved that Cedric had gotten up a study party. It had been so very comfortable to poke around in the library with kindred spirits who were not always overwhelming him with their beauty, their elegance, or their clever wit. And he had begun to have his doubts about the nature of his feelings for Lady Diana. Of course he adored her to distraction, but such an elevated emotion was rather exhausting to maintain forever.

Seeing that his uncle was a rather frequent visitor at Brook Street and that the ladies never lacked an escort, he became less assiduous in his attentions, slowly concentrating on the less exciting but less terrifying topics of classical antiquity, hoping desperately that Lady Diana would not notice a slackening in his interest.

She did notice, however, as did Lady Walden, and both ladies derived a good deal of amusement from watching Reginald come to his senses. His visits became less frequent. He sighed a good deal less, and his conversation, when he did call on the ladies, became far more rational—so much so that Boney stopped putting his head under his wing the moment the viscount appeared.

Chapter 26

"IT appears to me that the Viscount Chalford has at last awakened from his infatuation," Lady Walden commented one day as the door closed on Reginald, who had departed after the briefest of visits to return a volume of Epictetus Diana had kindly lent him.

"Yes." Diana looked up from the *Times* with a wicked smile. "Adoration is such an exhausting exercise . . . for all of us. I find I quite like him now that his ardor has cooled. 'Tis a pity that his father is continually after him to leave off this *queer start* of his, forego his books, and return to Winterbourne like a *good sensible lad*. Poor boy. In due time I am sure he will, and he will be as estimable a landlord and as dull a country gentleman as his father, but at least he ought to be allowed to pursue his interests in peace for the moment. Until now I had never thought to be grateful for Papa's lack of interest in me, but I can see there is something to be said for being ignored."

"Poor Geoffrey. He never should have been anything but a scholar." Seraphina nodded in agreement. "But he did love you in his own way, you know. If he hadn't considered you worthy of it, he would never have taken such care with your education. He was quite proud of your scholarship, you know."

"He was? He paid so very little mind to me that I hadn't the least idea." Diana stared wistfully out the window.

And therein lay a problem, her great-aunt thought to herself. There were very few people in Diana's life who *had* paid any attention to her. Certainly Ferdie Hatherill had not. To be sure, the Tottingtons had done their best, and Reginald, in his own besotted way, had recognized what a rare creature she was, but no one besides Seraphina had ever truly appreciated her quick and inquiring mind, her quiet courage, her independent spirit. No one had until now, that is, Seraphina amended.

Along with Lord Beardsley and Reginald, Lady Walden had also noticed a change in Justin as he escorted them around. The air of cynical boredom had been replaced by genuine interest and amusement. He had been unfailingly kind to them, an attribute that the shrewd old lady suspected had always been part of his nature but kept carefully hidden from a callous world that was only too ready to take advantage of such things.

In fact, the older woman suspected that despite the plethora of adoring women who flocked around him and the young sparks who tried to imitate his casual elegance and his offhandedly ironic air, he was a lonely person. There had been nothing cynical in the eagerness with which he shared books, pamphlets, and papers on the waterworks or other enterprises that the ladies might find useful. He had spent untold hours in their drawing room discussing all their various economic endeavors with the air of a man starved for intelligent conversation and rational companionship.

And then there was the way he looked at her niece. Seraphina smiled. It wasn't precisely the expression of an adoring swain, it was something deeper than that—a warmth that sprang from a realistic and genuine admiration for her unique qualities and a respect for her capabilities. And, if she weren't mistaken, there was a dawning tenderness there as well.

Lady Walden was not sure how much her niece was aware of all this, but certainly Diana had responded to it unconsciously. She had quietly blossomed under Justin's appreciative friendship, allowing her sense of humor to show and revealing a delightful whimsical side of her that even Seraphina had not known existed. Like Reginald, Lady Walden had intercepted looks between the two of them, and she had been highly gratified to see the intimacy they shared— just the way she and Thomas . . . Lady Walden sighed and glanced at the clock. "I must be going. I promised Mr. Pennyroyal I would have those papers read, signed, and delivered to him today, and I have not yet done so," she excused herself and hurried from the room.

Left alone, Diana continued to gaze out the window.

Wellington, who had been soundly asleep, stirred on her knee. She looked down at him and smiled. He was such a good little dog and already a devoted friend—a happy addition to the household.

How had St. Clair known she needed a puppy when she hadn't even known it herself? In some ways the man appeared to be omniscient. He divined the sorts of activities that she would find most amusing and invited her to share them with him, provided her with information and insight that he knew she would find most helpful, and offered stimulating companionship besides. She could say anything to him, and he was not shocked or bored as so many people were when she spoke of things that truly interested her. It was quite the opposite, in fact. Justin made her feel that he admired and applauded her for thinking and acting the way she did, and he did his best to encourage her to develop the way she wished to rather than the way society appeared to think she should.

Diana continued to stare out the window, a soft smile on her face. It was nice to have a true friend, she thought. Then catching sight of Boney, hitherto her most constant companion, she sighed. The bird had not been at all himself as of late. He spent most of his days clinging dispiritedly to the curtain, paying very little attention, and talking even less. Diana was becoming extremely worried about him.

Dumping Wellington unceremoniously from her lap and gathering a few select seeds from the untouched pile in Boney's cage, she went over to the curtain for what seemed the hundredth time in the past few days, calling softly, "Boney?" No response. "Boney?" Still no response. She moved closer to the curtain, and he retreated rapidly up toward the ceiling. Her shoulders slumped. He had been this way for nigh on a week, and Diana was beginning to despair. "Boney, please. I have some of your favorite seeds."

In her distress, Diana did not hear the drawing room doors open, nor was she aware of her visitor until a deep voice at her should inquired, "Diana? Why, whatever is wrong?"

She turned to find Justin looking down at her with such concern in his eyes that she couldn't help bursting into tears in the weakest way. "It's Boney," she wept. "He won't talk to me. He won't eat, and he hasn't come down from the curtain for ages."

"Oh, my poor girl." A pair of strong arms went around her and pulled her close. A gentle hand came up to stroke her hair. "Hush now. Boney is all right, I promise you," he soothed.

Diana remained in the circle of his arms for a moment, savoring the wonderful and surprising sense of consolation and security to be derived from being held close to a hard chest and having comforting fingers moving softly through her hair. Then admonishing herself sternly not to be such a watering pot, she sniffed determinedly and pulled away.

That was a mistake, as it gave the gentleman an opportunity to pull out his clean white handkerchief and dab the tears away so tenderly that it felt like a caress.

"There's a good girl. Now smile at me," he commanded, tipping her chin up to look deep into the dark blue eyes. Diana smiled dutifully, and Justin was seized by the maddest desire to pull her back in his arms and kiss away the tears that still twinkled on her eyelashes, tracing a line with his lips down to the delicately sculpted lips that curved most enchantingly. He wanted to hold her and promise her that he would take care of her forever, that nothing would make her cry ever again. It was but a fleeting, though, tantalizing thought and then he had himself well in hand. He released her gently. "As I was saying, I feel quite certain that Boney is fine. He is merely sulking."

"Sulking?" Diana repeated blankly.

"Yes. I believe he is suffering from nothing more than an ordinary case of common jealously. And, as you are the cause of it all, he is punishing you by ignoring you." Justin laid a kind hand on her shoulder.

"Me? But why? And of what or of whom could Boney possibly be jealous?"

Justin pointed to Wellington, who, having climbed back into the *bergère* Diana had vacated, was slumbering peacefully. "You must admit he is more easily held on a lap and petted than is a sharp-tongued bird, no matter how long you have been friends."

"Oh!" Horrified, hand held to her mouth, Diana gazed wide-eyed at him. "How dreadful, I never thought . . ."

"I am sure you did not," he replied gently. "But it is easily remedied. Where is some of Boney's food?"

"Over there in his cage."

"Good." Justin strode across the room and filled his hand

with seed before strolling casually over the curtain to stand directly beneath the sullen bird. "Hello, Boney," he remarked in a conversational tone. "I expect you must be quite hungry now, eh, old fellow?"

Boney tore his eyes from the passing scene below to gaze suspiciously down at Justin.

"That's a good bird." Slowly Justin opened his hand, revealing the pile of seed in the palm. "I quite understand your being miffed, but it won't do, old fellow. Don't let your pride get the better of you." Keeping his eyes fixed on the scene outdoors, Justin didn't betray by the least movement that he was aware the bird was cautiously making its way down one of the folds of the curtain. "It would be the greatest of pities to go hungry just to prove a point," he continued. Boney had reached his shoulder level now and hesitated just a moment before climbing on and inching his way down Justin's arm to the seed-filled palm. He pecked greedily for a few minutes, then cocked his head to fix Justin with a speculative stare.

"Yes, Boney, that's a good bird." Justin smiled reassuringly. Tentatively he stroked the parrot's glossy head. "Shall we go to see your mistress. She's very sorry, you know." Slowly Justin began to make his way toward Diana, still stroking the bird. He came to stop before her, and Boney flew up to his shoulder to begin rubbing his head against his protector's jaw, muttering to himself, "Good bird, Boney. Good bird, Boney." and pointedly ignoring his mistress, who stood quietly by Justin's side.

"He must be very angry at me, indeed, for he rarely has much use for visitors, and he certainly never showers them with such attention as he is now lavishing on you," she remarked thoughtfully.

"Yes, indeed," Justin agreed. "But he'll get over it once he sees how repentant you are."

Diana bowed her head, the very picture of contrition.

"Excellent." he chuckled. "Just remain that way for a moment. Now Boney, you see how sad she is? And you see, she is sad about you and not Wellington here." Justin had inched his way over to the *bergère* where the little dog was snoring soundly.

"Wellington," the bird repeated. The dog woke with a start

and looked around. Boney chuckled to himself. "Wellington," he reiterated.

The puppy sat up anxiously surveying the room.

"Come here, Wellington," Boney called in Diana's voice while his mistress and Justin exchanged amused glances.

Wellington leapt down and obediently trotted over to Diana, who was doing her best to keep a straight face.

"Sit," the bird commanded.

Looking expectantly up at his mistress, the puppy obeyed.

"Well trained, and a terrier, too, you are to be commended," Justin murmured his eyes dancing.

Boney darted over to the mantel. "Wellington come here," he commanded and again the dog leapt to do his bidding, then stopped midway across the floor to turn and look curiously at his mistress, who stood rooted to the spot struggling to contain her helpless laughter.

"Wellington, come here," Boney shouted as he swooped overhead on his way to the curtain. Wellington ran after him. "Come here, Wellington," he called again, flapping over to perch on the molding at the opposite corner of the room.

Delighted with the new game, Wellington raced after him. "Wellington." The parrot landed on his mistress's shoulder just as her dog, sliding on the polished floor, crashed into her feet.

Diana laughed. "I thank you for having restored harmony among the members of my household, though I very much fear it is at the expense of any peace and quiet that might have reigned here."

"Oh, 'tis nothing," Justin assured her. "If you had not lived in seclusion for so long, you would have recognized the jealousy for what it was."

"A mere nothing for you, I am sure, after years of soothing jealous mistresses," she teased.

"Vixen." He grinned stroking Boney, who had again alighted on his shoulder. "But truly," his expression suddenly became serious again, "if there is anything I can do to help you in any way, I beg you to ask it of me."

And the odd thing was, Diana thought to herself, he truly meant it. No one had really ever offered such a thing to her before, and she felt just a little overwhelmed by it. "Why, why, thank you," she stammered, "but I don't expect . . ."

"You'll be needing it," he finished for her. "I know. I am aware of just how self-sufficient and independent you are, but should you, by the most unforeseen turn of events, find yourself requiring assistance of any kind, do not hesitate to ask me. No doubt, I shall expire of extreme old age before such an unlikely situation arises, but in the meantime, I beg you to remember that the offer is made. I also came to ask if I might escort you and Lady Walden to Lady Topham's masquerade. I realize that it is a more frivolous entertainment than those to which you are accustomed, but you might just find it amusing. And with your educational background, you will undoubtedly create a far more arresting and authentic costume than most."

"I, well, I don't think, that is to say, I hadn't intended to go," Diana began doubtfully, "but . . ."

"Do join me," he urged eagerly. "I am sure it has been a long time since Lady Walden has attended such an affair, and I feel certain she would enjoy it."

When it was put to her that way, Diana could hardly refuse, and she found herself thanking him for his invitation. Though after her visitor had departed, she murmured to herself, Diana what were you thinking of? You must be all about in the head to allow yourself to be drawn into such a thing when you know how it will be—a crowd of overdressed people taking advantage of the license allowed by anonymity. Still, if she had Justin to share it with, it would be rather fun to watch.

Chapter 27

HOWEVER, in the succeeding days, Diana was to acknowledge the astuteness of St. Clair's observations. She and her great-aunt were enjoying themselves thoroughly as they set about deciding on the characters they wished to portray and the appropriate costumes. It was a challenge to select a persona that was enough like their own not to feel awkward but different enough to offer some degree of disguise, and they spent several happy hours poring through their favorite works of history, literature, and mythology in an effort to select the perfect thing.

There were so many choices that they might have deliberated forever had not Lord Beardsley appeared on their doorstep some days later, a perfect picture of gloom. Ostensibly he had called to present Lady Diana with a copy of George Graves's recently published *Ornithology*, which he did with a polite nod toward Boney, who was preening himself on the mantel. As the scientist was a favorite with the bird, he was rewarded with a brief hello before Boney returned to the arrangement of his feathers.

Well aware that a good deal more than ornithology was on the marquess's mind, Diana invited him to stop awhile. "We are quite ready for some serious conversation as, I am sad to say, we have been passing the time as frivolously as any of the flightiest members of the *ton* in trying to devise costumes for Lady Topham's masquerade. It is a very good thing indeed that you came to distract us, as we stand in danger of entirely destroying the nice tone of our minds. But something appears to have vexed you. I hope your observations are proceeding well."

"Yes. They are coming along splendidly what with the new equipment I have procured," Alan replied. He fell silent for some time and then in a rush of confidence burst out, "It's this deuced masquerade. My mother absolutely insists that I accompany her. I find social affairs of any sort to be a complete waste of time, and masquerades only encourage ordinarily stupid people to even greater heights of folly. But the plaguey things of it is, I must abide by my promise to escort her around the town if I am ever to be left alone to do my work."

Diana smiled sympathetically. "In the main I agree, but St. Clair has offered to escort us, and I must say that now I have consented, I am rather looking forward to it. 'Tis bound to prove a splendid spectacle, and one is less carefully scrutinized or gossiped about at these affairs than at others, and therefore may take the retiring role of observer without occasioning the comment that is bound to arise if one does such a thing in other situations. Besides, I shall know at least three sensible people there, and that is more than enough for me."

She thought for a moment before exclaiming, "I have it! We can all go as constellations, and thus be forced by the nature of our costumes to stay together. That way we can be assured of rational conversation and behavior. Knowing that I don't care to dance, you won't feel constrained to ask me, and I shan't be forced to accept. What do you think of that?"

"You might have an idea there," his lordship admitted cautiously. In truth, it did not sound so very bad. After all, he quite enjoyed Diana and Lady Walden, and one could always count on Justin to be amusing. "My mother is going as Mary Queen of Scots—does so every year. She won't be half pleased if I don't go as Darnley," Alan fretted. Then, taking courage from the thought that he would be among supporters, he continued boldly, "But she will just have to accept that. You might go as Andromeda, Lady Walden as Cassiopeia, and Justin as Perseus while I could be Orion; that is if it agrees with you," he concluded hesitantly.

"A splendid idea!" Diana and her great-aunt spoke in unison.

The marquess blushed a fiery red. "I'm glad you like it. But, indeed, I only meant to call for a moment as I must get back to my work." He rose hastily, somewhat alarmed at being the object of such approbation. However, at the door he stopped and turned around to add bashfully, "I do thank you ladies. I shan't dread the evening quite so much."

"Nor shall we." Diana rose also. "And thank you very much for the book." She rang for Finchley to show him out, but the marquess was already plunging down the stairs.

"Poor man," she remarked to her companion as she returned to her seat. "His mother seems a perfect gorgon. How much happier he would be if she were to leave him alone. There is something to be said, after all, for parents who are too absentminded to meddle."

Making his ways down Brook Street the subject of their conversation was thinking very hard indeed. Not that he paid the least attention to such things in general, but he seemed to remember that when he had complained in a passing remark to Justin about the masquerade, his friend had declared his firm intention of avoiding such a frippery affair at all costs—and Justin St. Clair was not a man to change his mind. It had not taken him long to think better of his resolution. Apparently the company of Lady Diana Hatherill could made even the most nonsensical of amusements worth attending—a most interesting state of affairs indeed.

In another part of town, someone very different from the marquess was arriving at much the same conclusion. For some time now Suzette de Charenton had been aware of her lover's abstraction. Of late, his attentions to her had been neither as frequent nor as marked as they had been in the past. Of course it could be attributed to a deadening sense of familiarity and the resultant boredom, but Suzette was far too experienced and far too wise to believe that. No, her intuition told her that another woman was responsible for the slackening of Justin's interest.

To be sure, he was as skilled and satisfying a lover as always, and when roused, was as passionate and sensual as ever, so she did not think that he found her any less desirable than he had before. No, this was a preoccupation that hinted that he was thinking about something or someone else. Of course, Justin had many friends and many other flirts, but until now no one had affected him enough to distract his attention from the opera dancer. Thus, it must be a relatively recent acquaintance, probably female at that. Suzette had her suspicions as to who it was—the woman who had so annoyed Justin by refusing to bend to his will—the woman she had seen at the opera who, unlike the rest of the female population, appeared to be un-moved by Justin St. Clair.

Ordinarily Suzette was far too wise a woman to tax her lovers, especially such a one as St. Clair, with other interests. But in this case, her curiosity was getting the best of her. And besides, for once in her life, she truly did care about her lover. Oh no, she was not in love with her handsome admirer—she was far too practical for such a silly notion—but Justin had been more than a lover. He had been a friend. He had recognized her as a serious artist and admired her for it. He had treated her as a human being instead of a beautiful face and an exquisite figure or a possession that would add to his consequence. And she in turn thought of him as something more than a conquest.

Leaning across a satin pillow after an especially passionate bout of lovemaking, the dancer smoothed back the dark hair that had fallen across his brow. "You are distracted, *chéri*. Is anything amiss?"

Justin started. To be honest, he had been thinking of the relief and happiness in Diana's face as she had laughed at Boney's antics. She had been so upset when he had arrived, and she had allowed him to comfort her. It was such a simple thing, but Justin felt more rewarded than he could remember feeling in a long time—more pleased than when he had convinced Monsieur Talleyrand to concede to the Russians on a small point. And now, here he was in another woman's bed thinking of how wonderful it had felt to hold Diana in his arms.

He must be all about in the head! Justin St. Clair had gone blithely from one woman to the next without a backward glance, and now here he was thinking about a pair of sapphire eyes and beautiful lips at what truly was a most inopportune moment.

Suzette saw the reminiscent glow in his eyes, she was sure of it. It had to be another woman. And this time it was not lust, but love. In the oddest way, she was happy for Justin. Suzette considered love a totally ridiculous and useless emotion, but she sensed that Justin, cynic that he was, had secretly longed for it, and had just despaired of ever finding it. Well, he had helped her and been a friend to her, the dancer decided, and now it was time to repay the favor.

" 'Tis the woman who made you so angry that you are thinking of, is it not?" She smiled impishly at him.

"What, Lady Diana?" The dancer's extraordinary perspicacity startled Justin out of his usual cautious reticence.

Suzette nodded sagely. "Me, I am a woman of the world. I can see she had reached the so imperturbable Justin St. Clair. Non, *chéri*, don't deny it. Me, I do not mind. I shall lose a lover of the most charming, but"—she shrugged her white shoulders—"there are others, and I am a practical woman. You have been the best I ever had and generous, too. Therefore, I wish you to find a woman worthy of you to love. I think that perhaps at last you have. And you are not the sort of man to have both a mistress and a wife, *hein*?"

Justin sat dumbfounded. Suzette was not given to idle chatter, and she was a shrewd woman. It had been her beauty and passion that first attracted him, however, it was her Gallic wisdom and her pragmatism that had kept him coming back. It was restful to be with her. She understood what life was all about, and asked for nothing from it except a chance to better herself through her work and to practice her art to the best of her ability. In some way, because he respected her so much for this, Justin wished he could give her more.

She sat looking him gravely, a hint of worry in her green eyes. "Don't be concerned about me, *chéri*. You know that I do not count on *mes affaires de coeur* to last or even to support me. Me, when I am too old to dance, I shall return to Paris and open a school for dancers so the world can see true ballet as she is supposed to be and not a bunch of silly girls looking for wealthy patrons."

"And you shall have it, Suzette," he replied with a crooked smile. "But that too will need wealthy patrons to support it, and I intend to be the first."

She grasped his hand and gazed deep into his eyes. "You, *mon ami*, are a very kind and true friend."

"And you do not have many of those I think?" He questioned her gravely.

"*Non*. Most people are fools that I do not waste my time on." She leaned over and kissed him. "Now be off. I must practice. She is a good woman, Lady Diana. She is proud. She looks after herself. I have seen her. She carries herself with an air of one who knows what she is about."

And that, Justin thought as he rode slowly home, was just the problem. Diana had even less need for anyone in her life than Suzette did, and he was fast coming to realize that he very much wanted to be a part of her life.

He had always led a rather solitary existence, surrounded by friends to be sure, but constantly focused on his interests, whether they were diplomatic or financial, rather than on people, and now, as Suzette had so cleverly pointed out, he discovered that Diana had become one of those interests. Not a day went by but that he wondered how she was faring. So many times he wished he could ask her opinion of something. So many times he wanted to share something with her. Not only was she interested in many of the things he was, she actually reflected on them and enjoyed discussing them as much as he did. At the same time, she added a slightly different perspective that was as original as it was refreshing and thus stimulated him to further thought.

So much of Justin's life had passed in idle amusement, not because he particularly wished to waste his time in an orgy of dissipation, but because there had been so little to challenge him in the empty life of the *ton*, and thus he had done everything to excess purely to make it as interesting as possible.

Now there was someone whose presence made anything interesting, whether it was a drive in the park or the discussion of income taxes, and Justin was filled with a desire to be the best, the most knowledgeable in every field in order to stimulate her in return. For she did seem to enjoy their time together as much as he did, didn't she? Surely there was a certain sparkle of enthusiasm in Diana's eyes that shone only for him and no one else, wasn't there? So often when she smiled at him lately, he was convinced it was a special smile she reserved just for him, wasn't it?

Suddenly Justin was seized with a horrible sense of doubt that he hadn't experienced since his first few awkward youthful encounters. What if he were just another man to her—someone as useless as Reginald, Ferdie, and her father had been? He couldn't bear the thought. You have become a coxcomb then, a nasty little voice in his head whispered, if you think that every woman is naturally smitten with you. Well, almost every woman had—until now.

By the time he reached Mount Street, Justin was in an

agony of doubt. So preoccupied was he that he almost stumbled over Lord Beardsley, who was in the act of knocking on his door.

"Why hello, Alan, what are you doing here?"

"Coming to call on you." Alan peered curiously at his friend. Justin was not usually one to belabor the obvious.

"Well, I am not at home" was the short reply.

"Whatever has put you in such a bad skin?" Really Justin was acting most unlike himself. The air of worried preoccupation was most unlike his customary cynical insouciance.

"I am being a bit of a bear, aren't I," Justin began ruefully just as Preston opened the door. "Do come and tell me what is on your mind."

"Well, it's this masquerade," Alan began as soon as the two were ensconced in large comfortable chairs with glasses of port. "I wondered if you had selected your costume yet. Lady Diana is thinking of going as Andromeda and Lady Walden as Cassiopeia. We wondered if you could be Perseus, and I shall go as Orion, or I suppose it could be the other way around, you could go as Orion and I could go as Perseus."

"Perseus, Orion?" Justin could hardly believe that Alan, misanthrope that he was, had actually come to discuss costumes to a masquerade with him. What or who had wrought this drastic change in him? Justin did not have to look far. Only Lady Diana could have made the event appealing enough to the marquess to make it palatable.

"Constellations, old fellow," Alan volunteered helpfully. Really, Justin was being singularly obtuse today. Something of major import must have occurred to make him so dull.

"I *know*, they're constellations. I'm not a complete nodcock. I am just surprised . . . well, that is to say I think you would make a much better Orion." He eyed his friend's massive figure, "Yes, I picture Orion as large and powerful while Perseus was, er, slighter."

"Really?" Alan was high gratified at this comparison, not that anyone would ever have been in danger of calling St. Clair's lean athletic figure *slight*, but despite his muscular physique, his considerable height did make him appear more slender than his fellows.

"Good. That's settled," Alan remarked abruptly. He eased himself out of his chair. "Must be on my way now—calculations I was in the middle of that I must get back to," he declared acting for all the world, Justin thought to himself in some amusement, as though they were going to boil over if left unattended.

"Well, off with you then." Justin rose as well. "I shall look forward to seeing you at Lady Topham's old fellow."

The door closed behind the marquess, leaving Justin alone with his unsettling reflections. Suzette was entirely in the right of it. Diana had rapidly become an obsession with him. Hardly an hour passed without his wondering what she would say about this, what she would think about that. Strolling down the street or riding through the park, he would catch sight of a slender woman with dark hair and quicken his pace in the hope that it would be Diana.

He couldn't remember when he had devoted so many of his thoughts to another person. Even in his salad days, when he had been in the throes of his first infatuation, the lady had rarely intruded into his preoccupation with horses and school pranks. Now the time he spent away from Diana's company seemed curiously flat and aimless. Was it, could it be love?

Never having fallen victim to that disquieting disorder, Justin could not be sure. Certainly he was not blind to the lady's faults as Reginald had been or as he had witnessed in other acquaintances in the grip of that emotion. He knew very well she could be stubborn and independent to a fault, rising to a challenge without the least consideration for her safety or her reputation.

Indeed, though he had never enjoyed the company of anyone more than he did that of Lady Diana Hatherill, Justin could safely say that he had never been so aggravated by anyone either. It was a very odd situation to be sure. Curiously enough he felt proud of her as well. That anyone could make Alan consider attending a social affair was momentous enough in and of itself, but that he should actually look forward to something as frivolous as a costume ball enough to consult Justin about it was nothing short of incredible. And it was all owing to Diana's gift for making whomever she was with feel relaxed and self-confident enough to be comfortable with the rest of the world.

In fact, Justin himself was surprised at his own pleasurable anticipation of Lady Topham's masquerade. Assured of felicitous company, he would quite enjoy watching the antics of the *ton* from the safety of a congenial group. It was a new feeling for one who ordinarily stood aside in proud isolation watching such affairs with cynical superiority.

Chapter 28

THE evening of Lady Topham's affair was unseasonably balmy with soft breezes wafting the scent of spring flowers and causing the hundreds of *torchères*, illuminating the impressive facade and the pathways throughout the splendid gardens, to flicker and dance, adding to the sense of fascination and enchantment as the most select of the Upper Ten Thousand made their way to the magnificent residence. Eyes behind masks glittered with excitement and intrigue, and smiles betrayed the eager anticipation of rare entertainment. Lady Topham was noted for her imaginative diversions whether it was flocks of rare birds released just as dawn was streaking the sky, brilliant fireworks, or fantastical ice sculptures in midsummer.

Slowly moving up the huge marble staircase to the brilliantly lit ballroom, Justin, Lady Diana, and Lady Walden were surrounded by pirates, shepherdesses, long dead kings and queens, and characters from every legend or myth one could call to mind. Surveying the crowd massed in the entry below them, Diana gazed in silent fascination at the vast array of costumes and headdresses. "It's as good as a play, isn't it?" she breathed. "And no one knows who one is, so one can observe as much as one likes without causing comment. Everyone is too occupied with discovering the identities of all the guests to remark on who is talking to whom, or to make one feel uncomfortable if one prefers not to dance."

Privately Justin thought that Diana with her slender elegant figure and graceful carriage was as easily identifiable as if she were without the dainty gold mask, which only lent an enchanting air of mystery to the beautifully inviting lips parted breathlessly beneath it or delicate dark eyebrows arched above it. Who else would have selected a costume so simple that it stood out among the rest of the gaudy company? Besides the flowing white drapery and daring gold sandals of Andromeda, every other woman appeared tawdry and overdressed.

Certainly Lady Blanche Howard, just arrived with the Duchess of Wrayburn and Lord Livermore, and catching sight of Andromeda, could have wrung Diana's neck, for the stark white of the costume, unrelieved by anything except the gold cords which fastened it and the gilded sandals and mask were infuriatingly conspicuous. The eye traveling over a surfeit of jewels and hues naturally fixed on it, and Lady Blanche though she might at first have been in doubt as to its wearer's identity, had no trouble recognizing the imposing figure next to her. Few men of the *ton* could boast the height and the powerful build of Justin St. Clair.

Blanche ground her teeth. Just a short time ago St. Clair had scoffed at the merest suggestion that he attend something as silly as Lady Topham's masquerade, and yet here he was escorting a woman who bid fair to become the cynosure of all eyes if the reactions of the gentlemen next to her and those in front and in back of her were anything to go by. They could not keep their eyes off the slim figure in white whose curves were so tantalizingly emphasized by the gold cord, and who was so obviously enjoying a highly animated conversation with her two companions.

"Who's that?" Lord Livermore, gazing raptly at Diana, gave voice to Blanche's thoughts.

"Oh, don't you know St. Clair's latest interest?" the duchess chirped gleefully, delighted to be one up on one of the *ton's* most knowing members. "That is Lady Diana Hatherill, poor Ferdie's widow. She ordinarily keeps herself quite apart from such amusements as this, but apparently Justin's legendary charm is too strong even for that hoity-toity young woman. They say he's quite devoted. Who would have thought he would pay the least attention to someone as blue as she is rumored to be. What a waste of a charming man! But, oh, look there. Have you ever seen anything as ridiculous as Lady Birdthwaite? Why, she is sixty if she's a day and dressed as a shepherdess." The duchess tittered happily behind her fan and renewed her grip on Lord Livermore's arm.

Meanwhile, Blanche was seething. That Justin should deprive her of his escort in favor of that, that *antidote* would have been beyond comprehension if it weren't so infuriating. How could he possibly prefer a reclusive bluestocking to an incomparable, she fumed to herself, forgetting entirely that Justin St. Clair had never voiced the least interest in escorting Lady Blanche Howard anywhere. All pleasure in the evening evaporated. Even the knowledge that she was clutching the arm of another of the *ton*'s most eligible bachelors and accompanied by one of its most sought after hostesses was of no comfort. Now the elaborate Egyptian headdress and daring gown of gold satin cut low across the bosom and enhanced by a glittering parure of enormous emeralds seem vulgar and overblown next to the purity of Andromeda's attire.

Blanche resolved to keep a careful watch on the trio, a strategy that was likely only to increase her distaste for the evening, as Andromeda was undoubtedly one of the belles of the ball. She was constantly surrounded by a crowd of Henry the Eighth's, cavaliers, monks, and pirates. Even the Marquess of Hillingdon made up a part of the admiring coterie. Ordinarily Lady Blanche Howard would not have been caught dead even being seen in proximity to such an eccentric as the marquess, but the fact that such a noted misogynist was clearly enjoying himself in the company of Lady Diana, even going so far as to waltz with her, only served to enrage the beauty further.

In fact, no one could have been more surprised than Alan to find himself at such an affair sporting a lion skin over his shoulder and a thick cudgel, but having committed himself, he entered into the spirit of things with more zest than he would have thought possible. As for his mother, she did not know what to think, torn as she was between dismay that her mild-mannered son had firmly refused to be Lord Darnley despite all her tears and sighs, and triumph that she had at last gotten him to acquiesce without having to resort to dire threats. She had still been trying to decide which of these conflicting emotions to give way to when they arrived at Lady Topham's. However, the decision was wrested from her by her son when upon their arrival, he had actually asked a female to dance with him, thus rendering the dowager marchioness speechless.

Speechless was also the word that could well have been applied to Lady Blanche. The final seal was set on her fury when some time later she observed Perseus and Andromeda slipping out through the French doors at the end of the ballroom. Pleading that her costume needed adjusting, Blanche excused herself from her own crowd of admirers and, after a quick trip to the cloakroom to ward off suspicion, unashamedly made her own way in the direction the couple had disappeared. When she reached the terrace outside the ballroom, however, Justin and Diana were nowhere to be seen, but there were numerous couples and groups of couples strolling among the gardens enjoying the fresh air and the moonlight.

Blanche gave up in disgust as she tried to distinguish her quarry among them. She already knew enough as it was. There was no real need to see further evidence that Lady Diana would stoop to any level to capture Justin St. Clair. Just wait until Blanche had discreetly spread the rumor around the ballroom that Ferdie Hatherill's widow was trying to ensnare another wealthy husband.

Indeed, Blanche knew very little, if any, of Lady Diana's history, but she knew enough to be sure that Diana had not been on the town until she had become Lady Diana Hatherill and that was all she needed, allowing her imagination to fill in as it would. Obviously Diana had made a match that had lifted her from obscurity the first time and was trying to do the same thing the second, Blanche remarked pityingly into a few carefully selected ears.

Meanwhile, blissfully unaware of the machinations they had set in motion, Justin and Diana were strolling along Lady Topham's carefully tended garden paths in a leisurely manner, conversing amiably on a wide range of topics.

Like Blanche, Justin had been well aware of the attention Diana was attracting the moment they arrived, even before eager partners had begun to cluster around her and, to his own disgust, he had fallen prey to a most uncomfortable attack of what could only be called jealousy, an emotion hitherto not experienced by the *ton*'s most eligible bachelor. Yes, he was delighted that she was so admired. It was about time that society appreciated her, but at the same time, he did not wish to share her with anyone else. He wanted to be the only man who could make her smile and laugh, the only one who could cause a sparkle of interest to shine in the blue eyes. Suddenly she was surrounded by a bevy of eager swains who hung on her every word. Entirely forgetting that he had been unmoved by such a situation several weeks earlier, Justin sought for some way to detach Diana from the group surrounding her so that he could have her all to himself. In what was a purely selfish move, he invited her to partake of some fresh air with him in the garden.

Blithely unconscious of the varied emotions that she had caused to seethe in more than one jealous breast, Diana gratefully agreed, for she had begun to find the crowd, not to mention the assiduous attention of her admirers, somewhat claustrophobic. A breeze fluttered her draperies and gently stirred the dark curls against one bare shoulder, caressing it in such a way that made Justin, his eyes glued to his companion, catch his breath. "How beautiful it is out here and what a relief after the stuffiness of the ballroom." Diana sighed with pure pleasure. "I do hope Aunt Seraphina does not feel abandoned."

"I sincerely doubt it. She and Lord Orpington were so engaged in their discussion of the many ills besetting the East India Company that I suspect they are not even aware of our absence. Besides, someone needed to rescue you from your importunate swains. One more dance and you would have been on the verge of exhaustion."

"Pooh." Diana laughed scornfully. "I am not such a poor creature."

"I know you are not." Justin turned to face her, gently removing her mask. "But do you know, sometimes I have the oddest wish that you were?"

"You do?" Diana's eyes were wide with astonishment. "But why ever would you wish such a thing as that?"

"Because," he reached out a hand to trace the line of her jaw, "then you might have need of someone like me to help you, and you might stop to think of me as often as I think of you." The hand brushed softly across her lips and then tilted her chin. "I find you are rapidly becoming an obsession with me," he murmured against the softness of her mouth, kissing her gently at first and then more deeply as he pulled her into his arms.

At first Diana was too surprised to react. They had been walking along speaking quite casually of the most unexceptionable things, when all of a sudden something had changed. She had felt it immediately in the way Justin looked at her. There had been an intensity in his expression that had not been there seconds before, and there was an unusual rigidity in his posture, as though he were holding something in it. The air around them felt charged with a certain energy, a sense of expectancy. Still, the kiss had come as a complete shock, for heretofore, there had been nothing in the least flirtatious in St. Clair's manner, and Lord knows, if anyone were skilled at the art of dalliance, it was Justin St. Clair. No, everything had all been very amiable, and then before she knew it, she was in his arms with his lips on hers evoking the most amazing responses in her—feelings she had no idea she possessed.

It was not as though Diana had never been kissed before. To be sure, there had been Ferdie who could be very sweet and appealing at times. After Ferdie, there had been one or two bold fellows who had hoped to offer some substantial consolation to a lovely young widow, but all of these had been the merest brush of flesh against flesh—something perhaps more intimate than a handshake, but certainly no more exciting.

But this, this was different. Diana felt weak and breathless, excited and exhilarated all at the same time. Her lips parted, and she could feel his breath mingle with hers. Justin's hands felt warm on her back as he moved them slowly down her shoulders to her waist. The silk of her costume was so thin, it felt as though they were caressing her bare skin as he pressed her closer to him.

Before, when Justin had consoled her over Boney's inexplicable melancholy, the strength of his body had been reassuring and, comforted by it, she had rested against him. Now it was quite the opposite, and she wanted to rub languorously against him like a cat. What was wrong with her? Diana felt like the veriest trollop, and worse yet, she suddenly found herself wishing he would lay her down on the soft grass and make violent love to her—she, who had borne Ferdie's perfunctory lovemaking as something one did for one's husband only out of wifely affection and a strong sense of duty.

Unthinking, Diana slid her arms around Justin's neck and pulled his lips firmly down on hers, sighing gently as she did so and melting further into his arms. His hands moved down her waist to her hips leaving a tingling feeling wherever they caressed her, and she pressed against him, reveling in the feel of him, the touch of him, the taste of him.

She had no idea how long they stood there wrapped in their own world, oblivious to everything but each other. Nor could

she imagine what might have happened next had not a shepherdess come tripping down the path shrieking with laughter
and waving a beribboned crook as an importunate young buck
tried desperately to catch up with her. They were closely followed by another giggling pair.

Brought swiftly back to reality, Diana freed herself and with
a shaken laugh turned to make her way back toward the house.
"Lady Walden, the others," she began breathlessly, "they will
be wondering what has become of us."

Justin was just reaching for her hand to pull her back when
a cheery voice behind them boomed, "Lady Diana, Justin. Are
they unmasking, then?" and Tony Washburne, his mask dangling from one ear and waving a bottle, came weaving blearily
along the path, the cowl of his monk's robe askew. He grinned
sheepishly at them. "There are so many monks in there, m'
mother won't know I've gone missing, so I figured I could
enjoy myself out here until the unmasking. But if they've already done it, the game is up and I must return. Don't want the
mater upset. Sweet lady, but got a fearful temper, you know."
He sighed lugubriously, and continued on his erratic way
lurching back and forth across the path ahead of them.

The moment had passed and heaving a sigh of relief, Diana
retied her mask most firmly into place and began to walk
briskly toward the ballroom telling herself that she was glad
for the providential appearance of Tony. Behind her, Justin
could do nothing but put on his own mask and follow her,
grinning ruefully to himself and vowing that the next time he
held her in his arms there would be no escape. He had hun-
gered for it too long, and she had felt too perfect there for him
to give up now.

Chapter 29

FORTUNATELY for Diana's peace of mind, the rest of the evening passed without incident. By the exertion of pure willpower she was able to last through it, though she was in a daze, not even evincing much interest when it came time to unmask. Fortunately, almost everyone around her was too caught up in it all to notice her preoccupation.

However, her niece's unusual state of mind did not escape the sharp eyes of Lady Walden. Observing Diana flushed and breathless after her supposed refreshing walk in the garden and remarking her subsequent air of distraction and the random replies she made to the questions put to her, Seraphina came to her own conclusions and did not press her for comments or conversation as they rode home. As Justin too had appeared rather subdued, the older woman allowed herself to speculate that perhaps something had transpired in the garden. She devoutly hoped that they had at last come to the recognition of their mutual attraction, which she had long wished for.

Alone in her bedchamber at last, Diana undressed herself and lay back against the pillows with a sigh. What precisely *had* come over her to make her behave in such a manner? Ordinarily she would have divined and forestalled St. Clair's advances, as she had so many others', with a witty remark and a change of subject. Had she wanted his kiss so much then? Recalling their other times together—his helping her dismount from Ajax, reassuring her over Boney's odd behavior—she was forced to admit, unwilling as she was to do so, that she was attracted to him. It was a lowering thought. Was she just another foolish woman joining the ranks of Justin St. Clair's conquests?

No, a voice inside her cried, this is different. And it *was* different, she told herself fiercely. She was not a coquette like so many who flocked around him. She did not enjoy flirting, nor had she thrown out any lures to him—quite the opposite, in fact. At first she had loathed him. But then as she had come to know him and to appreciate the keen mind behind the flippant remarks, the energy and lively curiosity that were so well hidden under the cynical and world-weary air, she had discovered that, despite his status as one of the *ton*'s most elusive, shocking, and sought after bachelors, there lurked a person very similar to herself, possessed of serious interests who was determined to live a life that was something more than the empty ones surrounding him.

And he, too, had seen something special in her and had sensed their kindred spirits. Diana was certain of it. Surely they could not have spent so many hours immersed in deep conversation if he had not truly felt she had ideas worth listening to. In fact, Justin St. Clair was one of the few people who made Diana feel as though she were actually accomplishing things in her life. Surely it took some mental and spiritual affinity and not some purely physical attraction for such a state of affairs to exist?

She rolled over on one side to stare into the fire that was still flickering in the grate. He had said that he wished her to depend on him. No one in her entire life had ever offered that to her before. How comforting it sounded! Of course, Justin St. Clair was quick-witted and articulate. He would know the words a woman wished to hear. But when he had spoken them, he had been strangely ill at ease, blurting the words out almost as though they were being forced from him.

In a curious way Diana had come to depend on him—not exactly in the way that he wished perhaps, but in a more subtle, intellectual way. If she came across some perplexing issue, she always knew at the back of her mind that he was there to help her think it through. He was more than happy to share knowledge with her from his vast experience, and could offer useful suggestions without making it seem as though he were telling her what to do. And she had quite gotten in the way of enjoying his escort. People leapt to do his bidding with an alacrity that poor Ferdie, or even she, was unable to command. It wasn't as though she truly needed him, of course. She managed quite well by herself and had been doing so for years, but after overcoming her initial resistance to the man, she certainly had been more comfortable and relaxed since she had allowed Justin St. Clair to become such an important part of her life . . .until now that was.

Now all she could think of was how it felt to have his arms around her and his lips coaxing hers into a response that she blushed to remember. And what was worse, she lay there wondering what it would feel like to have him in bed beside her now pressing her bare skin to his . . . Oh, it was too much! She must stop thinking such things, or she would never be able to face him with equanimity again. However, the most discouraging aspect of all was that she knew such episodes were so commonplace in Justin's life; that he wouldn't give it a second thought, while she could think of nothing else. Most likely he was in Mademoiselle de Charenton's willing arms at this very moment.

Blast! Diana hurled back the bedclothes, grabbed her candlestick, and lit it in the fire. She snatched up a copy of Ovid's *Metamorphosis* and returned to bed with it, determined at least to distract herself, if not study, until she was exhausted enough to fall asleep. It was an unfortunate choice as the ancient gods were an amorous lot, and it seemed as though every other page, someone was chasing after someone else. At long last, however, the lateness of the hour and the unaccustomed emotional turmoil of the evening had its effect, and Diana finally drowsed off into an uneasy slumber.

She was not alone in her insomnia. Contrary to Diana's unhappy conjecture, Justin was not in Mademoiselle de Charenton's arms but recalling their few moments together with just as much fervor and intensity as she was.

After dropping the ladies off at Brook Street, he had climbed out of the carriage, instructing the coachman to proceed while he walked home, hoping that the extra exercise and the fresh air would clear his head and tire him out enough to banish disturbing thoughts of Diana.

Again and again he pictured her with the white silk fluttering enticingly around her long slim legs, revealing a glimpse of a well-turned ankle, or the golden cords that outlined the swell of her breasts and the gentle curve of her waist. How perfectly she had fit against him, and how soft and firm she had felt beneath his hands as, all hint of her usual dignified reserve vanished, she had wound her hands in his hair and returned his kisses with such intensity.

He had sensed that underneath that cool collected exterior lay a passionate woman. She was too vital a person not to be. He had watched her eyes light up with enthusiasm when she was intrigued by something, he had seen her face flushed with the joy of physical exertion after riding Ajax, he had observed how she and her horse became one as they galloped along or sailed over a hedgerow, and he knew that underneath the calm, self-possessed bearing there was a sensual creature who only needed the proper encouragement to enjoy life to its fullest. Her complete unconsciousness of all this only made her all the more seductive. Yet at the same time, it rendered her terribly vulnerable, and Justin had been torn between the wish to tear off the thin silk of her costume and ravish her and the urge to wrap her tightly in his arms and defend her from all the evil in the world, including salacious fellows like himself.

He had never been so beset by so many conflicting emotions before, and the walk, along with several glasses of port, did absolutely nothing at all to relieve his embattled state of mind. What was he to do? He could think of nothing else but Diana, had thought of nothing else for days even before he had kissed her, and now after having done so, he positively ached for her in a way that he could never quite recall having ached before.

The few times in his life that he had wanted someone desperately, he had been able, if not to have her, at least to find a willing substitute who had soon assuaged his need. But this time it was different. He longed for Diana in so many ways—physical, emotional, spiritual, intellectual—that no one but she could possibly satisfy them. And seeking the satisfaction of his physical desires would have only exacerbated the others.

Justin stared moodily into the fire for what seemed like hours until, after cracking open the third bottle of port he was at last able to blot out the disturbing image of a goddess in white draperies from his mind and lapse into blessed unconsciousness.

Justin and Diana were not the only ones to quit Lady Topham's masquerade victims of a thousand disturbing thoughts. By the time the Duchess of Wrayburn returned Lady Blanche Howard to her residence in the wee hours of the

morning, the beauty was so seething with frustration that she
barely heard Lord Livermore begging her to drive out with
him the next day as he escorted her to the door. Almost snatch-
ing her hand from his reverent kisses, she hurried inside, so
eager was she to be alone someplace where she could at last
give vent to some of the fury consuming her.

That woman! Why she had no more claim to Justin St. Clair
than some trollop in the street. And she had practically made
Blanche a laughingstock. The entire *ton* knew that Lady
Blanche Howard was sure to capture Justin's notoriously
fickle attention, and woe betide anyone who had the effrontery
to thwart the wishes of one of society's incomparables.
Blanche ground her teeth as she revisited the scenes from the
evening. Justin St. Clair would discover that he had ignored
Lady Blanche Howard at his peril. As for Lady Diana Hatherill! The beauty hurled a Sevres figurine into the fireplace in
her bedchamber. Diana would rue the day she had set her cap
at Blanche's particular quarry.

There was a gentle scratch at the door. "What do you
want?" Blanche snapped as her maid peeked in cautiously.

"If you'll be excusin' me, miss, I only came to help you to
bed, miss," the girl pleaded hesitantly. Her ladyship was in a
rarer taking than the girl had seen her in many a day, and her
ladyship was one who had a temper and then some.

"Well, be quick about it then" was the curt reply.

The maid's soothing ministrations brought some degree of
equanimity to her infuriated mistress—enough so that at least
Blanche was able to think sufficiently clearly to devise a strategy for dealing with the meddlesome Lady Diana. She
schemed for some time, and then smiling slyly to herself,
Blanche climbed into bed secure in the likely success of her
nefarious plotting.

So confident was she of her own cleverness that surprisingly
enough Lady Blanche awoke early the next morning, thoroughly
invigorated and burning to put it to the test. She astonished the
entire household by arising at a most uncharacteristically early
hour and calling for a carriage to take her to Brook Street.

Ushered into Diana's presence, the beauty was delighted to
see the young widow looking quite hagged. Indeed, in the
harsh morning light, Diana didn't look at all the sort to win
even a passing glance from such a noted connoisseur of femi-

nine charms as Justin St. Clair. There were dark circles under the deep blue eyes, and her cheeks were quite pale, as though she had not slept a wink.

Good, the visitor remarked to herself with satisfaction. Then, pinning a look of sympathetic concern on her face, she crossed the room to where Diana sat listlessly in a chair by the fire, too abstracted even to read the newspaper that lay in her lap, declaring gently, "Pray do not get up. I am only here for the briefest of moments. In fact, I rather suspect you wonder at my calling on you at all, as we are hardly acquainted."

Taken entirely by surprise and thinking none too clearly as it was this morning, Diana remained seated in puzzled silence.

"I wonder at it myself, but I felt I must come," the beauty cooed, disposing herself in a chair on the opposite side of the fire. "I realize that though you are a good deal *older* than I," Blanche laid a delicate but unmistakable emphasis on the word, "you are far less accustomed to the ways of the *ton* and in particular those of St. Clair."

At the mention of Justin's name, some of the listlessness disappeared, and Diana unconsciously straightened up into a more attentive position.

"Justin and I have been friends this age and, fond as I am of such a naughty scapegrace, I do admit that I occasionally think he goes too far." Blanche took note with intense satisfaction of the delicate flush that was creeping into her unwilling hostess's pale cheeks.

"He is vastly amusing and a man who can never resist a challenge, as you undoubtedly know. I realize that I am far too inclined to be indulgent with him—he is so charming is he not—but when it involves the reputation of another woman, well, indeed, I think he goes too far."

At last Diana marshaled her wits about her. She knew the type of person Lady Blanche was, vain, greedy of admiration, and jealous of any attention that was not paid to her. The only thing that amazed Diana was that she, unpretentious Lady Diana Hatherill, had done anything to bring herself to the notice of such a person. Certainly she offered no competition to a diamond of such renown as Lady Blanche. Much as she hated to admit it, Diana could not at all like the possessive and self-congratulatory tone in the lady's voice when she spoke of

Justin. No one as independent as Justin deserved to be referred to in such a way. "You are all sensibility, Lady Blanche," she responded coolly, "but I quite fail to see what all this had to do with me."

"What?" Blanche feigned a start of surprise. "I was quite sure you knew of the wager. I only wished to warn you that people are beginning to talk, but if you . . ." the beauty paused dramatically.

"Wager? I have no concern with such things, and as far as talk goes, why, people will say whatever they will. I care very little for such mindlessness as the gossip of the *ton*."

It was Blanche's turn to redden. "You may think yourself above such things, Lady Diana," she sneered, "but no one is that powerful. Very well, if you wish to figure as a laughing-stock, I do not care, and Justin may go ahead and win his wager for all it matters to me. Though why he should consider the seduction of someone like you such a challenge, I have not the slightest notion."

Diana drew a quick painful breath. "Oh, *that* wager. Of course, I paid no heed to such a thing. As to *your* concern for *me*, why, that is far too kind of you. I assure you that neither the Bucklands, nor the Hatherills ever stoop to paying the least consideration to such vulgar things as *on-dits*, though I quite understand why *you* might. I thank you for your concern, but it is really quite unnecessary. Now, if you'll forgive me, I have an appointment I must keep." Rising to her full height, Diana gave the bellpull a sharp tug before sweeping regally from the room, leaving her visitor to gape in helpless fury after her.

How dare she, Blanche fumed. Here Blanche had only come to warn her off, and Lady Diana, not the least grateful at being saved from social ignominy, had stared down her patrician nose, delicately hinting that the daughter of a jumped-up peer had insulted her by proffering advice to a descendant of such illustrious lineage. It was too much! Without even waiting for the butler to appear, Blanche flounced out of the drawing room, down the stairs, and out the front door, letting it slam behind her. "Home, Hendricks," she snapped, climbing into the carriage without deigning to glance at the footman who helped her into it.

Meanwhile, an equally unwelcome visitor was descending

on a bachelor apartment in Mount Street. Puffing slightly, Alfred once again ascended the stairs to his brother's chamber, only to recoil in disgust at the sight that met his eyes.

Unshaven, cravat askew, hair tousled from a night spent in the armchair before the fire, Justin groaned at the sight of his visitor. "Not again, Alfred! More than twice in one Season and in the morning? It is really too much. After all, I ask so little of you."

With extreme difficulty, the Earl of Winterbourne held his temper in check. For all that he was a useless libertine, a hedonist, and a rake, Justin had, for once in his life, done his avuncular duty and tried his best to intervene in Reginald's affairs. Now, having gone to uncomfortable lengths to enlist his brother's aid, Alfred was going to have to tell him to stop.

"Well?" Sighing, Justin put a hand to his aching head. "What is it this time?"

Alfred settled gingerly on the only chair in the room not covered with reading material. "Er," he coughed uncomfortably. "I have come to thank you for your, er, work on Reginald's behalf."

"Think nothing of it." Justin waved a weary hand.

"No, no. I must give credit where credit it due. And you have succeeded in detaching Reginald from the har . . . er . . . Lady Diana. Why, would you believe it, he was even down at Winterbourne not long ago? He's a good lad, really, but young." Alfred chuckled with forced jocularity. "He'll come 'round. He's studying very seriously you know. Perhaps I have wronged him. It would only be natural—a parent's concern you know. I'm just not accustomed to thinking of him as an adult, I suppose. However, it is time he was considering marriage, and however well-off one is, it is no bad thing to bring a fortune into the family. They say that Sir Thomas Walden was as rich as Croesus, and after all, though the Bucklands are not a very powerful family now, they once were. Certainly the line is a very ancient and illustrious one."

Justin was fast becoming aware of the drift of his elder brother's ruminations. "How quickly we change our tune when a fortune is involved," he observed nastily. "But if its Reginald's marrying Lady Diana you're thinking of, Alfred, you can forget it."

"Now, now, Justin. I admit I have been rather too hasty about this, but I am willing to own up to my mistakes. I am sure the girl can be brought around," Alfred temporized.

"She can't and she won't," Justin snapped.

"Oh, come now, why not?" Alfred chuckled with false bonhomie.

"She can't because I'm going to marry her."

"You?" Alfred's jaw dropped.

"Yes, I."

"But you don't *need* a fortune," Justin's brother wailed. "You're already as rich as the Golden Ball!"

"And so are you, Alfred, except for your cheeseparing ways," Justin reminded him. "Incomprehensible as it may seem to you, I am not marrying Diana for her pecuniary expectations."

"But then what are you marrying her for?" the earl moaned in utter confusion.

"Because I love her, you dolt. Now if you know what's good for you, you'll leave me alone. I passed quite a night last night, and I've the devil of a head this morning." Not giving his brother a moment to recover, Justin rang for Preston, who appeared as if by magic bearing a steaming pot of coffee. "Thank you Preston," his master sighed with relief. "The earl was just going. Would you see him out?"

Closing his eyes gratefully, Justin sank back in his chair to consider all the possible implications of his own surprising announcement.

And it was surprising, coming as much of a shock to him as it had to his brother, but there it was. The cause of the vague feeling of nagging distaste for life, disgust even, that Justin had been suffering for some time had magically disappeared. That was it. He was in love with Lady Diana Hatherill. It was all abundantly clear. He didn't want her as his mistress. He didn't want her as a friend. He wanted her as his wife. He wanted to share his life with her, to have children with her, to grow old with her.

All of a sudden Justin's headache was gone. "What a fool I've been," he muttered to no one in particular. "What an arrogant impossible fool. I've been in love with her for ages, and I'm only just now realizing it." His ennui disappeared. Life seemed rosy and full of promise once more. "I must see her," he mumbled to himself, "before she writes last evening off as a mere flirtation. Preston!" he shouted.

Chapter 30

THOUGH enlightenment had struck in Mount Street, it was by no means in evidence in a slim house in Brook Street. There, with Boney perched on her shoulder and Wellington hard on her heels, Diana paced back and forth in her bedchamber alternating between fury and despair. How could he? Even such a heartless libertine as Justin St. Clair could not stoop so low? How could she? She, Diana, was not such a green girl as to fall for a handsome face and charm of manner. But Diana had, and she didn't know whether to be more furious with Justin St. Clair or Lady Diana Hatherill. At the moment, she hated both of them.

No. She did not. Diana collapsed on a hassock overcome with uncharacteristic tears. Very well, perhaps the kiss in the garden had been false, but surely their friendship, their camaraderie was not? Surely his present of Wellington and his kindness over Boney was not? But that is what makes him so irresistible, she thought to herself. He knows precisely what to do to please each and every one of us, from Mademoiselle de Charenton to Lady Blanche Howard to me. And he is so very clever, she admonished herself, more than a match for you, my girl. Overcome with misery, she wept while Boney clucked consolingly in her ear and Wellington licked her hand.

Finally, having cried herself to exhaustion, she pulled herself together and returned to the drawing room to continue her perusal of the morning's post, thankful that her great-aunt had gone to spend the day with friends in Richmond.

Gradually, as she forced herself to make sense of the morning's news and a number of bills and receipts from Buckland, Diana grew calmer and rational enough to wonder at Lady Blanche's part in the entire affair. Certainly, if the one time she had observed that lady and Justin together were any indication, Justin had no particular interest in the beauty. Come to think of it, of late he had been so much in Diana's company, he had had very little time for anyone else's.

And Diana could not think when she had enjoyed life more than when she was sharing it with Justin—catching his eyes, watching them crinkle with amusement as some absurdity of the *ton* struck him, or laughing with him at the follies and pretensions of those bent on leading a fashionable existence. So often she had found him looking at her in precisely the same way, smiling in wordless agreement over something or other, and had been flooded with the happiness of a companionship that she had never thought to find. Had it all been done to win a paltry bet, this sharing, this closeness? Diana flung out of the chair and began to pace again.

So wrapped up in her thoughts was she that she did not even hear Finchley enter the room or call her name until he was forced practically to shout in her ear, "Lord Justin St. Clair to see you, madam."

"Oh no!" Diana came to an abrupt halt. "I can't, I mean . . . oh do pray, tell him that I am not at home," she pleaded frantically.

"Too late," a cheerful voice observed as Justin, too eager to wait, strode into the room on the butler's heels.

"Oh." It took all of Diana's strength of character not to rush headlong from the room. "That will be all. Thank you, Finchley," she dismissed the loyal retainer who, struck by his mistress's uncharacteristic indecision, was hovering near the door.

The butler left them to face one another, neither one precisely certain as to how to begin. After years of dalliance with willing females, Justin was entirely at a loss as to how to proceed with one he wanted so desperately but of whom he was so unsure.

For her part, Diana had never been in such an equivocal situation. She did not know whether to launch into a furious and injured tirade at his perfidy, retire in dignified disgust, or to ignore the entire thing as though whatever Justin St. Clair chose to do was of not the slightest interest to her. Unable to make herself do any of these things, she stood there dumbly while Boney, now perched on the mantel, and Wellington, on the floor in front of the hearth, waited expectantly.

Finally Justin, trying desperately to interpret the lady's unreadable expression, began tentatively, "I came to thank you for allowing me to escort you last evening. I can't think when I have enjoyed myself more." Lord, he sounded like a schoolboy—even worse than his nephew. Taking a step toward Diana he tried again. "Diana, I . . ." There was a crash as Diana, backing up hurriedly, banged into the brass fender.

"It was most kind of you to take us, sir, but I must excuse myself as I have a most pressing engagement that I . . ."

"Diana," Justin possessed himself of her hands, "that is utter nonsense and you know it. You are no more dressed to go out than I am to attend a ball, and all this," he pointed to the mass of papers surrounding her chair, "does not look like the room of someone on her way to an appointment. Now what's amiss?"

She stared helplessly at the floor for a minute. "Why nothing is amiss. Why should you think anything is?" He re-collected her hands in his, but she snatched them away.

"Diana, I thought we were friends, you and I." Justin moved closer, repossessing her hands as he did so.

Without thinking, she looked up to find him regarding her steadily, his gray eyes full of tender concern. It was a terrible mistake. All of the hurt over his betrayal and her fury at herself over her weakness for him came flooding back. "Friends?" Her voice rose shrilly. "I wouldn't be your friend if you were the last man on earth—if my life depended on it. Your friend, your bargaining counter more like! Why should I be your friend? I would have more respect for myself now if I were your trollop instead of your dupe!"

Justin dropped her hands to grab her shoulders. "Whatever are you talking about? My trollop? My dupe? I came here to tell you I love you, and all you can do is shout at me and insult me."

"Well, if that isn't outside of enough!" she gasped. "*I* insult *you*? What did you win, sirrah, for making a fool out me? I hope it was a king's ransom. Was it not enough that you could take your winnings and go without having to come here and gloat over me?" She struggled fiercely to get away, but he only pulled her more closely to him. A tall woman, Diana had always considered herself to be strong as well, but she was completely immobilized by the powerful arms encircling her.

"Will you listen to me," he shouted. "I *love* you!"

"What of it?" she spat back. "I *hate* you."

Justin stepped back as if she had struck him, his eyes dark with anger, his face white and taut, but in her anger Diana barely noticed. "Oh yes, love is the merest game to you. A broken heart, a ruined life more or less is nothing to the great Justin St. Clair. And here I actually was foolish enough to think you liked me for who I was. I didn't even ask you to love me as so many silly women do. No wonder Lady Blanche warned me about you. Undoubtedly you did the same to her, too, only she, vain goose that she is, was merely annoyed at losing one of her vast number of admirers. I, on the other hand . . ." She paused at last to catch her breath.

"Blanche?" There was an arrested look on Justin's face. "Lady Blanche Howard? What does she have to do with anything?"

"She," Diana took a deep breath to stop the shaking in her voice, "she told me about the wager."

"Wager? What wager? You are talking a farrago of nonsense."

Justin's bewilderment was so patent that Diana hesitated. "You had a wager. She said that you did." Her voice faltered. "Didn't you?"

"I had no wagers with anyone, my love." He pulled her toward him. "Mistakes, I have made, I freely concede, but wagers—never. I admit the error of my ways. I first called on you at Alfred's behest because I thought you were pursuing Reginald. But the minute I saw you, I knew your were not. You were too honest, too sincere. I looked into your eyes and knew you to be a person of integrity. Oh, I could not admit that to myself, could not admit that I the infallible Justin St. Clair was guilty of an error of judgment. I could not admit so quickly that I had misjudged you so badly—my lamentable pride. But I never deceived you. You knew what I had come for."

"Later, perhaps, I was deluding myself, telling myself that I was keeping an eye on Reginald when really I was keeping an eye on you." He saw the flash in her eyes. "Not keeping an eye on you *that* way. I mean that I was attracted to you, enchanted by you, more enchanted than I had ever been by anyone before, and certainly more than I wished to be enchanted by any woman no matter who she was. I think that I was actually jealous of Reginald. There he was escorting one of the most beautiful and intelligent women in London to concerts and

exhibitions, sharing books and music with her in a way I'd
never dared to dream of, and he had just stumbled on it, while
I believe I have been searching for such a thing all my life. But
you loathed me—and with good reason. I had insulted you.
Furthermore, you considered me frivolous, a reprobate, a
wastrel even, but I took comfort in the fact that you seemed to
consider me an opponent worth fighting. At least I had that. At
the time, I don't think I was quite aware of all those things. I
only knew I couldn't keep away from you, and I hated myself
for it. I tried to put you from my mind, to lose myself in work
or Mademoiselle de Charenton, but it was no use. She recognized my obsession with you before I did." He looked down at
Diana smiling ruefully.

"It wasn't until you left for Buckland that it dawned on me.
I thought you'd eloped with Reginald, and I was beside myself. I told myself I was enraged because you had turned out to
be as duplicitous as Alfred and I had at first thought, but that
wasn't it. It was jealousy pure and simple. Then I arrived to
find nothing of the sort. There you were, as lovely as I had
ever seen you, carefree and happy in a way I had never imagined. It broke my heart to think of the years you had struggled
by yourself, and I wanted to sweep you off your feet then and
there and carry you away somewhere where I could lavish you
with every possible comfort. But I couldn't do anything but
give you the most meager advice."

Justin looked down at her searchingly. "I am begging you
now to let me do that, to take care of you, though I know you
are entirely capable of looking after yourself, to love you,
though you are so damnably self-sufficient that you don't need
anyone, to be part of your life, though I know that every other
man in your life has only proven to be an encumbrance." He
sensed her hesitation and was unprepared for the cold wave of
fear that washed over him and seemed to pool in the pit of his
stomach. He had been so ecstatic at his discovery that he loved
her, so happy that at last he had found someone to care about
as truly and deeply as he had always longed to do, that he had
not even allowed himself to consider the horrible possibility
that she might not feel the same way about him; and the
thought of facing life without her, now that he had found her,
was unbearable.

Diana was silent, too bemused by the intensity and variety

of emotions surging through her to respond. In the space of a few hours, she had been more exultant and more humiliated, more aroused and more despairing, more angry and more in love than she had ever thought possible, and she was not at all sure how she felt about it. Her life had been far less exciting but far more serene and predictable before Justin St. Clair had come into it. However, she had never felt so alive, so aware of all the possibilities around her, as she had in the past weeks. She had never looked forward so much to each day as she did now. In an agony of doubt, she stared at the floor.

"Diana?" Justin prompted softly.

"I don't know, I don't know," she whispered.

"It's all right, my beautiful love. Just tell me I have a chance. Just let me say I love you?" he begged.

She nodded slowly.

"Good." He tilted her face up to his and kissed her gently on the forehead, on each cheek, and then, slowly, lingeringly on the lips until he felt some of the tension go out of her, and she leaned against him with a sigh. He caressed the glossy black hair as she laid her head on his shoulder and held her close for a long silent moment while she absorbed the astounding revelations, the thoughts and emotions of the morning.

As she stood there with her head on Justin's shoulder, Diana felt some of the uncontrollable trembling subside. It was so comfortable in his arms, so perfect—as if after a lifetime of searching for it, she had at last found a haven of safety and security, someone else to depend on when she was too upset or overwrought to think clearly. And there was no doubt she was overwrought now.

Diana couldn't remember a time when she had been so much at the mercy of her own emotions and passions—love, lust, jealousy, rage, despair—emotions she hadn't even known she possessed. For a moment she longed to return to the comfortable sameness of her life, boring as it had been, before she had met Justin. Did she wish to risk feeling this way for the rest of her life—to be so happy one moment and so desperate the next? Did she want to have so much of her happiness bound up in another person? She was not at all sure she did. The emotional turmoil of the past weeks had been exhausting beyond belief, frightening even, and she had so much left to do that required her thought and energies—the repairs at Buckland, investment in the waterworks, a hundred little things. She could not afford to waste her time agonizing over her feelings.

Sensing some of the conflict that was tearing Diana apart, Justin deemed it prudent to intervene before she could retreat into the safety of her well-ordered but solitary existence. He looked deep into the worried blue eyes murmuring, " 'Tis a fearful decision, is it not, my love, to give one's happiness into another's keeping? But I, for one, can think of no one I would trust more to keep mine safe from harm than you."

As his words sank in, Diana realized with a start that, despite his vast knowledge of women, Justin was as inexperienced at this as she was. He was assuming just as big a risk—more, in fact, for he had never been married before, even to someone as inconsequential as Ferdie. "I . . . I don't know what to say."

"Just say you'll marry me," he whispered against her mouth. "Diana, I know very little about true love, never having felt it until now, but I do know that all the deliberation in the world is pointless when I feel the way I do—complete and happy with you, and lost and lonely without you. And I know that I could examine it forever, but I will never be able to explain to my mind what my heart has known for so long. I love you." He cupped her face in his hands and kissed it gently—the eyelids, the nose, and the lips slowly until they responded to his, and her body began to melt against him.

He slid his hands down to her shoulders, her waist, pulling her closer to him, his mouth more insistent now as her lips parted under his and her arms came up around his neck. The taste of her, the feel of her was magic. He could have held her thus forever and never tired of it. She *must* want him, she *must* care about him, please God. Panting slightly he lifted his head. "Diana, marry me?"

There was no question about it, the gentleman was not one to give up. The cautious voice at the back of Diana's mind urged her to doubt, to question, but her heart and body had given their answer long ago. Long before Justin had even kissed her, she had known, though she refused to admit it. She had known it every time she entered a crowded room and looked for him, she had known it when, not seeing him there, her interest in the affair had suddenly died completely. She had known it when just the sight of his tall figure striding purposefully along a street or into a room caused her to feel full of vitality and interest. She had even known that someone who had enough importance in her life to make her angry at him was a powerful force indeed. With a sigh, she gave in to the inevitable, to what she had sensed for quite some time. "Yes please."

"Yes please, what?" he prompted.

"Yes please, Justin, yes I love you, yes I shall marry you."

Sometime later, as she emerged breathless from his crushing embrace, Diana could not help giggling.

"What is it, my love?" he cocked a speculative eyebrow at her.

"Somehow I don't think this is quite what Lady Blanche had in mind."

"I hardly think so," he agreed, his eyes dancing. "But I have had it in my mind, and nothing else, for some time. Now be quiet and let us take up where we left off—the part where you said you'd marry me, and then I kissed you like this . . .like this . . .and like this . . ."